POWERFUL DECEPTION

JOCELYNE SOTO

The world that we live in is a very dark place. Everywhere you look there is blood looming. There are powerful individuals waiting for you to take your last breath. Powerful individuals that would strap you to a chair and let you suffer. It's those powerful men and women that took my father from me, the ones I'm going after. Starting with Dante Rosetti. He called the hit that took the most meaningful person in my life down. I will take him down, watch every inch of his life burn to a crisp, even if I have to pretend to be someone else entirely and lie my way into his life. I will destroy the man that everyone calls The Devil, and he won't see a thing that is coming his way.

CONTENTS

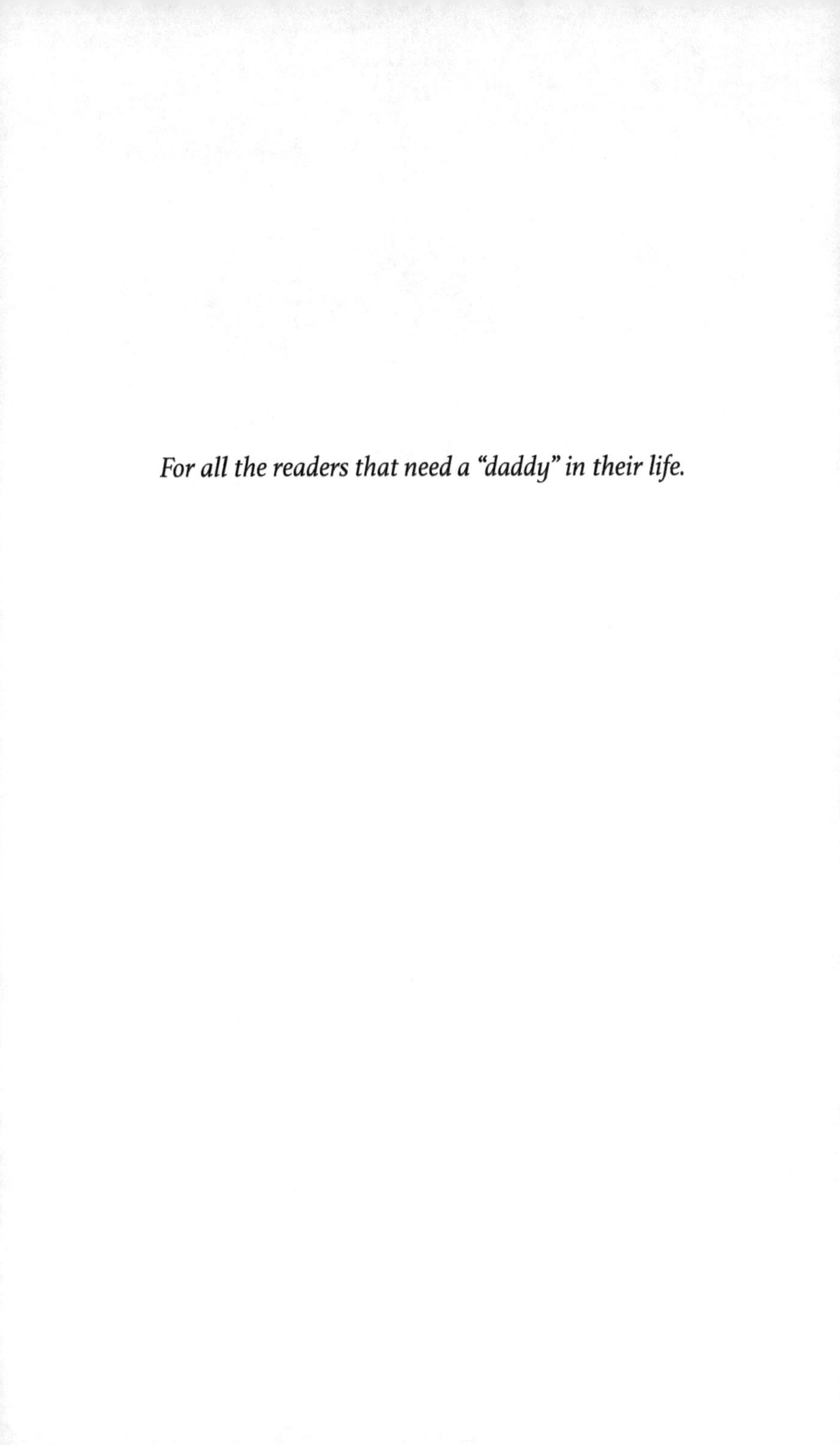

For all the readers that need a "daddy" in their life.

Author's Note

This story contains on page violence, gun violence and death by gun. If this is something that you are not comfortable reading, please do not continue.
If you would like more information about the content warnings related to this book, please visit my website for more information.
Thank you.

DANTE

This life has taken a lot from me.

The mother of my children and my wife, my own parents. Yet, it has left me standing.

Out of all the people that should still be walking this earth, I am not one of them.

In my lifetime, I've done a handful of bad things. More than most.

Things that would make people run for the hills. Things that would make people fearful of even coming within a hundred feet of me.

Things that make me a terrible, terrible person.

The type of person that parents warn their kids about when they go out late at night.

The person that cops tell the citizens of their city not to get into business with.

I'm a dangerous man and everybody who has lived within this beautiful yet dangerous city all their lives, knows it.

You see, the streets of the city of Chicago may be owned by some of the richest families in this country, but I run them.

There isn't a bullet shot that I don't know about. There isn't a cop that roams the streets that doesn't know my name. There isn't a drug trade that I don't have my hands in. Everything that happens within the two hundred and thirty-four square miles of the city of Chicago, I know.

I have a hand in every little detail that happens within the city's borders, and some people would be astonished to know just how far my reach goes.

People don't tend to cross me, yet the stupid ones try. Some I let, just out of pure enjoyment and to see how far they will go, and others I bring down before they get too close. Soon, though, there will be one person that will succeed in whatever plan they muster up to take me down, and when that happens, I will let them take my last breath.

I've done heinous things in my life, even I know that I deserve to be brought down for my crimes.

Until then, I will continue living up to my namesake that has been given to me by this city. By its people.

The way the people of the city of Chicago see it, the Windy City has two rulers. The king and The Devil.

I, Dante Rosetti, am The Devil.

And I live for anything and everything that comes with it.

Everyone be damned.

1

ARIANNA

Are you still considered an orphan if both your parents are dead before the age of twenty-four? Or do you lose that title the second you are no longer a child?

Because as I sit here in this pew, listening to Father John talking about how my father was a great man and loved by many, I feel like an orphan.

Especially since there is not one single person sitting next to me. There's not even a single person in my row.

No family members, no friends, no coworkers.

I'm alone. My last living relative, my last living parent, is in a wooden box a few feet from me, ice cold.

He shouldn't be ice cold.

My father should be sitting in his favorite spot on the couch with a can of beer in his hand watching whatever game is on. He should be putting on his uniform and going to work. He should be tinkering on that old piece of junk he has in the garage that he calls a car. He should be doing a whole lot more than being lifeless and ice cold inside a box that shouldn't even be his. A box that's rented.

Yet he is.

The only man that ever gave a shit about me, the one man that was my constant and would brighten every single one of my dark days, is in a fucking box.

At least he's with Mama because I'm a fucking orphan, no matter if the definition applies to me or not.

Mama died when I was twelve. A car accident took her, and her death was not something that I wanted to relive. Yet here I am. Reliving it.

It happened last Friday. We were supposed to grab some dinner after my shift at the bar ended. Poppa was supposed to meet me at the bar like he always did, and we were supposed to walk to the restaurant he always picked from there.

Dad was always on time, the detective in him not knowing how to relax.

So, him not showing up ten minutes before my shift ended was out of character. It threw me off that he wasn't there when I expected him, but I let it pass and waited. It was fifteen minutes after I had clocked out that I started to get worried.

Where was he?

I called his cell, no answer.

I called the house phone that he refused to get rid of, no answer.

I even called one of his closest friends, Tommy, to ask if he had heard from him. His response: he had no clue where my poppa was.

That right there made me worry even more. So, I went straight to my childhood home.

I moved out of the house when I was nineteen. All because I wanted independence. But the second I walked through the front door; I wish I hadn't.

Maybe if I hadn't moved out, the scene that was staring back at me wouldn't have been there in the first place.

Maybe if I was living there, I would have stopped whatever tornado had passed through.

The Chicago brownstone that my parents bought before I was born was in shambles. Every picture frame that was on the mantel or on the walls, was broken. There were bullet holes scattered all over the drywall, their casings scattered on the floor.

Nothing was in its place, and it looked like someone had broken into the house and robbed it.

And that's what I thought had happened, until I reached the living room.

I thought that I could handle anything. I thought that after I had witnessed my mother die in an accident, nothing would destroy me as much as that.

I was wrong.

So damn wrong.

The second that my foot crossed the threshold between the foyer and the living room, I stopped breathing. A sob formed in my throat at the sight before me.

My father occupied one of the dining room chairs. The very ones that I spent countless hours sitting in. His head was bowed, his body slumped, and every inch of him was covered in red.

Blood.

Dark blood. Not an inch of his olive skin was showing.

I held in my sob as I walked over to him. I called for him, I whispered for him to respond. Yet nothing happened. Not even a single pin hitting the floor could be heard.

When I was only a foot or two away from him, that's when I let out a scream.

My father's beautiful face was beaten in.

His eyes were open and bloodshot, and his legs and arms were tied to the chair.

My father was tied down and beaten to death, and all I could do was scream and cry.

After running to the garage and finding something to cut him free, I held my father's beaten body as tightly as I could, wishing that he would wake up. I wished that he would open his eyes and tell me that he was going to be okay.

That didn't happen.

So, I sat there for what felt like hours, crying, screaming, wishing that whoever came after my father would come after me too. They never did.

I think one of the neighbors must have heard my screams because soon, police officers were surrounding me and his limp body. I had no idea when they had arrived, but they did, and because my dad was one of them, everyone was on high alert.

One of Chicago's finest had been murdered, of course they were on high alert.

Everything after that is a blur of events. Talking to the

detectives handling the case, talking to the funeral director about a funeral I couldn't afford on my own, fighting with the bank about touching the funds my dad left behind.

Everything is jumbled up together and now here I am.

Watching his funeral.

I fucking hate it.

I hate being in this cathedral in the middle of Chicago, surrounded by people I don't know.

I hate that I have to sit here, like the good daughter that is mourning, and not as if my insides aren't screaming in agony, wanting to know who did this.

I hate every fucking thing about this whole situation and there is nothing that I could do about it but sit here and listen to a priest talk.

"Let's give one final moment of silence in memory of our friend, our brother, our son, and our father, Joseph Vitale."

As Father John bows his head, the entire church goes completely silent. Not even a cough sounds through the building. The only thing I'm able to hear is the rapidness of my heart beating in my chest.

I want to let out a scream to accompany the tears that are currently streaming down my face. I want to yell at everyone in this building to leave and let me mourn my father alone and not tell me how he's off in a better place, because he's not.

I want to run out of here and go find my father's killer and give them the same mercy that was awarded to the one man that has ever loved me.

But once again, I don't do that.

I just continue to sit here in this pew, waiting for this prayer to be over so I can continue to fight with myself as the funeral continues.

Because the funeral doesn't end here.

It doesn't end in this church that my father attended for years until my mother's death. A church that he hasn't set foot in, in twelve years.

No, Joseph Vitale was one of Chicago's finest in blue, and this funeral will continue with a progression involving every first responder in this city. And once the progression is over, I will witness my father's body be put in the ground to never see the light again.

I'm looking forward to that because then, then I will be left in peace and no longer will have to deal with the wives that look at me with pity.

To them, I'm the poor girl that no longer has her parents.

Once my father is in the ground, I will be all but forgotten by them. A distant memory they will only recall when they see me on the streets or when a picture of my father comes along the way.

To them, I'm nothing.

During this whole moment of silence, I don't bow my head or even take my eyes off my father's closed casket. I don't mutter the rosary prayer that I'm sure some people are saying in their heads. I stay that way until Father John clears his throat and says an amen into the microphone.

As soon as the amen is spoken, the music starts up, signifying the end of the service.

I still don't move. I still don't wipe away my tears and I still don't take my eyes off the wooden box.

In my peripheral vision though, I do see Tommy and a few of my dad's colleagues stand up from their seats and make their way to the casket. Then when they're in my direct line of sight, I see each of them taking their place as pallbearers.

Time to walk out of the church and act like I'm the strongest person in the whole fucking world.

Father John walks down the aisle, stopping right next to my pew, waiting for me to join him. The look of sadness as he looks down at me is not one that I miss.

Pushing down the ball of emotions that I have in my throat, I give him a nod and stand up, my eyes still never leaving the casket.

The two of us stand to the side as the men carry my father out of the cathedral and when Father John gives me the signal, I follow.

As I walk down the aisle of this old church, I can feel every single pair of eyes on me. I can feel as they stare at me and if pity was visible, I'm sure I would be able to feel that too.

But I ignore each and every one of them.

I ignore them until we reach the door of the church and step outside.

It's a cloudy yet humid September day in Chicago. It seems perfect for an event like this.

When the casket is walked over the threshold of the church, the bagpipes start to sound out. Police officers and first responders line the street and the sidewalks, standing in formation, all paying their respects to Detective Joseph Vitale.

I watch as Tommy and the rest of the men place my father just outside of the hearse and continue watching as the police commissioner and a few other officers approach it.

People start to congregate behind me and next to me. I can hear their whispers as we all watch the flag that was placed on top of the casket being folded up into a nice little triangle.

A flag for the fallen.

The whispers silence when the police commissioner, Commissioner Simmons, takes the flag and approaches me. With a salute and a bow of his head, he extends the piece of material to me.

I don't want to reach over and take it, but I reach my hands out nonetheless and take a piece of my father for safekeeping.

"I'm very sorry, Ari. I am very sorry that I couldn't protect him."

Yeah, I'm sorry too.

"Thank you, commissioner," I say giving him a small smile through the tears.

With one final salute, he takes his place again in formation.

The bagpipes seem to grow louder as my father's body is slid into the back of the vehicle.

But just because the bagpipes are loud doesn't mean that I don't hear the whispers that start back up again.

I hear each and every word that these people, who are just here to save face, are saying.

"I heard he was involved with the Italian mob. That he crossed them, and that's why they killed him," one woman voices.

"Really? I heard it was the cartel," another woman says.

"Nope," the first woman answers with a pop of her lips. "From what I hear, The Devil himself called the hit. I guess Detective Vitale was digging a little too deep into things for his liking. So, he did away with him."

"Wow. Unbelievable."

Yeah, unbelievable, because it is.

My father would never get involved with something like that, and as much as I want to turn and slap these two bitches for saying my dad's name in vain, I ignore them. They aren't worth my time.

But this wasn't the first time I was hearing that my father was involved with the Italian Mafia.

The rumor has been going around ever since I found his body. Shit, I even heard it as the coroner was putting him in a body bag.

Yet, even though I knew who my dad was and the type of person he was every single day, there is doubt forming in the back of my mind as I see the hearse door close.

What if the rumors are true?

What if my dad was involved in something dark, and death was the only way out?

Because what the woman said about The Devil himself being involved is something that I've been hearing all week.

The Devil.

I've heard the moniker but have no idea who the person is.

Are they really a he? I don't know.

I do know one thing though.

As the bagpipes ring out and I'm ushered to a waiting car to head to the cemetery, I know what I want to do.

I want to find out who this devil person really is. I want to know if they really did have a hand in my father's death, and I want to know the why of it all.

And if they are involved, if this devil person is really the reason why my poppa is dead, I want to make sure that they pay for what they did to him.

I want whoever called the hit, the one that threw every single punch, including the last one, to suffer just as much, if not more than Joseph Vitale.

I will not stop until my father's killer is behind bars, or better yet, dead.

That much I know.

That much I want.

2

ARIANNA

Saying you are going to do something and actually getting it done are two different things.

And sometimes, when you try to get things done a little too quickly, you end up paying the consequences. I'm paying those said consequences with the head pain I'm experiencing.

There is this pounding headache just above my left eyebrow that doesn't seem to go away.

I've taken pain medicine, drank water, and yet the headache is still there like a persistent telemarketer calling about your car's extended warranty.

Maybe the headache is a result of the countless hours that I've spent crying these last few days.

Maybe it's a result of me not eating anything but water and wine since the funeral.

Or maybe the headache is stemming from me spending the last twenty-four hours glued to my computer screen and not giving my eyes a break for more than five minutes.

I'm putting my money on the third one. That is, if I had any money.

My dad's funeral was three days ago.

After the church service, we drove to the cemetery, and my father was finally laid to rest after a week of agony.

The dirt hadn't even touched the casket before the two-faced people that attended the service started to leave. That, of course, included the two women that were talking about my father and what he might have been involved in.

Within ten minutes of the funeral ending, the only ones that were left standing by the hole in the ground were me, Tommy, and a few of my dad's colleagues. But soon after, they left too, and I was left alone, just like I wanted.

I stood by his gravesite until the sky turned a dark blue and the groundskeeper told me that it was far too late for a girl like myself to be out there alone.

I wanted to tell him that even in the safest place, even in one's home, something bad could happen. I knew it from experience. Take the man we had just buried for example.

He was in his home, probably living his life like it was any other day when someone came in and took everything away from him. Nobody is safe anywhere. What would make a dark cemetery any different?

But I didn't tell him that, just like I didn't slap the bitches at the cathedral. I just nodded and agreed when he suggested calling a cab to take me home.

It was when I got home that I realized just how numb I

really was. Even being alone wasn't enough to take the numbness away, so I brought out the wine.

For nearly two days, all I did was stay in my bed, watch random shit on TV, and drink. Eight bottles of merlot later, I knocked out, and when I woke up, the numbness was still there but so was something else.

There was this urge deep inside of me that told me that I needed to get to work. To start doing some research and find out who exactly killed my father. What exactly was he involved in that would cost him his life, or better yet, what would lead to such a horrendous death?

I started with a simple search for Joseph Vitale in the Chicago Public Library database. I thought it was going to be a simple search, one that would take me through his accomplishments as one of Chicago's finest, but that wasn't the case.

I found countless articles that mentioned Detective Vitale and talked about the criminals that he had brought down and the good he was doing for the Chicago Police Department. But in the last three years those articles went from being praiseworthy to downright disgraceful. There were so many opinion pieces talking about how Detective Vitale went from one of the most respected men in blue to being the most despised.

Something that just blows my mind because that wasn't the man that I knew at all. That wasn't the man that raised me and made me into the person that I am today.

What blew my mind even more was the fact that his name was being thrown around with those of thugs and known members of the Italian and Irish Mafia. There is even mention of him being associated with members of the Bratva in some way.

And now, hours later, here I am with a headache and not anywhere near close to finding who could have gone after my father. It could have been anyone.

Instead of answers, all I have is questions as to who my father really was.

As much as I want to say that those women at the funeral were wrong, everything I've found so far has told me otherwise.

He was, in fact involved with the wrong people, but why? What made him go from being one of the most respected men in the city to whatever he was at the end?

What was he digging into that he had to die for?

And how is it that the city of Chicago noticed that my father was changing into a different person and yet his own daughter couldn't? Did I see things and just turn a blind eye to them?

My dad had always been the most loving man. He did everything that he could to give me a good life after Mama died. He went to my school events, and when I told him I was going into bartending after college because I had bills to pay, he supported me.

Never did I see the man that the articles, these opinion pieces, described him to be.

I know deep down inside me that the man described in those articles was not the one I knew.

The way he was acting as a cop had to go deeper. It had to go so deep that it was changing the way that he was conducting his cases.

But what could change him in such a way?

The only reasoning that I can come up with is that it all stems from who he was associating with. And through all of my research, one name keeps coming up wherever I read.

The Devil.

Never a real name, never what he looks like, just the stupid nickname.

A nickname that people came up with to describe the person they say is the one that runs the blood-filled streets of the city.

Whoever this person is, people seem to think that they are the one that called the hit on my father. That is, if they didn't throw the fatal blow themselves.

But why?

In all the articles that I read through, there wasn't a direct connection between my dad and the so-called devil. There were connections between the thugs that my dad was supposedly associated with and The Devil but from what I can see, that was where the relationship ended.

As I sit here, rubbing at the pain in my temples, I realize something. Maybe I was looking for answers in the wrong places.

Maybe I shouldn't be looking for articles mentioning my father to find his killer. Maybe I should be looking into the people he was said to be connected with.

Especially this devil person.

I open my laptop, closing all the tabs and start with a fresh one.

My fingers land on the keys, and I hesitate.

I know Chicago may look like a great city, but I know what lies within the streets. There is darkness, blood and death everywhere, even if the city tries to hide it. Some very powerful individuals run this city and the citizens just turn a blind eye to it.

What will I find if I do this? If I let my fingers move and type out the names of the powerful individuals, I've heard for most of my life?

More blood? Skeletons?

I don't know, but I won't know until I do.

Ignoring the pain medicine that I have next to my laptop and the wine bottles calling my name, I take a deep breath. Mentally preparing myself for whatever is going to pop up when my fingers start to move and I hit the Enter key.

Putting aside all my fears, I start to type into the search engine.

I type in the first name that is currently over taking my mind.

The Devil of Chicago.

That seems like a good starting point as any.

Especially if he really is what people describe him to be.

The second I hit the search button, over a hundred thousand results pop up.

The first result grabs my attention with the heading "Who really is The Devil of Chicago?"

I guess I'm not the only one who is wondering.

As I click on it and wait for the screen to load, a knock on my door takes me out of the cloud I'm in.

I look over at the door, since my apartment is a small studio, as if I can see who is on the other side. My heart starts to beat fast in my chest, remembering who the last person to knock on my door was.

It was my dad only a few days before all of this shit started. That thought brings tears to my eyes, but I push them down.

Getting up from my seat, my whole body swaying in the process, I head over to the door.

Could it be my dad's murderer found me and is here to stop me from digging into the death?

Maybe it's the cops and they are here to tell me that they found whoever is responsible, making my research a moot point.

I'm almost hopeful of the second thought when I reach the door and open it, but that hope quickly disappears when I see a woman standing on the other side and not a detective.

At least I don't think she's a detective.

She's beautiful and from the way she is dressed, very well put together. Her honey-colored hair is half up and half down, the style fitting her face perfectly. She looks young and doesn't look like she belongs in my apartment building.

"Can I help you?" I ask, my voice sounding like it hasn't been used in days.

Thinking about it, I don't think I've said a word since the funeral.

"Arianna Vitale?" Even her voice is like honey.

"Yes?" There is a questioning tone in my words.

"My name is Ella Vincent, I'm with the Lane Family Foundation and I'm here in regard to your father's death."

The Lane Family Foundation?

What the fuck?

What does one of the richest family in Chicago want to do with me and my dad's death?

"What about my father's death?" I ask, on high alert now.

Ella gives me a small smile before she looks around the hallway. She must realize that she sticks out like a sore thumb, especially with that big ol' diamond that she is wearing on her finger.

"Maybe we can have this conversation inside?" she suggests, looking over my shoulder into my apartment.

I don't really want this strange woman in my space, but I still open the door wider and wave her in.

The second I close the door; I realize just how much of a mess the place is.

"Sorry," I mutter as I make my way to the small couch I have across from my bed.

"No worries. I know it's been a rough couple of weeks for you," she says, taking a seat on the couch, her back slouching a bit.

"Yeah, it has," I say, following her lead and taking a seat of my own before turning to her. "What does my father's death have to do with the Lane family?"

Growing up in Chicago, I spent the majority of my life hearing about the elusive Lanes. There are so many rumors about them that nobody knows what is true and what isn't. I do know that they own most of the buildings in the city and they do a lot to support the people that live here. Of course, I also know the patriarch of the family is Bennett Lane, who up until a few years ago was considered the city's most eligible bachelor.

Never have I crossed paths with the family and all I know about them comes from all the rumors and news articles that have been circulating around throughout the years.

I know my dad never met Mr. Lane. Or maybe he had since there is so much that I didn't know until recently. But that doesn't answer why the hell a person working with the Foundation is sitting on my couch right now.

"Mr. Lane heard about your father's death and unfortunately was out of town for the service, but he still wanted to make a donation to pay his respect," she tells me.

I watch as Ella reaches into her purse and takes out a white envelope before she extends it to me.

Wary, I take and open it as if confetti were to pop out the second, I slide my finger under the flap.

I take the piece of paper out and flip it over and the second I see that it's a check and what is written on the front, I feel my jaw go slack.

Five hundred thousand dollars and it's made out to my name.

The other shocking part? The check is coming straight from Bennett Lane himself and not from his foundation.

What the fuck?

"I'm sorry, but did Mr. Lane know my father?" I ask.

Maybe he did, and my dad never told me because who gives a random stranger half a million dollars?

I can feel tears stinging at the back of my eyes as I continue to look down at the piece of paper in my hands.

This amount of money can change so much.

"Their paths did cross a time or two. Mr. Lane is a big supporter of the Chicago Police Department and knew the type of detective that your father was. When he heard of his death, he wanted to do something to help."

Finally, I look up at Ella. "Giving me a check with this many zeros, is helping?"

Ella lets out a sigh. "Bennett, Mr. Lane, knows just how much pain comes with the death of a parent. He also knows of the struggle that one goes through financially to take care of everything that they left behind. He wants to make that process easier and the only way he can think of doing that is through that check."

"And if I decline his help?"

"Then I'm sure somehow that amount of money will show up in your bank account in the next couple of days."

I want to laugh at her words but the look on her face tells me she is one-hundred-percent serious.

Who the fuck is this family?

I look back at the check.

This amount of money can really help. Especially, to pay off the debt I acquired with paying for the funeral. As for the rest, my bank account currently sits at one dollar and fifteen cents, so I'm sure I can find something to do with it.

And like Ella said, I can pay off some of the stuff that my dad left behind.

Would taking this money be a bad thing?

Surely if Mr. Lane didn't want me using it, he wouldn't have offered this much.

I nod as I feel tears, those filled with gratitude and not those of sadness, roll down my cheek.

I look over at Ella. "Thank you. Thank you to Mr. Lane. He didn't need to do this."

She gives me a small smile. "He wanted to make sure that you were taken care of for at least a little bit."

"Thank you." I give her another appreciative nod.

"Of course," she says, standing up from the couch and making her way over to the door. Halfway through my small living room though, she turns back in my direction. "Can I speak out of turn, Miss Vitale?"

"Um..." Is she going to lecture me on how to use the money? "Sure."

Her whole demeanor changes. When she was sitting on the couch, she was relaxed but now it's as if she's ready to go into battle.

"I know that you may have a lot of questions when it comes to what happened to your father. The rumors circulating around definitely don't help putting those questions at bay, but if I could offer you a piece of advice, it would be this. Don't go looking into things that aren't meant for you. Especially not into anything that has to do with Dante Rosetti."

Dante Rosetti?

"I'm sorry. I think I'm missing something. Who's Dante Rosetti?"

As I ask the question a faint memory pops into my head from last year sometime when I was having dinner over at my dad's house and he got a call. I remember he walked out of the room to take it, but before he was fully out of earshot, I heard him say one thing, Rosetti.

Is it the same Rosetti that Ella is talking about now?

I look at Ella, and she turns to the table where my laptop sits.

Following her line of vision, I see that the link I had clicked on earlier finally loaded and opened up to a picture of a man. The picture looks like a mug shot, and a man with dark hair and an olive skin tone a bit darker than mine stares through the screen.

It's a simple picture, but it feels like there is nothing simple about the man in it.

I don't have to ask to know that this man is dangerous and shouldn't be crossed.

"That is Dante Rosetti," Ella states, taking me out of whatever trance that picture has put me in. "Only a few people know who he is, but some in Chicago know him as The Devil and you should stay away from anything that has to do with him."

The Devil has a name.

I'm faintly still aware that Ella is still in the room. I don't pay her any attention. No, I continue to look at the screen on my table as if it's going to change in a few seconds.

This is the so-called Devil of Chicago. Not only do I now have a name, but I also have a visual of what he looks like.

Now I can really dig. This is what I needed to start my journey to bring down those that went after my father.

And I will start with Dante Rosetti, because if the rumors are true and he's the reason my dad is dead, then he's the one that has to suffer first.

The only thing that I must do is figure out how to do just that.

How do you destroy a man that goes by the name The Devil, for everything that he has?

3

———

ARIANNA

Ella left soon after she told me who Dante Rosetti was.

When she said the word devil it was like everything around me was forgotten and I was only concentrating on that. I didn't even realize she had excused herself and left until I turned to ask her a question and noticed I was alone.

I had so many questions roaming through my head about Dante Rosetti that I wanted to ask but I missed my opportunity.

The article that I had clicked on before Ella showed up was no help. It was a puff piece talking about how they suspected that Dante Rosetti was indeed in fact the person they called The Devil. The person that ran all the crime rings in Chicago, but there it was merely opinions and nothing concrete.

Nothing that tied him to killings that happened in poor

neighborhoods around the city or even the drug trade, just suspicions.

I abandoned the article and looked more into who Dante Rosetti actually was.

From what I found, I know he is well-off and is a member of high society. I know he's Italian and is the owner of one of the most prestigious strip clubs in the state, if not the country.

On paper, Dante Rosetti is clean, too clean if you ask me but if Ella's warning was anything, I know that this man is the exact opposite of the person he portrays to be.

The man that goes by the name Dante Rosetti may have come out clean in my research, but the one that goes by the other name, The Devil, did not.

Police and reporters describe him to be the main crime boss in Cook County. The Mafia boss they say. The monster. The ruler of the underworld.

This man is tied to more than a hundred murders. He may have not pulled the trigger in all of them, but the police are certain that he was the one behind them. The one that called for them to happen. From the looks of it, people have been trying to bring down this man for years, and not once have they come close to succeeding.

Or even being able come up with evidence that tells them that Rosetti and the devil are the same person.

Looking through all the articles, I couldn't help but wonder if my dad was close. Maybe he was working on something that could bring this person down.

To bring Rosetti down.

And if he had gotten close to succeeding, then that has

to be why he was killed, right? He had to have found something that ultimately cost him his life.

The only way to find that out is to disregard Ella Vincent's warning and go after this man. Because the more I learn about him, the more I know that Dante Rosetti had a hand in my father's death. I need to find out for sure and if I am right, I won't hesitate to tie him to a chair and give him the same beating my last living parent received and leave him for dead.

How I will achieve that, I have no idea.

As of right now there are a few ideas swimming through my head, but the more I think about them the more the doubt of them actually working sinks in.

But I have to try.

I have to try to bring this man down because I'm sure once he is out of the picture, anyone else involved in this will crumble.

Dante Rosetti is the main character in this, so it's fitting that he goes first.

Step one in doing this, is getting out of the mourning cloud that my head is in and show the world I started living again even if I haven't.

And what better way to keep that act up, that there is life after losing a parent, than to go back to work?

When my dad died, Jimmy, the owner of the bar where I work at, told me that I could take off as much time as I needed.

With the money that Bennett Lane gave me, I don't have to go back, but if I didn't go back, it would raise a few eyebrows. I, Arianna Vitale, am not the type of person to just quit her job because of money. I have to be strategic about this and acting as if my life is somewhat normal is the way to go.

Besides the bar is what I like to call a watering hole for business-type men. Men that may know a thing or two about how one would find themselves involved with Rosetti.

From what I've seen and heard from these people, some of them are more than willing to talk with the promise of a young mouth blowing their popsicle behind their wife's back.

Even if I think that type of thing is wrong on so many levels, to get the information I want I wouldn't be opposed to using my body. I just hope that it doesn't have to come to that.

Yet that didn't stop me from leaving my apartment twenty minutes ago wearing a tight pair of jeans and a low-cut shirt.

Anything to help with getting the information I need, no matter how much self-respect I lose.

I pull open the door to the bar and instantly I'm met with the scent of greasy food, beer and loud music.

For a second, I'm back to the night that turned my world upside down. As much as I want to cry, I don't. I push it to the side and slap a smile on my face, and walk in.

As soon as my foot is over the threshold, a few of the regulars greet me and so do some of the waitresses. A few of them give sad smiles but I ignore them and continue back to Jimmy's office.

The door is slightly ajar, so when I knock and he sees that it's me, he waves me in.

"Ari, what are you doing here? I thought you would be out longer," he says, giving me a look of concern.

I shrug a bit. "I need a distraction, so I thought I would come and see if you needed some help for a few hours."

It's not a total lie at least.

Jimmy's face changes as a smile replaces the concerns.

"Of course, sweetheart. I was actually thinking about calling you in because we've been a little swamped, but I didn't want to take away from your time. Work however long you want today."

Jimmy is a nice guy and definitely not what you would expect him to be as a bar owner. He's like the neighborhood grandpa, always looking out for his employees.

"Thank you, Jimmy."

"Anytime. If you need someone to talk to, I'm here."

I give him one final nod and make my way back to the front to get started on my shift.

Or should I say, my recon?

One of the waitresses, Cora, sees me as I tie on my apron and approaches me with a big smile.

"How are you sweetie?" she asks before taking me in a tight hug.

The warmness of it takes me by surprise but I realize that this is what I've been missing these last few weeks. A hug from someone that cares about me. Maybe not on the level of my dad, but still cares, nonetheless.

So, I bask in it for a few seconds longer than needed.

"I'm getting better," I say when she lets me go. "I

needed to get out of my own head though, so I thought that I would come in for a few hours."

Cora placed a hand on my shoulder and looks down at me with a sad smile. Everyone looks at me with a sad smile nowadays.

"Well, I'm glad you're here. Why don't you work on tables eleven through fifteen and we'll see where the night takes us?"

I give her a curt nod. "Sounds good."

Right away, I get back into the groove of things. The thoughts of what happened the last time I worked, are still playing on repeat in my head but it's nothing that I can't smile through.

At least I think I'm smiling through them.

A few regulars do stop me to give me their condolences and I try my hardest to not let the tears roll on through when I hear their words.

About three hours after I arrive, Cora tells me to take a quick break, so I grab some food from the kitchen and situate myself in one of the booths in the back corner.

It's as I'm eating my fries when a conversation between a woman and man catches my attention.

Most of the time I'm not one to pry into what people are saying but when I hear what they are talking about, I'm all ears. More so, given the information that I've been seeking.

"He's having the interviews at *Perversa*," the male says in a hush tone.

Perversa.

I know that word. I've seen it countless times in the last few days.

It's the name of Dante Rosetti's club.

They are talking about his club.

Fuck, I knew coming to the bar was going to be beneficial, but I didn't think it would be this quick.

My insides want to jump for joy, but I keep myself in control and listen to the rest of what they say. Especially if it has to do with that club and Rosetti.

"Really? I would have thought that he would have had them somewhere else," the woman interjects.

"Would you want a strange woman in your private space? I wouldn't. I think he's smart for having them there. Vets the ones that are serious about the position," the man tells her.

I'm trying to piece all the information together, but whatever they are talking about is just jumbled up pieces

Is *he* in this conversation, Rosetti? It has to be, right?

"I guess you're right. Think I should apply?" I can hear hope in the woman's voice, like this is her moment to shine.

"To tell you the truth, you may have the experience, but to work under Dante Rosetti is a hard feat. Especially with this type of position. I say you skip this one."

The woman lets out a loud sigh that even I can hear. "But I'm sure it's good money."

The man snorts. "I'm sure it is, but..." He pauses and for a few seconds I think that I missed what he said but then I hear a whisper. "You don't want to be working for The Devil."

A chill runs down my spine when I hear the words. I don't know why, but it does something to me, and I don't know if it's a good or bad thing.

"Yeah, that is true. I feel bad for whatever girl he picks," the woman muses in a normal voice.

"Whoever it is, that person and every single person that interviews for the position has balls. I wouldn't even be able to make it through the doors of *Perversa*." I swear the guy shudders as he says the words.

What can possibly be so bad about a strip club? I've never been, but it can't be so bad that it would make a grown man shudder.

"Do you know when he's doing it? I may know a friend that would be interested in applying. She knows how to work with those types of men."

"This Friday. I think she has to call *Perversa* and speak to an Evelyn about it, but that's all I know," the guy answers her, and then he shifts the conversation to something else.

My food is all but forgotten as I piece together everything that the pair had said.

Dante Rosetti is interviewing women at his club this coming Friday.

He's probably looking for new dancers for his lineup and since it's the most exclusive club there is, he is only hiring one.

This could be my chance.

If I interview, there is a chance that he could pick me, and I would have a direct line to him. I would be able to get close enough to come up with something to put an end to him.

I've worked in a bar for years and I know a thing or two about showing off my body for tips. There might be a chance that I can get this position. If it doesn't work, then I will come up with something else, but for right now, this is it. This is all I got.

This is what I have to do.

With my mind set, I grab my plate and head to the restroom to look up the number for the club.

As I reach the back door, I come up with a plan.

I will interview with Dante Rosetti, I will show him I'm the best girl for the job. Then I will keep my fingers crossed that he picks me.

And if he does, I will work to bring him down from the inside out. I will hit him where it hurts, and he will never see a thing coming.

Just like my father never saw his death coming.

Dante Rosetti will be the first to pay for his actions, and it will be at my hands.

Once he's down, I will move on to whoever else had a hand in my father's killing.

Hopefully this works.

4

ARIANNA

It's Friday.

It has officially been over one week since I buried my father. I'm struggling emotionally and mentally and all that I want to do is call him and ask him about his day.

But I don't have the ability to do that anymore. I don't have the ability to pick up the phone and call my dad just because I want to hear his voice or to tell him about everything that's on my mind.

Because it was taken away from me.

To distract myself, I've been trying to concentrate on other things. Work has been one of them, but a close second has been figuring out what to do with the check that has been burning a hole in my wallet.

That second one was a little hard, but after a while I was able to figure something out. It was hard to see the number dwindle but in the end it was helpful.

With a small percentage, I paid off the small amount of

credit card debt that my dad had and whatever was left on the mortgage for the brownstone.

Paying off the house was something I debated over. I never want to step foot through the front door ever again, but I couldn't just let the bank take it. It was my childhood home. It was the last place I saw my parents happy. So, I'm going to keep it until I figure out what to do with it.

Another small percentage of the money went toward my rent for the remainder of the year, and to pay off all the debt I acquired from the funeral. The rest was put away for safekeeping. At the moment there was no need for it.

Especially if I start a new job.

Because today is Friday and there is an interview looming.

Today is the day that interviews are being held at *Perversa.* On top of wanting to call my dad and the money, this is the third thing that has been on my mind.

This one overpowering the first two.

I spent hours trying to find any information I could about Rosetti and who he is and the type of relationship he may have had with my dad.

But I came up empty.

So, I put my concentration somewhere else. The interview.

I had called the club after hearing it from the man at the bar, and weirdly enough it was easy to get through and talk to the woman named Evelyn. All I had to do was tell her my name and tell her if I had a college degree, which I do.

When she asked me for my name though, I froze,

debating if I should give her my real one. She was connected to Rosetti after all, maybe giving it to her would set off alarms. So, I decided not to, and I gave her the name Arianna Amato. Amato being my mother's maiden name.

After that she just gave me my time slot and told me to wear something somewhat professional. It was right before she hung up that I asked what the position was, and she told me that I would find that out during the interview.

That part I found strange. If the couple at the bar knew what the position was, why couldn't I?

But I didn't get to ask that because Evelyn hung up a few seconds after.

The process of actually getting an interview was surprisingly easy. You would think if you were going to be interviewed by an elusive mob boss that there would be a lot more hoops to jump through to be able to get in.

After the phone call, I tried to look up the position online. I just wanted to be somewhat prepared, but I couldn't find anything.

There was nothing talking about the club holding auditions for new girls and I didn't hear anybody else at the bar say another word about it.

I even tried to ask Cora if she had heard anything, but she shut me down the second I said the club's name. She told me to stay as far away from there as I could, that sure the money was good but that type of place would eat me alive.

I should have listened to Cora.

I should have also listened to Ella Vincent and stayed

away, because now I'm standing outside of the club late in the afternoon feeling as if I'm about to burst into flames.

Not because of the nature of the club itself but because I feel like the second I step in, people are going to look right through me and see me as a fraud.

I am a fraud. I'm only here because I want to take down the owner, not to work.

Am I a foolish person for thinking that this might be a logical plan?

Do I really think that I can take down a powerful man by inserting myself into his business?

I'm just a twenty-four-year-old girl, for crying out loud.

As I watch people walk past the front door of the establishment, I contemplate if what I'm doing is even a safe idea.

I shouldn't insert myself like this. I should just let the police take care of finding my father's killer and making sure whoever it is, is put behind bars for the rest of their lives.

They must already have a list of suspects and without a doubt have to have Rosetti at the top. Because who else would want a respected detective dead?

They should be taking care of this, they should be inserting themselves into this world, not me.

But maybe instead of playing executioner, I can find information that will not only put Rosetti behind bars but countless others as well. Maybe I can help the police put the bad people away once and for all. Even if I want to tie each and every one of them to a chair and torture and watch them suffer just like my dad did.

And maybe by doing this, I will find something. Maybe I will find something that pins Rosetti to all of this because my gut tells me that he is the one that wanted my dad dead. He's the one that called the hit and maybe even delivered the fatal blows.

Maybe...

"Are you going in?" a voice says from behind me.

After jumping a bit at the proximity of the voice, I turn to see a woman dressed as if she's going to a business meeting standing about two feet away from me.

On the call Evelyn told me to dress somewhat professional and as I look at the lady in front of me, I see I'm clearly way underdressed.

My somewhat professional consists of new black suede knee highs and a black dress that has no real shape to it that hits just below my knee.

"Going in where?" I asked as if I don't know what she's talking about. Of course, I know, but my mind is so boggled with the thought of taking down Rosetti that I can't think straight.

"Into Perversa," she replies, her eyebrows bunching a bit in confusion. "For the interviews?" The woman looks me up and down as if she is assessing me. "Is that not the reason why you are standing outside?"

"Um..." why am I having trouble with words? "Yes, I'm here for the interviews. I'm just trying to work up the courage to walk in. Jitters and all that." I throw a weird chuckle out at the end.

She nods. "Understandable, why don't I walk in with you? To help with any jitters you may have."

Is this woman the house mom or something? Is it her job to stand outside and make sure that every person that is here today goes to the right place?

I could walk away from her, but I find myself giving her a nod. "Yes, thank you. That would be very helpful."

She waves for me to follow her in.

"Arianna, right?" she asks as she holds the door open for me.

There is no going back now.

"Yes, but everyone calls me Ari," I say, walking through the door and being instantly engulfed in darkness.

We're in a hallway and I can't even make out where the woman is until there is a knock somewhere and another door opens.

"It's nice to meet you, Ari," the woman says once I can see her again, a smile on her face. "I'm Evelyn."

So, this is Evelyn.

I don't know why but when I pictured her, I saw someone much older, maybe with a head full of grays, but this woman looks nothing like that. Her hair is in a sophisticated bun without a strand out of place and most likely in her early to midforties. She is absolutely gorgeous. I bet there are countless women that want to look like her one day.

Evelyn directs me through the second door that is being guarded by two very intimidating men. I swear they both snarl at me as we walk by.

They calm down when after Evelyn tells them what I'm here for and they give me a quick pat down.

"Are you the manager of the club?" I ask her as we walk

through yet another hallway that looks as if it's covered in velvet.

"No, I work for the owner."

"Oh, okay." If I wasn't freaking out about this already, I sure as hell am now. This woman works for Rosetti and for all I know she knows who I am and is planning to kill me just like they did my dad.

I really didn't think this whole thing through.

"You have nothing to worry about. I'm sure you will do fine, it's just a simple interview," she throws back when we reach the end of the second hallway.

Another door opens and we finally walk into the club.

Online it said that this club was the epitome of class and opulence but seeing it in person is a whole different experience.

It's dark, but not dark enough to not see all the leather, the reds and the crystals. If I didn't know this club was owned by Dante Rosetti, I would find the place breathtaking.

I think this is the one strip club that I wouldn't mind dancing in. There is no doubt in my mind that the girls that dance here make thousands each and every night.

"A simple interview," I whisper mostly to myself.

An interview with someone that most of the city of Chicago fears, doesn't scream out "simple."

Evelyn continues to guide me through the main portion of the club, and I finally notice that there is nobody here. That seems a little odd given that it's a Friday.

"Is the club closed?" I ask Evelyn as she guides me through yet another hallway.

"It doesn't open until ten this evening," Evelyn says before she opens a door that leads to a room that does not match the rest of the place.

It looks like a living room, covered in all white and gray.

The vast contrast of this room has me feeling more nervous than walking past the reds and leathers.

I look over at Evelyn and she just gives me a smile.

"Wait here, let me see if he's finished with the last interview before I bring you in." She excuses herself and heads to a dark wooden door on the opposite wall. She knocks before stepping in and shutting the door behind her.

Taking a deep breath, I take a seat on one of the cream-colored couches and try to relax as best as I can.

I really should have listened to Cora when she told me to stay away from this place. I have no idea what I have gotten myself into.

Never in my life have I heard of a strip club having auditions like this. I always heard that they were on stage and that you had to show whoever was hiring what you can contribute. I've heard that you have to show every inch of your body.

But given the way Evelyn is dressed, this interview must be way more sophisticated. This isn't any normal strip club, it's for the elite and the powerful.

Fuck, I think I'm going to puke.

The door opens and Evelyn comes out with a bright smile.

"Okay, he is ready for you," She says a little too brightly for the situation.

I give her a nod and stand up from my seat, smoothing down my dress in the process.

"Remember it's just a simple interview. You have nothing to worry about, you will do great."

The way my heart is beating, I have everything to worry about.

"Are you not coming in with me?" I think having her in the room will stop me from puking all over the place.

"I will walk you in but then it will just be you and Mr. Rosetti for the remainder of the interview."

Of course, it will be.

I try to ignore the tightness in my chest as she opens the door and waves for me to walk in before her.

I'm about to enter a room that is occupied by one of the most powerful individuals that the city has to offer.

I can do this.

I can do this.

Please God, let me do this.

Taking another deep breath, I enter the room and once again I'm astonished by the vast contrast between this room and the one I was just in.

The other room was light and had a home feel to it.

This room, this office, feels cold and everything about it makes me feel unwelcome. It does have the same gray color scheme but this one is much darker and very much looks like a businessman uses it daily. If I can think of one thing to say about this room, it's that I hate it.

I hate it so much and I have no reasoning behind it.

There is a clearing of a throat somewhere and when I look around, I see him.

Dante Rosetti, the man that I've seen in countless articles online, is sitting on a leather chair in the corner, with his right foot propped on his left knee and a crystal glass in his hand.

The pictures that I've seen of this man do not do him justice. The more I look at him, the more I can see things that the pictures don't show.

I can see that his eyes are a light brown that doesn't match the darkness of his hair.

I can see that his jaw is profound and his skin looks as if it would be silky smooth.

He's older than what he looks in the pictures, but he still looks too young to be a crime boss or a Mafia man. This man has to be in his mid to late thirties. He could even be younger than that.

I swallow once more as he brings his glass up to his lips and takes a drink, his eyes traveling up my body in the process.

I let out a shiver at the action, but not from fear. I can't explain it but all the fear that I was feeling when I walked into the room a few seconds ago is completely gone.

The fear should still be there, because there is a possibility, a large one at that, that this man knows who I am. There's a possibility that he can kill me the second Evelyn leaves because I came looking for answers when I shouldn't.

"Mr. Rosetti, this is Ari Amato," Evelyn says, walking into the room before turning to face me and for the first time I take my eyes off the man. "This is your last interview."

The room goes still for a few seconds before Rosetti moves and places his drink on the small table next to him.

He throws a nod in Evelyn's direction. "Thank you, Evelyn. I will let you know when we're done here."

"Of course, sir," she says with a smile before she turns to and leaves.

She leaves me in the same room as the one they call The Devil.

The fear is back.

"Take a seat, Ms. Amato," Rosetti directs me, extending a hand over to the couch that is across from his chair.

Without showing any fear, I do what he says, placing my purse on the floor next to my feet and facing him straight on.

"I apologize for this type of interview, Ms. Amato. Given the business that I run I have to be very careful with the type of people I let inside."

My shoulders relax a bit as he continues to use the name Amato and not anything else. He doesn't know who I am. I'm taking that as a good thing.

There is also something about his voice that has me relaxing into the couch even more.

"That is something I understand very well, sir." I try to

give him a smile but I'm not sure if it comes out as a friendly one.

"How old are you?"

"I'm twenty-four, sir." I say and I get a nod in return.

"And are you okay with working late nights?" His face shows no emotion, as if he is sick and tired of all these questions at this point.

I nod. "Yes, I am very okay with working late. However late you need me, I will be there," I say as if I'm dedicated to any job that this man offers me.

I will be, just as long as I get the information I want in the process and see him get brought down.

He gives me a nod before taking his drink in his hand once again and taking a sip.

"Then should we talk about your qualifications?" he says, his rough enunciation causing a shiver to roll through my body.

"Yes, of course."

This is the portion of the interview where the outfit I chose comes to play. This is a strip club after all.

I mentally prepared for this part. I just should have mentally prepared for only him and me in the room and not more people.

I give Rosetti my full attention, not once taking my eyes off his as I stand up to full height.

A dark eyebrow lifts up in question, but I continue with my motions.

Placing a hand on my strap, I lower it in the most seductive way I can.

Once the strap of my dress, that is a scoop neck, is at

the top of my breast, I move to the next one, never taking my eyes off the man in front of me.

I don't know if he likes what he sees, because his face shows no emotion.

So, once I lower the second strap, I pull the top of the dress down to reveal my fully bare breasts.

This is what causes a reaction.

First, it's the glass that gets slammed against the table, then it's Rosetti standing from his seat and then it's the yelling.

"What the actual fuck do you think you are doing?!"

5

DANTE

When Miss Ari Amato walked into my office, I thought my eyes were playing a cruel joke on me.

Or should I say when Arianna Vitale walked in?

Why she used a fake name is beyond me.

I may be a recluse but did this woman really think that I wouldn't know who the fuck she was the second she walked into my office?

Given who her father was, given my relationship with him, of course I knew. I've known her name and seen countless pictures since I met her father almost twenty years ago. She's not as forgettable to me as she may be to others.

The world must have wanted to torture me having Joseph Vitale's daughter within a few feet from me. Having her not only in my club but in my personal space. Seeing her walk in was like a punishment for each and every sin that I have ever committed in my life.

Why was Joseph Vitale's daughter in my office at the moment? I have no fucking idea. From what I know she had no clue about my dealings with her father but maybe her old man's death is causing her to dig into the life he lived these last few years. I wouldn't put it past her. From what he told me of her, she's a very smart girl.

Maybe she thinks I'm the reason the man is dead.

Or maybe she's here for the actual job and I'm just assuming the worst of her.

I was thinking that. I was thinking that she was really here for the job but then she stood up. She stood up, and her shapeless dress fell to her knees and her eyes never left mine.

Then she started to push down her dress. At first, I thought that she was just adjusting the strap like I had seen countless women do before, but then I took in her seductive manner. I saw the way her body swayed as if there was music playing in the background.

Now her eyes bore into mine as she continues on to the next strap and I don't know what it is about this girl, but I'm fucking captivated.

Every one of her movements, I watch like a hawk, not wanting to miss whatever she does next.

Her eyes seemed to be filled with fear but also with lust. She's enjoying being watched like this.

She is moving to lower the neckline and for a second, I contemplate letting whatever she's planning on doing to continue.

I contemplate demanding that she get on her knees

and let me stroke myself to the visual of her chest and then finish off by giving her a glistening pearl necklace.

Her tits look like a fucking handful and I want to mark them as mine.

But just as quickly as those thoughts arrive, I push them away when I remember why exactly we are currently in my office.

I remember who her father was.

The glass of scotch that I have in my hand, shakes at the amount of force that is exuding from my grip and when I slam it on the table, it nearly shatters.

Without even thinking, I'm on my feet looking down and I can feel anger starting to boil within me.

"What the actual fuck do you think you are doing?!"

My voice vibrates through the room and instantly Arianna's eyes grow wide with surprise, and she starts to cover herself up with her hands.

"I'm sorry? I thought I was interviewing for the position." Her voice shakes as she says the word, fear clouding her eyes even more. All signs of lust gone instantly.

I move closer, towering over her small, curvaceous frame. "And what exactly do you think this position is?" I say through my teeth.

"To be a dancer here or a bartender, at the very least," she says, stepping away from me.

That's why she's dressed the way that she is. A black dress that cuts at her knee and leaves everything to the imagination and don't get me started on those boots. The second I laid eyes on them, I was picturing them pressing against my ears while I ate her pussy raw.

Her clothes are definitely a change from what I've seen the other women I met with today wear. And here I thought she was making a statement, not because she was auditioning to be one of my strippers.

I try to hold my anger back as much as possible. I feel the urge to protect her, to get her out of here. Thinking of how Joseph wouldn't want her here. Or even for me for me, for that matter.

"Well, it's fucking not. Did you even bother to ask Evelyn when you called or when she brought you in what exactly you were interviewing for?"

Arianna shakes her head, and I have the urge to grab the glass on the table and throw it against the wall for no reason other than I'm pissed she's here

"How the fuck did you hear about this position?"

Only a select few knew that I was looking for someone. Because of how protective I am of the subject, I stopped Evelyn from even posting the listing online. I needed someone that I could trust and not someone random off the streets that thought that they could get in bed with me.

Is that what sweet Arianna wanted? To get in bed with me? Is that why she's here? Daddy's death must have cost her a fortune and maybe sleeping with me was a way to pay off that debt.

Well, it's not going to fucking happen. No matter how much I want her to lower her arms and let me ogle at her chest.

I need to fucking forget about her tits.

I need to remember who she is and how I can never

touch her. Not because of who she lost, but because of who I lost.

"I heard some people at the bar I work at talking about it. And since I'm in a tough place financially, I thought I would look for something that would pay better."

Tough place financially. I was right, I guess. Her father's funeral did put her back. Either way, I can feel my jaw tic, which causes her to cower back even more.

"Put your dress back on," I throw out before heading over to my desk and calling for Evelyn.

The sooner Arianna is out of here, the better.

I had one Vitale involved in my business, I don't need another.

"Yes, sir?" Evelyn says through the phone intercom.

"We're done," I grunt out, not even letting her respond before I release the button.

I look over at Arianna and she has finally covered her chest and has her arms wrapped around herself in a protective manner.

"Can I ask what the position really is?" she throws out, her voice sounding a lot smaller than it did when she first walked in.

"No, you cannot," I answer.

"Please? Maybe I could still be of help in some way? You never know, maybe I really am qualified for the position."

I can't help but snort. "You're a qualified nanny?"

That takes her by surprise. "A nanny?"

"Yes, a fucking nanny. These interviews weren't for new

dancers or bartenders for the club, Ms. Amato. I was looking for a new caretaker for my children."

I use the fake name that she gave because if I use her real one that will just cause her to throw questions at me that she shouldn't know the answers to.

Though I do suspect that she is here for more than just finding another job.

Because what a fucking coincidence that only a few weeks ago a cop comes up dead, my name gets thrown around in the mix of possible assailants and now his daughter is here for a job?

There is definitely more to this, I know there is.

"Oh," Arianna voices, like she doesn't know what else to say. "I didn't know you had children."

"It's not public knowledge," I tell her through gritted teeth.

There are people in this city that think they know every fucking detail about me, that they know the type of man that I am.

Yes, I'm a killer. Yes, people should be afraid of me, and yes, I hold secrets, but that doesn't define who I am outside of the city limits.

They don't know I'm a father or that up until early this year, I was a husband.

And I will keep it that way until the day I die.

"Oh," she says again, cowering deeper into herself.

My attention moves from Arianna to Evelyn, who just walked into the office looking surprised that I finished the interview earlier than expected.

"You can escort Ms. Amato out. We're done," I tell her

before taking a seat at my desk, waking up my computer in the process.

"Are you sure?" Evelyn asks and when I look at her, she has an eyebrow raised at me.

Look, Evelyn is a few years older than me, so she thinks she has this ability to tell me when I'm wrong. She calls it a big sister looking out for her little brother.

We're not related, and I see it as a fucking pain in the ass.

"Yes, I'm sure, Evelyn. Escort Ms. Amato out." I swear if I have to tell her again, I'm going to grab something and throw it against the wall.

My assistant gives me a nod and then turns her attention to our guest.

"Wait," Arianna says, walking over my desk.

"I can be a nanny. I have my CPR certification and I have a degree in child development. I also babysat all through college." As she speaks, she bites her bottom lip in the process. Out of fear or nervousness, I don't know.

"Babysitting and being a nanny are two different things, Ms. Amato," I throw back at her.

"I know but I can learn. I can learn to do the job that you need me to do." The way she says the words tells me that she wants this job a little too much. Like my suspicions are right and she's here for something other than the job.

I'm already shaking my head before she finishes. "I'm afraid that this isn't a 'learn as you go' type of job, Ms. Amato. I need someone with actual experience, not someone that is going to call me every time one of the kids' cries. Now I'm asking you to leave, I have work to do and this conversation with you is just setting me back."

She looks at me with brown eyes that have so many questions floating in them. It makes me wonder if she actually has the balls to ask them.

After a second or twenty, she finally moves her line of vision somewhere else and gives me a nod.

"Thank you for taking the time out of your day to meet with me," she says before she starts to walk to the door.

I don't say a word, I just concentrate on whatever spreadsheet I have open on my computer screen.

I think that I'm finally free of her presence when she speaks again. "I'm really good with kids, Mr. Rosetti. My experience working at a bar may not be a good way to prove that, but if you need references, I can get them for you. I'm not saying that you have to hire me, but it is an option, especially if you've interviewed a number of people and still haven't found one. Goodbye, Mr. Rosetti."

There are words at the tip of my tongue that I want to say as I watch her leave the office with Evelyn behind her, but I don't.

She may be right.

In the last three weeks I've interviewed close to fifty individuals for this position and not one of them has seemed right.

There were a few people that I thought were contenders but when I looked deeper into who they were, they quickly were taken off the list.

Maybe I should hire Arianna, but I have a feeling that if I hire her, it will come and bite me in the ass.

Joseph wouldn't want that.

No, he wouldn't.

Shaking my head, I get to work looking over the numbers from the past month for the club.

I'm able to get through five pages before my door flies open and Evelyn comes storming in.

"Why in the world would you end that interview early?" She sounds angry. Evelyn is always angry with me. That sweet voice she uses when people are around is just an act to get under my skin.

I don't look at my assistant as I answer. "Did you vet Ms. Amato before bringing her in here?"

"Yes, I ran the number she called from, and she came back clean. Name discrepancy aside," she snaps out.

I look at her with a raised eyebrow. "Well maybe if you had done a better job, you would have known that she thought that she was here for a dancing position, not to be a fucking nanny."

Evelyn's mouth falls slightly open. "Did she…?"

"Did she strip? She started to. I saw her fucking tits before I stopped the interview. I thought that you were vetting these people."

She lets out a sigh and actually looks apologetic over this. "I'm sorry. She asked what the position was, and I just told her that she would find out today."

I grind my teeth at her answer.

"Don't do it again. Now let's move on and get me another list of people for the job." I turn back to my computer, dismissing her, but she doesn't move. "What?"

"Maybe Ari was right. Maybe you should go in a

different direction with this. We don't have anyone yet. We can give her a try and if she doesn't work out, we start over."

Who is this person and what the hell has happened to my agreeable assistant?

I want that person, and not the one standing in front of me.

But I'm tired of this shit, so I ignore her comment.

"Get me a new list of people for the position," I say through my teeth to drive my point.

Evelyn looks at me for a few seconds as if she is thinking of challenging me, but she gives up quickly.

"Yes, sir." She turns to leave but I stop her before she can step through the threshold.

"If you see Honor, can you please send her in?"

Evelyn gives me a scowl but nods either way and is on her way.

I shouldn't have requested Honor and I didn't need Evelyn's facial expression to tell me that, but after being tormented by Arianna's full tits, I need a distraction.

Honor, one of the main girls here at the club and someone that doesn't mind the no-strings-attached shit, is the perfect distraction.

Within five minutes of Evelyn leaving, there is a knock at my door and Honor walks in with her tiny outfit for the night.

The woman wastes no time, dropping to her knees instantly next to my chair and soon I'm enjoying the feel of her warm mouth around my dick.

It may be no pearl necklace, but it will do.

6

ARIANNA

I run out the door before Evelyn can tell the security guard to let me through. I don't even turn to thank her for giving me the opportunity to interview or for being just a nice woman in general.

Even if I ruined it before it could even start.

Because of course he was looking for a nanny for his kids and not for a new dancer.

As I walk down the street, I can't help but think that I was foolish for even thinking that I would be lucky enough to be in the same room as Rosetti, let alone be able to work for the man.

The plan was stupid from the very beginning. Why I even thought that someone like me would be able to get close enough to destroy a man like that from the inside out is way beyond me.

Like I figured out before I walked into the club, I should let the police handle my dad's case and let them figure it out for themselves. Let them figure out that it might actually be Rosetti who was behind it.

That's what I should do, but why is my mind already working up ways to get back into proximity with him?

Because being that close to him made you feel something you never have before.

It really did.

The whole way to my apartment, that thought circulates in my mind. Being in the same room as Dante Rosetti, made me fearful and nervous of course but there was something else that I can't pinpoint.

Was it just curiosity about the man sitting a few feet away at play?

No, it was something else.

The way he spoke to me, the way his eyes traveled down my body assessing me when I first walked in and the way his eyes bore into me when I pushed down my straps, it felt almost powerful.

That was it.

It was power. I felt powerful being in that room and getting that kind of attention from him, even if it was for a few seconds.

I don't know if the feeling of power came from the man or from what I was doing, but I want to feel that again.

That's why as I step foot into my apartment building and make it up to my place, I conclude that I very much want to try to insert myself into Dante Rosetti's life again. At least, just one more time.

I walk into my small apartment and stand against the

closed door and replay what happened in that office not even half an hour ago.

Fear was running through me.

Nerves were spewing off me like it was fresh sweat.

Everything about the man sitting in the leather chair with a glass of scotch in hand was daunting. Just being in his mere presence should have had me running out of that club and never looking back.

But then he spoke.

His words traveled through my body, and it was as if they ignited something. I knew it in that office, but I didn't know what it was until now. His words were simple, they were words said in any typical interview yet the way his voice curled around them burned into me in a way that I will never forget.

Like I said, it felt powerful.

And that power only grew when I stood up and his eyes took me in.

For a few seconds, I saw how he looked at my bare breasts. I saw how his fingers twitched a bit as if they wanted to reach out and touch me.

I saw how his eyes went from showing indifference to showing heat and lust, telling me that he liked what he saw.

That's what I hold on to as I make my way over to my bed. I keep the visual of his eyes on my chest in my mind and forget about taking down the man for everything he is. I'll forget about it for a few minutes.

For a few minutes, I won't concentrate on how much I want to destroy Dante Rosetti, and everyone like him. I won't think about how much I want to see him burn alive. Or even coming up with a plan to do just that.

No, for a few minutes, I will picture him sitting in his chair and me doing what I walked into that office to do.

Strip for him.

I ride dress up my thigh as I sit on my mattress, slowly caressing my fingertips against my exposed skin.

Even with the lighting, his light-brown eyes captivated me.

His stare pulled me in.

And his tough exterior made me want to follow through.

I grab at the hem of my dress and pull it over my head, leaving me in the only good pair of satin panties I own. I wore them for encouragement. I leave them on.

My knee-high boots also stay on as I stand up and sway my body a bit as if I were back in that office with no music playing.

I hum as I sway and soon, still with the thought of Rosetti in my head, I begin to touch my body. First my breasts and then moving my hands to my ass and giving my ass cheeks a good squeeze.

Then I move my hands to my front, and I touch myself against the delicate skin.

I slide my finger along my folds, wetness already coating my hand.

I circle my fingertips around my clit and a moan fills the small space.

My hips continue to sway, and my fingers continue to move.

As I continue to do what I am, a thought in the back of my mind creeps up, telling me that I shouldn't be doing this. I shouldn't be fantasizing about this. About him.

Yet here I am.

I'm fantasizing about the man that could have possibly killed my father.

And I fantasize about him until I'm panting, my legs are shaking, and my orgasm covers my fingers.

Tonight, I fantasize about my father's possible killer, tomorrow I will come up with another plan to take the fucker down.

7

DANTE

I look at the time on my phone screen and see that it's just over five in the morning.

It's almost time.

Finishing up the last of my run, I power off the treadmill, slide off the conveyor belt, and head to the fridge I have down here for some water.

As the cold water travels down my throat, I check the time again and see that it's getting closer.

I chuck the empty water bottle into the recycle bin and make my way out of the home gym I have in my basement and head upstairs.

The second floor is completely silent when I reach it.

Once I step onto the threshold, I stand there, unmoving, like I do every single morning and wait for the call to start up.

Like clockwork, right at five seventeen, the cries sound out.

Angel, my nine-month-old son, is awake.

Letting out a sigh, I head over to his room, the one that is next to mine and across from my daughter's. Walking in, I see his little body is already up and standing and when I turn on the light, I see the tears that are running down his full cheeks.

I waste no time going over to his crib and picking him up before grabbing a blanket and taking him over to the rocking chair in the corner.

Grabbing the fresh bottle, I placed in the warmer when I woke up an hour ago, I feed him and silently hope that he goes back to sleep.

This is a routine that we have been doing for the last seven months. Ever since my wife died in a car accident.

A car accident where our two children were in the back seat.

It was just after the new year when it happened. Angel was born two months before and Angelina was taking him to his doctor's appointment.

There had been ice on the roads from the night before. I had told her to reschedule the appointment or at the very least let one of our security guards take her since I couldn't.

She was a stubborn woman, always saying how I needed to let her keep her independence. I think that day she said something along the lines of not smothering her more than she was. So, I conceded.

I let her go to the appointment by herself and because Alessandra, our daughter, never left her mother's side, she went too.

I was at the club, dealing with a new liquor distributor when it happened. The second I got the call, all the blood in my body drained and I felt as if my world had just ended. I didn't even let the person on the other end of the call finish speaking before I was rushing to the hospital.

For an hour, I didn't know what the actual hell was happening. All I knew was that someone was dead when the paramedics had arrived at the scene and I didn't know who that was.

I argued with countless nurses and doctors until I was let back to see my family. That's when I was told that Alessandra was in surgery to repair a bone in her leg, Angel came out just fine and Angelina was the one that had died.

My parents had died when I was twenty-three and now my wife was gone thirteen years later.

The feeling I felt when I heard those words wasn't a feeling that I had ever felt before. And it was something that I never wanted to feel ever again.

I was told to mourn, but I couldn't. I had my children to take care of.

Alessandra not only had a broken leg, but also a cut that went the length of her face. I had to make sure that she was taken care of on top of Angel's needs.

I gave myself until the day after the funeral to mourn and then I had to get into the headspace of raising two children by myself.

At first it was a struggle. I was used to depending on Angelina when it came to things like the kids' schedules, what type of diapers and formula to buy and now that she was gone, it felt like I had to learn everything again from the very beginning.

For the most part it has only been the three of us, with Evelyn popping in and out on occasion, but as the days go by and the club busier than ever, I realized I need help.

That's where the fucking nanny interviews come in.

I brushed it off when Evelyn first suggested it about five months ago. After Alessandra was sent to preschool with two different shoes that didn't fit her last month, I had her set the interviews up.

Evelyn was right, I needed help. But like anything else, there was a catch. I wasn't just going to pick just some random stranger off the streets. I wanted someone that knew what the hell they were doing and was able to pass a damn background check. With who I am and the type of life that I live, I needed to be extremely vigilant with who I was bringing into my house.

Yet weeks later, I still have no nanny, and the only one I'm considering showed me her fucking tits during the questioning.

Tits that I'm not ashamed to say were in my dreams last night.

Angel lets out a small burp and drops the bottle from his mouth. He looks up at me with eyes that look so much like his mother's before cuddling deeper into my hold and falling asleep once again.

"*Dormi mio angioletto, ti proteggerò.*" Sleep my little angel, I will protect you, I say as I glide the back of my finger against his cheek.

He's not even a year old and he has already gone through so much.

Keeping his body close to mine, I stand up and place him in his crib once again.

I place a kiss on his small head and leave the room to let him sleep for a few more hours.

Before heading to my room to change for the day, I peek into Alessandra's, to make sure her brother's cries didn't wake her.

I half expected for her eyes to be open and staring back at me, but she is fast asleep, as if she hasn't a care in the world.

Out of my two children, Alessandra worries me the most. Her leg has healed up fine, but the scar on her face will forever be with her. The scar isn't what I'm most worried about though. She will grow into a beautiful woman, just like her mother and that scar will make her the strongest person that she can be.

What has me the most worried is the fact that she hasn't said a word since Angelina died.

At four, my little girl should be talking my ear off as she tells me about the adventures she's had during her day. Yet she isn't.

It's as if the accident stunted her speech. Every doctor has told me that nothing is wrong with her, that she will talk when she wants to.

But I'm starting to doubt them.

I'm starting to doubt that I will ever hear her voice again.

With one final look at Alessandra, I close the door and let her sleep.

I go get dressed and get my day somewhat started before the kids are fully awake and I have to get Alessandra ready for school.

Once I have a cup of coffee, I head into my home office and start up my computer.

Most people in Chicago would tell you that Dante Rosetti spends his days planning his next kill. If he's not planning a kill, then he is planning on more ways to steal from people that don't deserve it.

If they saw what I really did in a day, they would be fucking baffled.

All they see is a thirty-seven-year-old man that has ties to the Mafia and is known for being a little trigger- happy.

Are they right?

Partly.

Do I have ties to the Mafia here in Chicago? I'm the fucking Mafia here in Chicago. I'm one of two kings that this city has, and the people only see the bad that I do and never the good.

I will say though, I do a lot worse than good.

And one of the good things is *Perversa* and all the money that it brings to the city.

I opened *Perversa* over fifteen years ago. I was twenty-two and had money in my pockets from some of the jobs I was working for the Falcone *famiglia*.

Alberto Falcone was my mother's brother and up until about ten years ago was the mob boss that ran all of Chicago.

Alberto was fucking ruthless, some people comparing him to the mobsters from the forties. The bastard was killed when a Molotov cocktail was thrown into his car as he was pulling out of the driveway.

What a glorious day that was. And no, I wasn't the one that threw the cocktail, though there are days where I wish I did.

Years before his death, I had branched out from under the wing that was my mother's family. I did jobs for them here and there but nothing to get me a seat at the table with the boss and his soldiers. I was mostly involved out of respect for the boss's sister.

I had always wanted to open up a club that was so elite that even the richest of the rich had to pay to be able to step through the doors. When I finally saved enough money, Perversa was the first thing I brought to fruition.

It took everything that I had in me to get the place started. Blood, sweat and tears.

Within a year we were the talk of the town and had Chicago's elite asking for access to the most gorgeous girls that the world had to offer.

The success of the club was something that Alberto hated and hated it even more because he knew that I was making money without him. He knew that if I continued, I would soon become more powerful than he could ever think of.

You see, Alberto saw me as a threat, especially when I became of age and would never show him any respect.

My father always saw Alberto for who he was and so did I.

And if I had even an ounce of respect for the man, that disappeared the second that my parents died. Alberto called a hit to take me out because he didn't like that his men were interested in the type of business adventures I was involved in. So, he thought that he would earn his men back by having me killed, but he failed.

He had someone shoot up the house that he thought I had bought for myself, but in reality, I had bought it for my parents.

Like Angelina, they died before the paramedics arrived.

After that I hated the bastard and I distanced myself from him and that life even more.

That is until the fucker died three years later, and because he had no living heir, his men, his family looked to me to take over the family business.

I wanted to say no, but after taking a few weeks to think about it and seeing the benefits that life would bring, I agreed.

I agreed to be the new crime boss of Chicago and the Falcone Family was extinguished and replaced with the Rosettis.

For years, making money and getting rid of people that crossed me was the only thing that I had to live for. That is until I met Angelina six years ago. She was the daughter of the family's consigliere. She was a few years younger than me and beautiful and I was enthralled by her right away. We started seeing each other and within the year we were married, and the king of the underworld had his queen.

We were the perfect pair. People said she was the light

to my darkness. That is until the darkness took over and the light was taken away never to be turned on ever again.

Now here I am, a powerful Mafia boss, running a few businesses, completely wifeless and trying to raise two children by himself.

The business can die tomorrow, and I wouldn't care, as long as the kids are taken care of, that's all that matters.

As for the Rosetti *famiglia*, I'm sure that if I died tomorrow, my second-in-command would be happy to take over. He sure as hell would deserve it, especially after dealing with my exasperating ass for almost ten years.

A phone ringing takes me out of my own head. Shaking my thoughts away, I grab my phone from where it sits on my desk and see that it's an unknown number.

Fucking great.

I check the time before swiping at the answer button. I guess I'm not the only one that starts their day at a god-awful time.

"Rosetti," I answer, not even bothering to be polite.

"I'm setting up a meeting," the voice on the other end says.

I don't even have to fucking ask who it is. There is only one person that calls me at this time from an unknown number. The other king of Chicago.

"For what?" I ask, not wanting to deal with this shit.

"Doesn't matter. Can you meet or not?"

"When?"

"One month from today. Eight in the morning."

I look at the calendar that I have lying across my desk

and nod. "I just need to find a babysitter and I will be there."

The fucker has the audacity to let out a snort. "You still haven't found a nanny?"

"Some of us aren't as lucky as you."

"Whatever you say. Are we good with this or not?" the king throws out.

I roll my eyes. Not like I have a choice. When the king calls, you run. "We're good."

The line goes dead as soon as I say the words and instead of going back to what I was doing, which was basically nothing, I dial Evelyn.

As the phone rings, I know that I'm going to regret the moment that she answers.

"Yes, Dante?" Evelyn says after the third ring. She is the only one besides my underboss, Lorenzo, that I'm completely fine with calling me by my given name.

"Hire her," I say, no greeting, nothing. Just a command.

"Hire who?" Evelyn muses, as if she doesn't know exactly who I'm talking about.

"Don't play dumb, Evelyn. It doesn't suit you. Hire the girl. You know which one. Make sure you find out every detail on her. Anything that her father didn't tell us. I don't need the shit that I do in my own house landing on the front page of the Tribune."

"Will do, sir," she hangs up without another word.

Doesn't anyone know how to be fucking polite anymore when it comes to ending a phone call?

As I place my phone back on the desk, I can't help but

hope that I didn't make a stupid decision in telling Evelyn to hire Arianna Vitale to be my kids' nanny.

And if I did and it comes back to bite me in the ass, I was thinking with my dick and not with logic.

But maybe it would be a good decision.

Maybe with her as my employee, I will find out why she was in my club in the first place with a fake name.

There's a reason behind it because a woman like that doesn't seek a job at my place of business just because they want to.

Especially when that woman's father was just murdered, and my name has been listed as suspect number one.

8

ARIANNA

Some people would say that the best time to visit Chicago is in October. It's not too hot, still somewhat warm but the winter air is slowly coming in and people aren't crowding the streets as much.

Some would also say that Chicago is the most beautiful city in the world.

Those people are wrong on both counts. Don't get me wrong, Chicago is a very beautiful city, but that beautifulness is clouded by the darkness that surrounds it. The darkness that plagues the city is the most dangerous in the country.

That little tidbit is always overlooked.

The people that visit the city daily, tend to not see the drug deals that are happening in every corner. Tend to not hear about the murders that are happening every night. Tend to ignore the sirens that ring out almost every single minute of every day.

Perceptions are clouded at the thought of exploring a new place, a new city culture. For tourists, the city is perfect but for those who have lived here for longer than half their lifetime, they know the real truth.

They know about what really happens on the streets and who not to get involved with.

They know not to cross someone that goes by the nickname The Devil.

What the people that have lived here half their lives don't know is that even someone that goes by the name of The Devil, has enemies.

As far as Dante Rosetti is concerned, you would think that his biggest enemy is the Chicago Police Department. I thought that, because who else would want to take down the man? Besides me, of course.

CPD was the only logical enemy that I could think of for Rosetti and anyone else who is a part of his Mafia family. Yet after spending more hours of my life trying to find another way to infiltrate his, I found another.

Roberto Gallo.

From what I can find, Gallo and Rosetti were once connected. Apparently, they were both involved with Alberto Falcone, the Mafia boss that was at the head of the table before Rosetti took over.

I was able to find out, by asking customers at the bar, that Gallo has had it out for Rosetti for the last ten years or so.

I was so able to find out that even with the power Rosetti has over the city, Gallo was still able to build his own operation. Maybe not as big as the one that Rosetti has built in his years in power but still somewhat notice-able, supposedly. I've never heard of this man or there being another Mafia family in the city, but I could be wrong.

The second I found out about Gallo, my plan to bring down Rosetti diverted a bit.

If I'm going to do this, if I'm going to take down Rosetti and make him pay for something I know in my gut he did, working with the CPD isn't going to help. They aren't going to let me get my hands dirty. They will also most likely never be able to get incriminating evidence.

But Gallo can.

So, I started to set my plan in motion. I would find meet with Gallo and then together we would find a way to insert me into Rosetti's life. Once I'm there I will figure out a way to bring him down.

And maybe Gallo could also help me with the list filled with unknown names that follow after him.

I just had to get in front of Gallo.

Weirdly enough, finding out where Gallo does busi-ness was easier than walking into Perversa. I honestly think if Evelyn hadn't found me out front, I wouldn't have been let in.

Apparently, it's well known that Gallo owns a Laundro-mat, so clever, at the edge of Little Italy.

So, I decided to take my shot.

Today is Sunday, a whole week and some change since my disastrous meeting with Rosetti and I thought it would be a good day as any to do my laundry.

And what better place to do it than at the laundromat Mr. Gallo owns. From what I hear, he's always there, so this is a better chance than any.

That's why I'm currently lugging a duffel filled with dirty clothes on the blue line to see for myself if Gallo does in fact reside at his place of business.

As I sit here on the train looking out at the city skyline, I can't help but feel a small ping of sadness in my chest.

Every two months like clockwork, Dad and I would take this very train to Little Italy all because he wanted Italian lemonade. I always suggested that we take his car but every time he would tell me that he wanted to experience the city by train. That it was faster and that we could spend more time together. I never told him no.

Now here I am heading to Little Italy by myself and I fucking hate it. He should be here with me, making me laugh, pointing out something random through the window.

Instead, I'm on my way to speak to someone to help me not only prove who his killer really was but to also bring that person down.

Closing my eyes, I try to take as many deep breaths as I can to push the feeling of loss away. I miss my dad and every day it gets harder and harder. Some days I feel like I am able to move on but then I get memories like the one I just had, and it hits me like a dump truck all over again.

Once I'm calmed down a bit, I open my eyes and concentrate on what I'm supposed to do.

Head to the Laundromat.

Hopefully meet with Gallo and come up with a plan to help me prove that Rosetti is my father's killer.

And then when that is all set and done, come up with something to finally rid this city of its devil and the other bad people in it.

Because it's the bad and powerful people that make this city such a horrible place.

I'll mourn once Rosetti is behind bars or in a box, but for right now, I have to concentrate on the task at hand.

Fifteen minutes later, the train is arriving at my stop and I'm dragging the duffel off the car and heading to the Laundromat that's across the street.

Convenient, I guess.

I make my way over to the storefront and when I step foot into the building, I find nothing special about it. It's just a regular self-serve laundry facility. Nothing screams out that a crime boss making a name for himself owns the place. Not even the old lady that is behind the service window.

Maybe I'm at the wrong place.

I pull out my phone from my back pocket and quickly Google Gallo's name. I wait and a few seconds later, this Laundromat pops up.

Huh, I guess I am in the right place.

Also, shouldn't Gallo be more vigilant about people knowing he owns the place? At least Rosetti had security guarding the doors.

Walking deeper into the place, I start putting my stuff into the first available washer.

Once my quarters are in and the machine is running, I

make my way over to the window. Maybe the old lady knows where I can find Gallo.

"Excuse me," I say as I knock against the window to grab the woman's attention.

She turns to face me and looks at me like I'm the first person that has approached her all day.

"Can I help you?" she asks, her eyes a bit wide with curiosity.

"Um..." What do I say? That I'm looking for the guy that also wants Dante Rosetti dead? "I was wondering if Roberto Gallo was around?"

Instantly the curiosity in her eyes disappears and it's replaced with wariness.

"Why are you looking for him?" Her old eyes narrow, looking at me through the window as if she can burn me for even mentioning Gallo's name.

I square my shoulders and step closer to the window so that the other individuals in the place don't hear my next words.

"I need to talk to him about someone named Dante Rosetti."

Did I have to name-drop? No. I'm sure that I would have been able to come up with something that would have gotten me in with Gallo.

But the way her eyes open up a bit, tells me that I did the right thing by mentioning Rosetti.

The woman looks at me for a few seconds longer before she gives me a curt nod and leaves her place at the window and heads somewhere in the back.

My eyes follow her retrieving figure until I can no

longer see her, and I can't help but ask myself if I should continue standing here or find a way to go after her.

I don't have to contemplate for long because within two minutes the lady is coming back with her head held high and a look of indifference on her face.

"Go to the door by the soda machine and knock three times," she tells me before looking away and down to whatever she was doing before I approached her.

It takes me a second to register what she said. When the words finally sink in, I have to contain myself before giving the woman a nod and doing exactly as ordered.

At first glance someone that isn't paying a whole lot of attention will never see the door next to the soda machine. It's somewhat hidden in plain sight, blends in with its surroundings.

I stand in front of the door, and I hesitate to bring up my hand and knock against the wood.

Do I really want to go this route? I can back away now, finish my laundry and never look back.

But if I do that, Rosetti will never pay for what he did. He will never go through the same pain that my dad went through when he was tied to that chair.

With a silent fuck it, I raise a closed fist and give the door three knocks.

Knock.

Knock.

Knock.

My hand shakes more with each knock that I give. Lowering my hand, I stand there, waiting for whatever is supposed to happen next.

As I stand here, I can feel the hairs on my arms stand up, and sweat rolling down my back. Standing here is freaking me out more than when I was about to walk into Rosetti's office a week ago.

I almost convince myself to back away and never step foot in this place again, when the door swings open.

A man in a dark suit stands in the entryway, eyeing me as if I were a piece of meat on a dinner plate and he is assessing if I'm good enough to eat whole.

The man is trying to look scary, like the men at Perversa, but this guy has nothing on Dante's men. Those men can eat this guy ten times over. This man standing in front of me looks like a dodgy banker that steals from his clients.

Is this Gallo?

"Last name," the man orders, his voice making me jump a bit.

"Vitale," I say to him, an eyebrow rising in confusion.

He gives me a curt nod before slamming the door in my face. Once again, I'm standing here dumbfounded and not sure what to do.

Do I knock again? Do I really leave for good this time?

No, I won't leave. I didn't leave when I was almost shitting my pants standing in front of Perversa and I'm sure as hell not going to leave now.

I raise my hand again to knock but before my fist makes contact, the door opens once again with the same man standing in the entryway.

"Come in and stand against the wall. I need to search

you and also take your phone. We can't have you recording anything that is said in the room."

Okay then.

I step into the room and without warning, my front is pushed against the wall closest to the door and the man starts patting me down. A little too roughly if you ask me and when I feel his hand glide against my ass, I know he is doing it for his enjoyment.

I try to push the bastard away from me, but he doesn't budge. He just pushes me into the wall even more with one hand while the other moves along my body in an aggressive manner.

When a moan escapes him, I realize just how bad of a decision this was. I should have left. I should have never come to Gallo. Who knows what is going to happen to me here.

A scream is about to escape when the bastard finally relents and let's go of me, his hands finally dropping from my body. His hands may have stopped touching me but as I turn, I can see his eyes still perusing me like I really am his next meal.

"Phone," he orders, stretching out a hand for the device. A hand way too close to my breast.

Without taking my eyes off the man in front of me, I grab my phone from my back pocket and hand it to him.

He takes it and slides it into his jacket before waving me to follow him. Following him down the short hall, I feel more terrified being here than I was walking through Dante's club. It should have been the other way around.

The man, who I'm guessing is Gallo's bodyguard, walks

up to a door, knocks twice before opening it, and waves me in.

Wary, I walk in, sweat coating my hairline, and I meet the beady eyes of another man. I don't know what I expected when it came to Gallo, but it sure wasn't this.

A man making his name as a crime boss should look put together. Should exude power but the man sitting behind the desk is nothing like that.

His gray hair is standing in all directions and his suit is wrinkled as if he slept in it.

I expected a whole lot more from Dante Rosetti's enemy, but I guess that's what happens when you run your business out of a Laundromat.

"Miss Vitale."

I cringe a bit at the sound of his voice, it makes my skin crawl and not in a good way.

"What brings you to my business establishment?" the man behind the desk voices, placing folded arms on the wooden top.

"Are you Roberto Gallo?" I ask, trying to keep the nerves running through my body at bay.

The man shrugs. "That depends. Why are you in my Laundromat spewing Dante Rosetti's name?"

Straight to business. "Because I need help bringing him down and I hear you're the man that can possibly get the job done."

He looks at me as I say the words. He looks at me as if he is trying to figure out if I'm being truthful as to why I'm here.

Maybe he's trying to figure out if Rosetti himself sent me and this is just all a game.

Finally, after what seems like the longest minute in the world, he gives me a curt nod.

"I'm Roberto, now take a seat and tell me why you want Mr. Rosetti dead."

I take a seat in the chair in front of his desk, and I tell him. I tell Gallo about my father and how he was murdered, and I tell him how I know in my gut that Rosetti was the one that called the hit. Gallo agrees.

"It sounds like the fucker. I bet he got off on it too, the sick bastard."

After that, Gallo tells me that he will gladly work with me to figure out a way to get me inside. He even agreed to get me identifications with the name Arianna Amato on them to make it more believable.

The only thing that was left up in the air was the how and the when. Once we had those things somewhat figured out, we would be set, and we would be able to bring Rosetti down.

The one thing that we did figure out was how I was going to pay him for his time. Of course, this wasn't going to be free, and I expected that but that didn't mean that I didn't balk at his need for five thousand dollars. It hurt, but I agreed to the amount. If I didn't have the money that was donated by the Lane Foundation, I would have walked out.

Not even twenty minutes into me walking in and meeting with Gallo, I'm excused. All with a promise to deposit the money into an account he gave me and a burner phone that came with the orders of only using it when I've learned something pressing.

Like if I find a way to infiltrate Rosetti's world, if I find any information about my dad's hit. I'm supposed to go to Gallo first and he will know what to do.

Does that part freak me out even more? Yes, yes it does, but if it what needs to be done then I will do it.

I finish my laundry and put everything back into the duffel and start heading back to my place.

It's when I'm sitting on the train that my phone starts ringing with a call from an unknown number.

Given the meeting I was just in, I answer.

"Hello?" There is a slight shake in my voice as I address the person on the other line.

"Is this Arianna Amato?" a woman's voice says from the other end.

A woman and she used the name Amato. This couldn't be Evelyn, could it?

"This is her."

"Oh, hi Arianna, this is Evelyn, Mr. Rosetti's assistant. I'm calling you because I wanted to see if you could start the position tomorrow?"

Start the position tomorrow?

"I'm sorry, I'm a bit confused. Position?"

"The nanny position. Mr. Rosetti would like you to start tomorrow."

Is he that desperate for help that he is going to hire *me*?

"I thought that after..." The interview where I flashed the man my chest, I want to say. "After the disastrous inter-view, my chances were gone."

"Mr. Rosetti is a hard man to please but nonetheless he thinks you are right for the job. Are you still interested?" Evelyn asks.

Hard to please feels like an understatement.

This is it. This is the opening I've been waiting for, and it's being handed to me like a piece of cake.

There is no hesitation in my voice when I answer.

"Yes, I'm still interested and yes, I can start tomorrow."

9

ARIANNA

I should have thought this through a lot longer than just a few seconds. I should have told Evelyn to give me a few days to think about the offer and not jump right in.

But I didn't and now here I am standing in front of a black metal gate that protects a mega mansion at six in the morning on a Monday.

After I agreed to take the job, Evelyn sent all the details I needed to get started.

The children's names and ages. Their daily schedules, their likes and dislikes. Everything that I needed to know about the two of them stared back at me on the screen. It felt like I was reading a résumé for two little people. Reading all the information on the train was a bit over-whelming.

Evelyn also requested information, things that any normal employer would ask for, and wanted it as soon as I arrived at the house this morning. Except that I'm using a fake name.

So as soon as I hung up with her, I took out the burner phone that Gallo gave me and shot him a message.

I told him I had an in with Rosetti and I needed an ID and whatever else he can get me that had the last name Amato. He asked me for my information and within an hour, I had an ID and social security card in hand.

I couldn't believe just how real they looked.

As soon as I had the items, I started to get ready for my first day as Dante Rosetti's nanny.

What does one wear to be a nanny for one of the richest men in Chicago? I have no idea, so I pulled out the best black slacks and nicest blouse that I had.

And once my outfit was picked out, I tried to sleep and well that didn't go so well.

Since my dad died, I haven't been able to sleep much. Every time I closed my eyes during days leading up to the funeral, I would be back in the brownstone and see everything all over again. I can count on one hand how many nights I slept for more than five hours. It's gotten better since then but last night it was as if I was in the middle of it all over again.

I tossed and turned and every time my eyes closed, I would see Rosetti standing over me, telling me that I was going to meet the same fate that my dad did. If it wasn't that then it was him telling me that he knew what my plan was and that I will never succeed.

Now here I am, standing in front of the man's property, telling myself that I need to do this.

That I need to insert myself like this and hopefully find a way to take this man down. If not for me then for my poppa.

Taking a deep breath, I push my fear aside and push the intercom button on the gate keypad.

It rings for a few seconds before a male voice sounds through.

"Name," the voice orders.

I clear my throat. "Ari Amato."

"Full name."

I roll my eyes at the command but answer anyway. "Arianna Amato."

There is silence for a few seconds before the voice comes through again.

"Please hold up a photo ID to the camera."

I guess when you're someone in power, you have to go through these measures. Unless you're Gallo.

I do as I'm told, crossing my fingers behind my back in the process, hoping that they don't notice that it's a fake.

There's silence again and then the voice speaks.

"The gate is going to beep and open up. Walk through and wait. Do not go farther onto the grounds. Someone will pick you up shortly."

The voice fades out and just like it said, a beep rings and the gates open.

Stepping through the gate is like stepping into a whole different world. The grounds that surround the house are endless. There is green everywhere and it's breathtaking.

It reminds me of a castle that could be owned by the

royal family. My mind is blown that a place like this, a home like this, can actually be found in Chicago.

I've read a lot about Rosetti and his business this last week or so, but never did I think he would live in a place like this.

I want to take my time and explore it.

But that will have to wait, since a black SUV pulls up next to the now-closed gate.

A bodyguard steps out and opens the back door for me. I hesitate for a second but get in nonetheless and just as quickly as it showed up, we are making our way to the house. Or the main house as the guard called it when speaking into a phone.

The main house can't be seen from the gate so when it comes into view, I see that it's breathtaking. Instantly, I love everything about it, and I haven't even stepped foot inside yet.

I have to stand on the front steps for a minute just marveling at it.

If it looks like this at dawn, I wonder what it looks like when the sun is brightly shining.

How can someone that goes by The Devil live here?

This French château style house, it's beautiful and definitely made for royalty.

I guess in a way that is what my new boss is. Chicago royalty, but of the evil kind.

The front glass paneled door opens, taking my attention away from the exterior of the house. I look up and see Evelyn standing in the doorway.

She gives me a bright smile that tells me that her day started hours ago.

"Arianna. Welcome. I'm glad that you are here." Evelyn holds out a hand for me to shake and I do.

"Ari. You can call me Ari, and I'm happy to be here."

Evelyn's smile brightens up even more. "Ari. Why don't you come in and we can go ahead and get started?"

With a nod, I follow her into the house, and just like with the outside, I fall in love. It's like a damn dream and I have to keep my gasps contained as I walk deeper into the house behind Evelyn.

I try to take in where everything is but the more I see the more I know it's going to take me a few days to get the lay of the land.

"Do you plan to wear heels all day?" Evelyn asks, looking over her shoulder at me.

I stop and look down at my clothes, then look over at what she's wearing. It's almost identical.

A nervous chuckle escapes my lips. "No. Sorry. I didn't know what else to wear and I didn't want to come off as unprofessional."

Even though I'm lying about who I am and why I'm here, I still want to be taken seriously.

I have to treat this just like any other job.

Evelyn gives me a small smile. "I'll send someone out for some clothes. That way you're more comfortable."

"Oh, it's fine. I can totally work like this." I profusely shake my head, not wanting to take any handouts.

"I insist. You deserve to be comfortable on your first day."

I want to argue, but after a reassuring squeeze of my hand, I concede and take her offer.

We head into a room that turns out to be an office, her office and she has me sit down to fill out all the appropriate paperwork.

My hand shakes when I write Amato instead of Vitale. Never in my life have I used my mother's maiden name like this.

Once that is done and Evelyn has the copies of everything, she gives me a very detailed list for each child. More detailed than the list she sent over last night.

Everything that there is to be known about a one- and four-year-old is in my hands.

"If you don't mind me asking, where is their mother?" I ask, curiosity getting the best of me.

This question has been bugging me for a few days now. I understand that rich families use nannies all the time, but I found it odd that it was Dante looking for one, and the children's mom wasn't involved.

Evelyn's eyes saddened a bit. "Mrs. Rosetti is no longer with us. She passed away a few months ago."

"Oh."

I didn't know that Rosetti was married, let alone that she had died.

My question all but forgotten, Evelyn continues to give me a rundown of the job. She goes through every single detail, including my housing.

"I'm sorry, housing? I'm supposed to live here?" I ask, confused.

Evelyn gives me a nod. "After this first week, if everything goes well, you will move in. That way, you are available whenever needed. You will have some days and nights off of course, but Mr. Rosetti thought it would be best that the nanny moves in to ease the process in a way."

Ease the process.

How the fuck is living under Dante Rosetti's roof easing the process? I'm already terrified of the man and if I live under his roof, he has a better chance of finding out who I am.

This is for the kids, not for you.

Right for the kids.

The kids that I have to look after, the kids that I have to take care of and spend every day with. The kids that I will, without a doubt, get close to and will destroy in the end when I take their father away from them.

That last part is why I should have said no to this job. Why I should have hesitated more than what I did.

Ultimately, I'm here to take down Rosetti, to find something incriminating to put the bastard behind bars or to burn him to a crisp. This has been about him and only him and his kids should never be involved.

Yet here I am, about to become their nanny for the unforeseeable future.

I'm such a horrible person.

But I need to do this.

I need to get revenge for my father, and I can do this, do this job and not get overly attached to two children I haven't even met yet.

I can. I know that I can.

And moving in would be good in helping with what I need to accomplish.

"Right. Sorry, it took me off guard." I try to give Evelyn a smile, but I don't know if it comes off as genuine.

She gives me a reassuring smile back and goes back to giving me the run of things.

I have access to most of the main house. Evelyn gives me a map of it and tells me which rooms are a no-go.

The master bedroom.

The office on the second floor.

The basement.

Places within the house that are solely for Rosetti, I'm guessing.

"I know it's a lot, but I think that within the next few days, you will get the hang of things. Especially with your education."

Right, my education.

I may have used a fake name on my paperwork, but I didn't lie when I told Rosetti about my degree.

There was a time in my life when I wanted to be a teacher. It was a month or so after I graduated that I decided that teaching wasn't the route for me, and I became a bartender.

Now here I am about to finally use my degree by becoming a nanny for a Mafia boss.

"You're right," I tell her truthfully. "I'm just a little nervous about taking on a new job."

"Don't be. You'll do great." She gives me a genuine smile before looking down at her watch. "It's almost time to start getting the kids ready for their day. Should we go introduce you to them?"

I nod and give a smile even though everything inside of me is churning with dread.

I'm really doing this.

My breathing is erratic as I follow Evelyn through the house again and up the stairs, and it becomes even more when we walk into a nursery.

The nursery doesn't affect me much.

No, what's affecting me is the man wearing a suit sitting on a rocker in the corner with a baby in his arms.

And it's affecting me even more when his eyes meet mine and I fucking swear, the world stands still.

His eyes bore into me, and I can feel them deep inside of me.

In a different world, I would have said this man is absolutely gorgeous, even more so with a baby in his arms. In that world I would let him do what he wants to me.

But I'm not in that world and as I stand here feeling his stare, I swear he can see right through me.

Fuck, why did I think this was a good idea?

10

DANTE

"You better be right about this," I say through my teeth as I stand next to Evelyn as we watch Arianna interact with my son.

As much as I hate the fact that a woman, one I know lied about who she is, is watching over my kids, Evelyn was right.

I need more help than what I had. I needed someone to concentrate on only the kids and not on the million other things they had to do on top of that.

But like I said before, I sure fucking hope it doesn't bite me in the ass.

"I will be. You'll see. She is perfect for the job." She gives me an overly sweet smile and I swear I see her eye twitch trying not to roll her eyes.

"You know, if you weren't like a sister to me, I would fire your ass for bringing an unqualified woman into the interview."

Evelyn shrugs. "What's done is done. Look at her with

Angel. He loves her."

My eyes move from my assistant to the two individuals in the room.

Angel and Arianna are sitting on the floor together and my son is laughing like there isn't a strange woman sliding a toy truck to him.

"He's not even a year old. He doesn't know who she is. Of course, he's happy." The kid would be happy if I put him in a pile of mud and left him there all day.

"You stress too much," Evelyn throws at me, the eye roll finally escaping.

I grab her by the elbow and walk her down the hallway, away from prying ears.

"You seriously want me to trust a twentysomething year old twat, one that lied about her name, to be around my children? Because I'm not, I'm not going to fucking trust her until she proves herself. Until then, of course I'm going to fucking stress too much, as you put it."

I don't tell Evelyn that something at the back of my head is telling me that Arianna is here for something other than being a nanny. Why else would someone that thought she was interviewing for a dancer or bartending position accept a nanny position?

She has to be here because she wants answers. That's the only logical reason.

"Would it make you feel better if I say I'm running a background check on her?" She raises a perfectly sculpted eyebrow at me.

"You should have done that before the fucking interview," I say through my teeth.

Evelyn lets out a sigh. "I did, and all I was able to find was the bare minimum. Name, phone number, address, place of employment. I wasn't able to dig deeper until I had all the other information. Now that I do, I'm doing a thorough check, but I don't think that anything serious will pop up."

Especially if her father had anything to do with it, I don't voice.

Joseph Vitale was someone that I have known since I was a teenager. He was one of the only individuals in the Chicago Police Department that not only knew me as Dante but also as The Devil himself. Our relationship changed a lot throughout the years, but he was always there. That is until he got himself involved in shit he wasn't supposed to and ended up paying the price with his life.

The bastard.

I told him that was going to happen.

Now I have his daughter in my fucking house and she either knows her father and I had some sort of connection, or this is the biggest coincidence in the world.

My gut has told me from the very beginning that it's the former, but I'm not going to call her out on it.

If she wants answers, let her ask them. Joseph would have wanted me to tell her.

And if she wants to take me down, then she can fucking try, I'm not going to stop her.

Everyone but my kids would be better off if Dante Rosetti was in the ground six feet deep.

I hear footsteps and when I look up, I see Arianna approaching with Angel on her hip.

"As soon as you have something on her, I need to know," I whisper to Evelyn, not taking my eyes off the new nanny.

I have to remind myself that she's Joseph's daughter and possible the enemy.

"Yes, sir," Evelyn whispers back before turning to our guest, planting a smile on her face. "Ari, is everything okay?"

Ari. God, why does it irk me to hear the nickname?

Also, why the fuck is she dressed just like Evelyn? Shouldn't she be in casual shit since she will be running around?

"Yes, everything is okay," she says nervously to Evelyn, not meeting my eyes. "I just looked at the time and I was wondering if it was time to get Alessandra ready for school?"

I look down at my watch, and I realize she's right.

"Fuck," I mutter, turning on my heels and walking over to Alessandra's room, acutely aware of the footsteps behind me.

I open the door to my daughter's room and let out a sigh of relief when I see that she is already awake and sitting up in the middle of her bed.

"Good morning, *gioia mia*," I say as I sit on her bed and place a kiss on her head. "Did you have any bad dreams?"

On top of not talking, Alessandra occasionally wakes up from nightmares. When she does, she runs directly to my bed and stays there until morning. I've talked to countless doctors about this, but they all say that we won't know what is causing them unless she talks about it.

She hasn't, and everything in me is telling me that she never will.

I know they are about the accident, but I won't know for sure unless she tells me.

Alessandra shakes her head and before I give her a smile, she looks over my shoulder and whatever she sees, makes her eyes go wide.

I don't have to turn around to see that she is looking at Arianna. She must have walked into the room behind me.

Letting out a sigh, I lift Alessandra up into my arms, stand and turn to face the nanny.

I watch Arianna as I approach her with my daughter. I watch her to see her expression when she sees the scar that travels across the little girl's face, expecting her to gasp in surprise when she sees it.

Everyone gasps when they see it.

But as I continue to watch her, there is no real surprise and there is no gasp. She just looks at the little girl in my arms with interest and not directly at the scar.

"Alessandra, this is Arianna. She's going to pick you up from school and take care of you and your brother when *Papi* can't."

That causes Alessandra to finally take her eyes off the nanny and look at me.

Her eyes, so much like her mother's and brother's, look at me in question.

She's curious about the new woman that is in her room and holding her brother. She wants to know what I mean when I say when I can't take care of them. So many questions flow through her grayish-blue eyes and I would kill to hear them being spoken.

But of course, she doesn't speak.

Alessandra looks at me until her eyes have said enough and she leans her head into the crook of my neck, holding her little body tightly to mine.

I rub at her back and when I look up again, I notice that Arianna has a small smile playing at her lips.

Does she have other smiles besides that one?

I hold in my scoff.

Why do I care? She's my employee. I shouldn't care about the type of smiles she has.

She meets my eyes for a second before turning to Evelyn and handing Angel over to her.

I watch as she approaches me and Alessandra and when she's a few inches away, she puts a delicate hand on my daughter's back.

At the movement, Alessandra detaches herself from me somewhat.

Again, with curiosity in her eyes, she looks at me before she looks down at the woman that she's going to be spending a lot of time with.

"Hi, Alessandra. It's nice to meet you. My name is Ari," Arianna greets her with a bright smile.

I guess she does have other ones and I think I like seeing this one.

Alessandra doesn't do anything, she just continues looking down at Arianna.

The silence doesn't halt Arianna from continuing their interaction.

"Would you like me to help you get dressed for school? Ms. Evelyn told me that you wear a pretty skirt every day."

It takes a second, but Alessandra finally answers with a small nod.

Arianna looks at me with eyebrows furrowed, silently asking me if she's saying yes to the help or yes to her wearing a skirt.

"Alessandra doesn't speak. She can but she hasn't spoken since her mom died. In order to know what she's answering, you have to ask more yes or no questions."

A contemplative look crosses her face before she gives me a nod and yet another fucking small smile.

Enough with the fucking small smiles already.

"Do you want me to help you get dressed today, Alessandra?" Arianna asks.

Time stands still for a moment and I'm about to tell her that I will dress my daughter when Alessandra nods.

She nods and Arianna's face transforms into another bright smile, and I have to take a second to figure out what the fuck just happened.

Alessandra doesn't let anyone but me dress her in the mornings, but she is letting this complete stranger do it.

What the fuck?

Without hesitation, my daughter goes to Arianna's outstretched arms and she starts getting ready for her day.

When the two of them are in the bathroom brushing their teeth, I turn to Evelyn who is smirking at me from the doorway.

I can hear the "I told you so" radiating from her body from where I stand.

"I don't pay you to stand around and smirk at me," I tell her which just earns me another smirk before handing me my son and leaving to do whatever she does this early in the morning.

Breathe. Relax. You know you would be lost without Evelyn.

Sure, but the woman sure knows how to get on my goddamn nerves.

Footsteps take my attention away from Evelyn and when I turn to I see Alessandra and Arianna come back into the room. My little girl has her hair done in two pigtails and already in her preschool uniform.

"Is it okay if I take her to school?" Arianna asks, a nervousness to her tone.

For the first time since the club, I get a good look at the woman in front of me.

Her dark hair goes just past her shoulders and her face has minimal to little makeup. The way she is dressed ages her and doesn't make her look like the twenty-four-year-old that I know she is.

She's young and I will admit beautiful and if she wasn't the new nanny or if I didn't know who her father was, I would suggest something else entirely. Like a proposition that will let me spend a large amount of time between her thighs, because fuck, even in the clothes she's wearing, the curves she has are mouthwatering.

It's a minute into the perusing of Arianna, I remember that she asked me a question.

Thankfully, she is looking over at Angel, who is giggling in my arms, and she didn't notice that I was ogling her or my hesitation in answering her question.

"I'll take her," I say a little too roughly and she takes notice.

So much so that she puts even more distance between us, and her eyes grow a bit wider.

"I'm sorry," she stutters out. "I just offered because Evelyn stated that was one of the jobs I had to do. I apologize if I interpreted it wrong."

I should feel bad.

I should feel bad that I scared the woman that is trying to make things easier on me by offering to take Alessandra to school, but I don't.

At least not a big part of me doesn't.

She's still a stranger. She is still here for a reason and until I find what that reason is, I won't trust her. Not fully anyway, especially when it comes to my children.

"It is a part of your job, but I don't trust you," I tell her, keeping it truthful. Placing Angel on the floor, I take a step closer to her. A look of fear coming through her eyes.

"I haven't trusted you from the second you stepped foot into my club. You may be the nanny, but you are here for a reason. A reason that will not be hidden for very long. I will find out, and when I do, you will pay for every one of your actions."

I pull back and I swear I see her shiver at my words.

Without another word, I grab Alessandra's bag and her hand and walk out of the room.

Arianna is scared and she should be.

Nobody messes with me and gets away with it. Even more so if it happens in my own house.

11

ARIANNA

You will pay for every one of your actions.

Those words brought a shiver down my spine when I heard them, and they still do four days later.

Dante knows that I'm here for a reason, and when he finds out what that reason is, I will possibly be in the gravesite next to my parents.

Maybe I won't even make it that far.

Maybe my body will be cut up into tiny pieces and scattered in his massive backyard, never to be found.

If I'm lucky, it would be the former because then I would be back with the two people that loved me the most.

But until that day comes, I will continue to do what I've been doing these last four days and that's take care of the man's kids.

Which I'm great at if you ask me.

I may not have become a teacher but I'm great with

kids and I like spending time with them, so that's making this job a breeze.

It also helps that Angel and Alessandra have been okay with having me around, if the way their eyes brighten when they look at me is any indication.

In the very short amount of time that I have spent with them, I've come to know that both kids are vastly different.

Angel, though he's only nine months old, is very happy and giggly and loves anything that has wheels. He has the same eyes as his sister and every time he looks at me when I feed him, I get lost in his gaze. I never knew a baby could be so hypnotic with his gaze. His little babbles of words bring a smile to my face every time that I hear them. I spend most of my day with him, so I feel like we've developed a bond of some sort and it's only been a few days. Angel, in a way, has accepted me, but he's a baby, I'm sure he would have accepted anyone that showed him love and affection.

Alessandra, on the other hand, is vastly different from her little brother.

When I first laid eyes on the little girl in her father's arms, she left me speechless. She's a beautiful little girl, with big blueish-gray eyes that are a complete contrast to her dark hair and olive complexion. Her eyes captivated my attention first and then it was the scar that went from the edge of her hairline to the tip of her jaw.

The scar, even healed, looks nasty but it doesn't take away from the little girl's beauty, it only adds to it.

As much as I wanted to gasp in shock when I first saw

it, I didn't, and I think that's what helped me gain Alessandra's trust a bit.

I showed her kindness and warmth and for that little bit she trusted me to help with her hair and get her dressed. But I didn't get a smile from her. I've tried though. Every chance I been with her these last three days, I've tried to make her smile and laugh or even to say a small word, all to no avail. All I've able to get from her are curious glances.

Like she wonders why I'm here.

She doesn't hate me, I know that much so that's a good sign.

And hopefully it stays that way, especially now since today I'm finally picking up Alessandra from school and not her dad.

Never did I think that getting approval to pick up a kid from school would be such a chore but of course, the mob boss made it one.

I have yet to earn his trust. Sure, I'm here picking up Alessandra, but I'm only here because Dante had some pressing business to take care of.

At least, that's what Evelyn told me when she asked for me to come here. I don't even think that Dante knows that I'm here, but I don't give a shit.

He's taking care of "pressing business," which most likely means that he's off killing someone, so he doesn't have a say.

Looking at the time on my phone, I see that it's almost time for me to go grab Alessandra.

I open the back door to the black SUV that Evelyn said

was at my disposal, but said SUV comes with two armed guards that both turn when I open the door.

My hand freezes on the handle when they do. I feel like I'm a kid again and got caught doing something bad.

"I'm just going to go in and grab Alessandra," I say, my voice going up an octave.

The guard sitting in the passenger seat, Bruno, lets out a grunt and steps out of the car to open my door wider.

I give him a nod as a thank you.

"Angel is sleeping. I will be back before he wakes up, I promise," I explain and all I get is another grunt in return.

Grunts.

I've been surrounded by grunts these last four days. Grunts from the bodyguards, grunts from Alessandra, and grunts from Dante.

Alessandra, I understand completely.

The guards, well I expect them to be hard even with me and the kids. As for Dante, I get the feeling that on top of not trusting me, he also doesn't like me, and not liking me must mean not talking to me.

That man is a bastard and a half, a hot one at that but I can't wait until I find something to bring him down.

In the meantime, I'll concentrate on his kids.

That thought has me churning inside.

It's only been four days, and I already care deeply for them. I don't know if it's because I've spent countless hours with them or what, but I feel this kinship with them, that, at times is making me overthink everything.

Like maybe I should quit my job tomorrow and figure out another way to do this.

Or just stop this all together.

Then the kids won't get hurt by my actions and won't lose their second parent and become orphans like I did.

I can walk away right now, but I don't want to.

I need to see this through. I have to continue this, if not for revenge than to stop another daughter from going through the same pain I am.

For right now, I will treat this like as any other job, giving it my all, and I will try to not get more attached to the kids than what I already have.

If that's even possible.

Shaking my head, I put a smile on my face, forgetting my though process and walk into the building.

When

I reach the classroom that Evelyn directed me to, I'm instantly thrown into the world of the most put-together women and their perfect children.

Everyone in the room looks pristine and dressed as if they had just come from the country club. Then there's me, wearing skinny jeans with flats and a Chicago Dark Knights T-shirt that has seen better days.

I stick out and I know it when all the adults stop talking and turn to look at me.

My cheeks heat up, so I turn away from the country club moms and look around the room for Alessandra.

I find her at a table by herself coloring, not giving the world any attention. Or is it that the world is not giving any attention to her?

Looking around some more, I see all the other kids

playing with at least one other person. Alessandra is the only one that's by herself.

Ignoring all the stares that I'm getting, I approach her and crouch down to her level.

"Hi Allie, how was your day?" I ask her and at the sound of my voice, she turns to face me.

Her eyes brighten up when she sees me, and it looks like she wants to smile, but she doesn't.

"I hope it's okay that I'm the one to pick you up today. Your *Papi* had to work. Is it okay that I'm here?"

I use the word *papi* for Dante, a word that I've heard him use a few times. Maybe by me using it, Alessandra will warm up to me a bit more.

As for Allie, well her name is beautiful, but it can be a mouthful, and she doesn't seem to mind it.

The little girl gives me a nod before going back to her drawing. Her concentration tells me that the piece of paper in front of her is her very own masterpiece.

"Excuse me?" a voice says from next to me.

Looking up, I see a woman with hair up to her ears looking down at me and given the paint-stained apron she has on, I would say she's the teacher.

"Yes?" I ask, not getting up from my position.

"Are you Arianna? Ms. Evelyn informed me that there was someone new that I had to add to the pickup list, and I just wanted to make sure."

I give the teacher a smile. "Yeah, that's me."

She gives me a nod. "Would it be possible for me to get a copy of your identification? We need to keep a list of everyone. It's a rule the school has."

Without hesitation, I hand my ID over and she takes it to get a copy, the whole time, the country club moms are looking at us.

I continue to ignore them as I get Alessandra ready to go and wait for the teacher to come back. It's when I'm grabbing Allie's little cardigan that one of the country club moms approaches.

The scent of her overly floral perfume tells me that this isn't going to be a pleasant conversation.

"You must be the new Mrs. Rosetti. It's nice to meet you, I'm Helen Baker," the lady, who I'm guessing is the lead country club mom, says.

Mrs. Rosetti?

"It's nice to meet you," I say, giving her a nod. "But no, I'm not Mrs. Rosetti. I'm just the new nanny helping out."

Helen fake gasps as if that is the hardest thing to believe. "Oh, you're the help. That's good. For a second, I thought that Dante had downgraded, no offense. You're just so..." she stops and looks me up and down before she continues. "So bland. You do look sensible enough to be the nanny."

I swear if my dad hadn't taught me to keep a good composure when someone is bad-mouthing me, this woman would probably have two teeth left.

Instead of lunging at her, I plant a closed-lip smile on my face and give her a response as eloquently as possible.

"Well, I'm glad that you think I'm sensible enough. Now, if you would excuse me, I have to get this little one home."

Thankfully the teacher comes back with my ID and

tells me I'm all set before saying her own goodbye to Alessandra. Who, by the way waves enthusiastically at her teacher before she takes my hand.

Helen watches the whole thing, not moving an inch to head back to her country club friends. When I sidestep her to head to the door, she cuts me off, smiling as if I'm her best friend.

"I was going to tell this to her father if he stopped by today, but I think I'll tell you, and you can pass the message along." Helen leans in, taking my elbow in the process.

"What message?" I can feel my eyes narrow at the woman in front of me, just waiting to hear whatever she's about to say.

"I think he should look into taking Alessandra to a child psychologist. I think she needs help, you know, mentally. And maybe even a plastic surgeon for that scar."

If I didn't have the need deep in me to punch her before, I sure as hell do now.

Who the fuck does this woman think she is? And with fucking audacity.

"Excuse me?" I hear the bite in my tone, and I know she hears it too, but she brushes it off as if this is just an everyday topic of discussion.

"Didn't you see that not one child was drawing her? She's an outcast, and he should look at getting her help."

This bitch.

I grab Alessandra's hand a little tighter as I step closer to Helen so she can hear me and nobody else.

"Or maybe she isn't an outcast, and the kids here are

pretentious little assholes that take after their mothers. Maybe they should be the ones to go to therapy. That way they can learn to be better people and not treat others as if they are less than them because of something small on their face. So fuck your message and fuck you for even suggesting such a thing."

Her gasp rings through my ears as I place a smile on my face and walk Alessandra out of the room without another word or second glance at Helen Baker.

I'm fuming by the time I get back to the car and strap Alessandra into her car seat. It gets even worse as we drive back to the house.

How can a woman, a grown fucking woman, with kids, nonetheless, say things like that? Especially about a child.

Something has to be seriously wrong with you to suggest that a child, one that isn't yours, needs not only therapy but fucking plastic surgery, right? That lady is the one that needs therapy because fuck, who even does that?

Alessandra is perfect.

Yes, I've known her for only four days, and I don't know this beautiful little girl fully, but what I do know, I wouldn't change. Not even the fact that she doesn't talk or her scar.

I'm so pissed that I want to tell the driver, to turn back so I can beat this lady up.

Fuck it. She's next on the list. After I'm done here, I'm taking Helen Baker down but fuck her.

She will pay for disrespecting Alessandra like that.

When we reach the house, the anger has not dissipated enough, my blood still boils thinking about it. And even through my blood boiling, I'm somehow able to get both kids upstairs, not even waking up Angel in the process.

But the anger has blinded me enough to not notice when someone joins me as I change Alessandra out of her school uniform.

And I know this only because he speaks and breaks through the under-the-breath muttering that I'm doing.

"Arianna." The deep voice takes me out of my angry stupor.

I jump a bit, meeting his gaze in the process.

For a second, I just look at the man in front of me. He's wearing a black oxford that accentuates every inch of his wide shoulders and chest. For a second, I forget everything. Why I took this job. I forget about the anger from the preschool but then the man clears his throat and I'm brought back to it all.

I'm brought back to the anger and even remember the fact that I wasn't supposed to be the one that picked Alessandra up from school.

"Look, I know you're probably pissed that I picked your daughter up from school since you don't trust me and all, but it wasn't my idea. It was Evelyn's, so take it up with her and throw your anger in her direction. I'm already reeling from my adventures at school today, I don't have the patience to deal with your mood."

I tell him as I put Allie's shirt in the hamper and fold up her skirt and put it on top of her dresser.

"Adventures?" Dante asks as I go pick up Angel, who has finally woken up.

I ignore his question. "I can't believe that you let your

daughter deal with those types of people five days a week. The audacity of some of them. I swear if I ever see that Helen chick again, I will beat her face in."

There are a few more colorful words that I want to say, like bitch, but I keep them in because there are kids in the room.

"Helen Baker?" Dante asks as I bounce Angel on my hip.

I let out a frustrated sigh. "Yes. That *B*," I say instead of the complete word. "Who does she think she is? Suggesting that Allie needs to see a psychologist and a plastic surgeon. Alessandra is perfect, and she doesn't need suggestions from Helen Baker. I can't even believe she had the fucking audacity to come up to me and tell me that."

Dante doesn't say anything and when I turn, I see that he is looking at his daughter with his jaw ticcing a bit.

He's pissed.

At what, I don't know. It could be at me for doing something he didn't want me to do or it could be at Helen.

Honestly, it could be a toss-up.

I decided to deescalate the situation.

"Look, I'm sorry I went to pick her up. If you came in here to yell at me, can you at least wait until I end the day? That way I can drown in wine."

Dante takes his gaze off his daughter and then turns it back to me.

We look at each other for a few seconds before he lets out a sigh.

"I didn't come in here to yell at you."

"You didn't?"

Maybe he's here to fire me because he found out who I really am and why I'm here.

That has to be it.

Why else would he actively seek me out? He hasn't in the last few days.

I mentally prepare myself for him to destroy me, to rip me apart and leave me just like he left my father.

"No." He pauses, and I realize I'm not ready for what he's about to say. "I actually came to find you to tell you that you are moving in tomorrow night."

12

DANTE

If you ever get to ask a Mafia boss what he likes to do in his free time, his answer may surprise you.

Some will say that they like to count their money.

Others will say that they like to go to their favorite coffee shop and interact with people.

For me, I would tell you two things. My number one thing is to spend time with my children. No matter the time of day, as long as I am near them and have an eye on them, I am happy.

The second thing I like to do is sit in my suite at Perversa and look down at everything that is happening in my club.

Like I said, surprising, but I take pride in my club. I've worked hard to get it where it is today.

From the outside, most people wouldn't expect for the establishment to have more than one floor. Especially with how the windows align.

What people that have never been here before don't know, is that I own not only the building but the whole entire block. The club not only spans one floor but four, with the rest being used as storage and housing for some of my dancers and bar employees.

The first floor is the main section, the place where the people pay a hefty sum to be able to step inside. The floor where you are able to experience some of the most beautiful women that you will lay your eyes on.

Floor two is filled with private rooms that can only be rented out by the elite members. The rooms that they have to pay even more money to rent out. They are meant to give the club member a closer look at the dancers or to hold a private event but never touch.

Number one rule of Perversa, you touch no one. I don't give a shit how drunk you are, you don't touch my people.

The third floor is for those that want to experience the most beautiful male dancers that people will ever see.

My goal with Perversa was to cater to everyone so I knew that male dancers were a must.

The fourth floor is the dressing room and a place for the dancers and employees to destress during working hours.

As for the housing that I offer, I wanted the people that work for me to feel safe, especially if they didn't have a place to live and had to work late hours. It's not mandatory for them to live here, but it's an option offered to them for a very small fee.

Then there is my suite, of course. The place that I go to

in my free time when I'm not with my children or dealing with business.

I come here to de-stress and in the last seven months, that has meant a number of things.

Sometimes it was just to drink and make sure that everything is running smoothly on the first floor.

Sometimes, especially in the last three months, de-stressing meant calling Honor in here to give me a helping hand. That was the only exception to the no-touching rule and Honor was always on board with what I had in mind.

But tonight, the means of de-stressing is slightly different. Tonight, there won't be any heavy drinking, no calling in Honor to get on her knees. No, tonight I have other plans to get rid of the stress and anger boiling inside of me.

Plans that might be slightly darker.

One of the benefits of being the owner of the most exclusive club in the city is knowing its members. Some are politicians, some are police officers, and some are parents from your child's school.

It's only been a few short hours since Arianna started to babble about what Helen Baker told her at school concerning Alessandra.

When I first walked into the house and I noticed that Evelyn was there and not Arianna, I was pissed.

From the very beginning, I told Evelyn that I didn't want Arianna picking up my daughter from school because I didn't trust her. And it's true, I don't.

I didn't trust her not to have an ulterior motive, one that included her being alone with my children. For all I knew, she was planning on taking them away from me to hurt in some way.

When I was finished dealing with the shit show happening with my men and arrived home and noticed she wasn't there, I about lost it.

But then when I heard her arrive and take the kids upstairs, a part of me relaxed but I was still pissed off.

So, I followed her and was going to confront her when she stopped me. Something in the way that she talked to me and the way she was handling the kids made me stop.

During the last few days, I've kept my distance from seeing her work. I didn't want to get angry or be irrational, so I let Evelyn handle it.

But earlier today, I saw something that I didn't expect to see and that was how much she cared.

I saw it in the way that she moved through the room and always kept an eye on each kid. Better yet, I heard it when she told me about her interaction with Helen Baker.

She was angry because of the woman's words but she was more pissed off at the fact that they were directed at Alessandra.

Arianna Vitale was just as mad as I was and for some reason that stumped me to the point that I forgot about my anger toward her. So stumped that I invited her to move a few days early, versus firing her on the spot for doing something I told her not to.

Now hours later, the woman that may be in my home for reasons unknown, is moving into my house and I'm in my suite waiting for my guests to arrive.

Guests that I didn't give fuck about seeing until I heard Arianna ramble off, then a plan came to fruition.

Being an owner has its benefits and I'm taking advantage of this one.

And given who I am, I have ears everywhere. How else would I know that Helen Baker had planned to bring a group of her friends here tonight for a bachelorette party?

A bachelorette party she had to pay ten grand to have in my club.

I look at my watch and I can't help but smirk at the fact that my fun is about to begin.

Standing up from my seat, with my scotch in hand, I walk over to the two-way window that overlooks everything and wait for the bachelorette party to arrive.

One thing I know about the moms at Alessandra's school is that they are always on time, even to a fucking strip club.

Like clockwork, I watch a group of nine women walk in, all with a look of awe on their faces.

All of them except Helen, since she and her husband come here at least every two weeks.

I keep my eyes on them as they get escorted through the first floor and head to the elevator.

Once the group walks out of view, I continue to watch out of the window until I hear the knock ring throughout the room, not even ten minutes later.

"Mr. Rosetti, the party is all set." The guard that escorted the group for me to the proper location, tells me.

I give him a nod. "Thank you."

A nod of his own gets thrown in my direction and he leaves.

It's time to pay our special guest a visit.

I finish off my scotch and button up my suit jacket before making my way out of the room and head down the hallway.

The music that circulates through the floor surrounds me like a cloud and it does so until I knock on the designated door and get let in by the guard inside.

I take shit seriously here and each one of my private rooms has a guard standing inside to protect all my dancers.

The guard gives me a nod, closing the door behind me.

As soon as I walk in, I watch as nine heavily intoxicated women cheer on one of my best male dancers, as he performs for them.

My presence doesn't catch anyone's attention, that is, until Todd, my dancer, gives me a slight nod before going back to his routine.

It's the nod that makes the one and only Helen Baker turn to me. Forgetting all about Todd and her friends, Helen comes over to me with a big smile on her face as if I'm about to give her the prize money.

"Dante, I wasn't expecting to see you tonight," she says, reaching up and placing a kiss on my cheek as if we are old friends.

We aren't. I barely tolerate the woman on school grounds, and my club is no different.

I give her a nod. "I heard that you had rented out a

room and I thought I would stop in and see if anything was needed."

Lies on top of more lies.

"Oh, that is sweet of you," Helen says a little too excited. "We must be very special if the owner himself is stopping in to check on us."

"Special indeed," I say to her before moving the conversation in a different direction. "There was actually something that I wanted to talk to you about. Do you mind if we step out real quick?"

That grabs her attention. "Oh, what about?"

"Just a school thing," I say as I open the door a bit and wait for her to walk through.

Helen hesitates for a second, and if I were more caring, I would say that she's a little terrified to follow me out of the room, but she does it, nonetheless.

I close the door behind us, putting a barrier between us and her friends, the hallway empty of any spectators.

"What is it that you wanted to talk about?" There's a shakiness in her voice, the fear bleeding through.

I don't answer her, instead I close the distance between us, pushing her back until she is against the wall.

"How about you going up to my nanny and telling her that my daughter not only needs to see a therapist but also a plastic surgeon?"

Helen lets out a little gasp, as if she was shocked that I know what happened today.

"She's the nanny, Dante. You can't believe everything she says."

She's right on that one, but I don't tell her that. I also don't tell her that I have my doubts about said nanny.

"Do you really believe that if she didn't tell me, I wouldn't have heard it from somewhere else? You must severely doubt my abilities, Helen."

I watch her throat as she swallows. She must be nervous or scared of what this conversation is going to turn into.

She should.

"If I didn't say it, someone else would have."

A chuckle leaves my mouth at her statement. "Maybe you're right."

"There is nothing you can do about it anyway. The words have been said and I'm not one of your employees that you can fire." The confidence that this woman has is fucking astonishing.

Does she have any idea who the fuck I am?

I think it's time I show her.

Pouncing on her, my right hand goes to her throat and my other goes to cover her mouth. I don't usually get this close to women, especially ones I despise but this bitch needs to learn not to mess with me.

"I can do everything that I want about it. Like banning you from this club permanently, or better yet, I can get your husband fired from his job. He works at the Lane Enterprises, does he not? All it would take is a phone call letting them know that his wife is verbally abusive to children, and he's gone."

My grip around her neck grows a bit tighter and Helen lets out a whimper.

Those two things may seem minuscule but with people like the Bakers that are all about appearances, those two things matter. I can do a lot worse to a woman like this, but I don't see any reason for trying.

"I can do everything and anything to destroy you and your family, Helen. So keep my children's names out of your whore mouth and nothing will happen. Do you understand?"

Another whimper escapes her before she gives me a nod.

I could tighten my grip on her right now and leave her limp on the club floor, but I don't.

Instead, I step back and readjust my jacket, letting her catch her breath.

There is no reason to stay, so I leave the poor excuse for a woman to go back to her party.

"I guess the people are right, Dante Rosetti really is The Devil."

Arianna is right on one account; this woman has some fucking audacity.

"Sweetheart, if The Devil was standing in front of you, you wouldn't be going back to your party with just threats. You would be limp on the floor and not one person would know what happened to you. Continue to run your fucking mouth and maybe that will happen."

Without one final look in her direction, I turn and leave her to her own accord.

My work for the night is done.

Now to deal with my new roommate.

13

ARIANNA

If you would have asked me during my father's funeral where I thought I would be in two months, I would have said in my apartment being a hermit.

Never, and I mean never, would I have thought that I would be in the position that I'm in. Currently moving into Dante Rosetti's house, and as his nanny of all things.

But here I am at two in the morning, trying to organize my things in a room that is two times the size of my studio apartment.

It's been two weeks since Dante told me that I was moving in.

Was I surprised? Hell yeah, I was.

I thought that he was going to fire me, that he had found out that I lied and was going to kick me out on my ass.

Yet the words "moving in" came out of his mouth and I was dumbfounded.

So dumbfounded that I stood there with my mouth

open, not being able to say a word. Not even when he took Angel from me and took him and Alessandra downstairs.

I wanted to fight him on it, tell him that I wasn't going to move in.

But Evelyn told me at the beginning of the week that it was going to happen. I couldn't fight it, I was going to move into the Rosetti manor whether I liked it or not.

Then I thought about it, for a long minute, I thought about it, and I realized that moving in might actually be a good thing. A great thing even.

I wanted inside Rosetti's life and I thought I was doing that by being just the nanny, but I could do it better by being the live-in nanny.

By moving in, I could get in deeper and find things that may be harder to find otherwise.

Moving in was a good thing, and I was going to grasp it as long as it was handed to me. And Dante was handing it to me.

The poor bastard, he doesn't know what's coming for him.

Well, I don't know either, but still.

After I concluded that I was moving in, I went downstairs and told Dante yes. It wasn't really a question, but I still agreed to move in.

For the rest of the night, I watched the kids while he went to the club, and I got together with Evelyn to plan out everything.

Like which room in the humongous house was going to be mine.

To my surprise, she put me in the last empty room that

the second floor had to offer. It was its own separate wing, but it was still close enough to the kids if they needed anything at night.

The day after, I brought over only my essentials, because I wasn't going to empty out my apartment for this, and officially moved in.

As to why I'm barely unpacking three weeks later at two in the morning? Because the kids have kept me busy.

Sure, I spend twelve hours a day with them for a week, but that's nothing compared to watching them twenty-four seven.

Okay, I'm not watching them all day, Dante does take over after a certain time on nights that he doesn't go to the club. It's still a lot more than the first five days.

So, I'm finally making my new living quarters actually look livable.

My bathroom is done, and so is my closet since I didn't bring many articles of clothing. Now I just have my bedroom left and the small living room area left to finish.

Yes, my room has a living room. If it had a kitchen I would never want to move out.

I look over at the bed and I sigh at how tempting it looks. I just want to crawl under my covers and fall asleep, but I have to power through.

Tomorrow is my day off and I need to finish this tonight so I can sleep in and then go over to the cemetery to visit my dad.

Something that I haven't done since he died.

But tomorrow I'm making myself do it. Tomorrow I will get a cab or call an Uber and I will go to the cemetery.

Because tomorrow is his birthday and I owe him that much. And maybe after I visit him, my head will be clearer.

Maybe then I will have a clear plan on how to take down Dante once and for all, and if I could do it without hurting his children, even better.

Because what I thought would happen, did. I've gotten attached to Alessandra and Angel and its scary how quickly it happened.

Ever since I realized just how much I cared for them, I've been trying to come up with a different plan that would move everything along faster.

I have yet to come up with anything.

Hopefully going to visit my dad's gravesite will help me a bit.

Fuck. Well, there goes my mood. I went almost a whole day without thinking about why I'm really here and bringing pain to the kids and now I feel depressed.

I need sugar.

Giving up on my room for the moment, I slip on slippers and head downstairs to the kitchen in just my t-shirt.

Maybe I can grab some of the kids' fruit snacks since that's the only sugar Dante lets them have.

I should start sneaking in sugary stuff and hide it in my room, I bet the kids would love it. Some cereal, powdered donuts and peanut butter cups are definitely needed. Maybe I'll stop by the store on my way back from the cemetery tomorrow.

Concentrating on my sugar-filled grocery list, I get to the kitchen and turn on the light, illuminating the room.

The second I do, though, I see that I'm not the only one up at two in the morning.

We meet each other's eyes at the same time, and I think it might be the shock of finding Dante down here that makes my eyes wander.

And by wander, I mean they wander down his chest. His very naked, broad chest. A chest with more muscles than what I've ever seen on anyone.

Then my eyes wander some more, down to his stomach, which is flat and has ridges going across it. Abs. This man has abs.

Isn't he almost forty? How does he look this good? This man is making my mouth water.

Oh my god, did I just think that? Did I really just think that Dante Rosetti, the man that possibly killed my father, was mouthwatering? What is wrong with me?

It's not the first time that thought popped up.

Being in his presence makes me want to cover up a bit more. I'm definitely not wearing nanny attire.

"Arianna." His deep tone reaches my ears, making my eyes move away from his naked upper half.

"What?" I say, with some raspiness.

Him being shirtless is really affecting me.

Who wouldn't be? This man is gorgeous and one that would know how to make a woman scream. Even if he is the meanest and baddest in of all the land.

"I asked why you were up so late," he says putting a container of ice cream on the counter.

Ice cream?

The man that doesn't allow his kids to eat sugar, besides fruit snacks, is eating ice cream? With that body?

Focus, Ari,

"I um…" I can't think of anything coherent to say. "I was unpacking, and I thought I would come down for a snack."

He gives me a nod before he leans against the counter behind him, crossing his arms against his chest. "I thought you unpacked weeks ago."

Are we having a normal conversation? If we are, this would be a first.

I shake my head. "I've been putting it off, and well, I didn't realize how much it would take to be a live-in nanny."

Dante nods again, not looking at me while he does it. "Because you've never been a nanny before."

His comment comes off more as an observation than an accusation.

"Yup. Because I've never been a nanny before." I want to roll my eyes, but I don't. He's right, I never have.

"But you have a degree in child development." Another statement and this time he does look at me.

I give him a nod. "There was a point I wanted to be a teacher."

"What changed your mind?" he asks, looking at me with genuine curiosity.

I don't know what is happening here, but I don't hate it.

"I graduated and I saw how much life depended on having money. So, I went to the one place where money was always flowing and ended up liking it." I give him a shrug like not pursuing something that I wanted to do most of my life wasn't a big deal.

"You could have gone into stripping."

I snort. "Would you have hired me as a dancer?"

He pauses for a long minute, looking me up and down. Appraising me like he's never really seen me before.

In a way the look reminds me of when I first walked into his office at the club.

The appraisal makes me want to shield myself, but I keep still.

"No," Dante says after a minute.

Well, then.

"Thanks for the confidence boost," I say to him a little too sarcastically.

At my comment, I think he is going to call me out for using a sarcastic tone with him but when he lets out a snort, I'm taken by surprise.

The smirk he wears also takes me by surprise.

"You're a very beautiful woman, but a strip club, especially one like Perversa, is not a place for you," he tells me, keeping my gaze. "Your beauty would run that place to the ground."

A small gasp escapes me as I hear the last words leave his lips.

Your beauty would run that place to the ground.

That small sentence is playing over and over in my head, and I can't think of one thing to say in response .

This man, this man that is such an enigma, a man that could kill me with a simple movement of his arm, a man that possibly killed my father, called me beautiful. And instead of running away scared, I'm standing here marveling at his words. Hoping to hear them again and again.

I open my mouth to say something, but nothing comes out.

Eventually, I just say the first thing that comes to mind. Putting the thoughts of his words away, for now.

"Where did you get the ice cream?" My voice is a bit high pitched, which causes Dante's smirk to get slightly deeper at my uneasiness.

"I have a stash hidden in the back of the freezer." He says proudly, nodding toward the freezer that blends into the wall.

"Seriously?" Who hides ice cream?

"Seriously." Dante nods.

"Why?"

"Because if I don't hide it, then my kids will eat it and I won't get a drop."

Okay, who is this man and where did the hard mob boss that people call The Devil, go?

"Can I have some?" I ask, liking the back and forth that's happening between us.

Dante nods and gestures me toward the pint that he had put down on the counter. I take the invitation and walk over to where he is standing.

All of this feels weird.

For the last three weeks, all my conversations with Dante have been solely me speaking and him grunting or saying yes or no in return. I think this is the first time since he told me to move in that I've heard a full sentence directed at me.

And the more I experience it, the more I like it.

I really need to get my head checked.

Grabbing the pint of ice cream, Moose Tracks, I might add, I take the spoon and place it in my mouth.

This is exactly the type of sugar I needed.

I take a few more spoonfuls and as I go back for my fifth one, I turn slightly and notice that Dante is watching me.

More specifically, my mouth, which is currently wrapped around the spoon that was in his mouth not even five minutes ago.

A blush creeps up my cheeks when I realize it and I embarrassingly put the spoon back in the container before setting it on the counter.

"Well, that satisfied my sugar craving," I say, not looking up at him. "I'm going to head back to my room and finish unpacking."

I scurry away from him and I'm almost halfway through the kitchen entrance when Dante stops me.

"Good night, Arianna," he says, and when I turn, I see his eyes filled with sincerity.

I get lost in his gaze for a second before I respond. "Good night, Dante."

Not Mr. Rosetti, like I've said every day for the last three weeks, but Dante.

Without another word, I leave the kitchen, leave my boss behind, and head back upstairs.

Once I'm behind the closed door, I let out the breath I was holding.

Tomorrow, I have to not only clear my head about the Rosetti children, but also their father.

Because just one conversation at two in the morning and I'm feeling the way I felt after my disastrous interview.

Powerful.

Power with the way he looked at me. Power with the way he talked to me so freely and without anger or irritation.

And just like after the interview, I like it.

I like it so much that I want to experience it every chance I get.

I want to experience everything that Dante Rosetti has to give and that right there is the most dangerous thing I could ever want.

More dangerous than wanting the man dead.

14

———

DANTE

The hot water hits my bare back, not doing anything to relieve the tight knots that line my shoulders.

Knots that are there because of I got a call from a detective. A detective that wanted to talk about my whereabouts the day Joseph Vitale was murdered.

Knots that are there because I'm seriously thinking about taking my daughter to see a therapist to help her to find her voice again.

Knots because I can't stop thinking about the fucking nanny and wanting to feel her pout around my swollen cock.

The latter gives me the biggest knot of all and it's not just in my shoulders.

Here's the thing about Arianna Vitale, I found her attractive the first time she walked into my office. There is no denying that. Even in her shapeless dress, I wanted to explore every one of her curves.

And when her tits were on display, I wanted to mark them as mine.

I feel this pull toward her, one that even having Honor blow me after that interview, was not enough for me to put the urge for her to bed.

Then she started working for me, and the urge continued to grow, so I put as much distance between the two of us as I could.

I didn't look in her direction.

I didn't speak to her directly.

I even called Honor into my office a few times so that I could fuck the thoughts of my nanny out of my mind.

I kept my distance.

All of that continued when she moved in, and I was doing great, until we came together in the kitchen a few nights ago.

Until she came down from her room at two in the morning in nothing but a shirt that barely covered her ass and found me in the kitchen.

And yes, I fucking noticed that the shirt didn't cover much of her thighs. More so, when she came to where I was standing and placed her mouth on the spoon.

All I wanted to do was lay her across the counter, raise the shirt up and cover her pussy and tits in ice cream and to lick it off.

Who knew that watching someone eat ice cream could give you a half chub.

But it did.

It also didn't help that I liked talking to her even if it was for a few short minutes. Hearing her sarcasm and seeing her blush at my words, made me go from chub to full mast.

I almost let my dick take over my thinking for a bit. I know for a fact that I wasn't thinking when I told her that she was beautiful and didn't belong in my club.

It's that look that she gave me when she heard my words that is currently circulating through my mind.

Her hair was slightly wild. Her lips looked full, and her eyes looked wide. She looked like every one of her twenty-four years of age. Then I saw her blush and I couldn't help but wonder if it traveled all over her body. I saw the way her breath hitched, and her shirt lifted a bit more along her thighs.

That image is what is making my dick hard to the point of pain.

Even when I close my eyes, all I see is Arianna and the urge grows even more.

So much so that I find myself sliding down my hand until I grip myself tightly.

Hard stroke after hard stroke, I work myself trying to release the pressure my cock is currently experiencing.

My hand slams against the marble tile that lines the shower walls, a moan escaping when I tug at my balls and let my imagination run.

I picture the dark-haired beauty with the doe eyes kneeled in front of me with her mouth wide open.

I picture the tits that were on display in my office all those weeks ago, glistening from the water, waiting for me to give them attention.

Then as I fuck my hand, I picture pounding into her

delicate pussy and watching her as she drains me and when she's close to finishing, it's my name on her lips.

It's at the fantasy of her yelling out my name that I explode into my hand. Cords release out of me, and it feels like it's never going to stop.

I lean my forehead against the marble, recovering from my fantasies.

Dirty fantasies that involve the nanny.

A twenty-four-year-old nanny at that.

If I don't go to hell for the shit I've done in my life, I might go for this.

15

———

DANTE

Sometime after my release, I switched the water from scalding hot to ice cold. All because Arianna was still in my mind and all I wanted to do was to go find her and bring her into the shower with me.

To not let that happen, I took the coldest shower that I have taken since I was a fucking teenager. Given the circumstances, it won't be the last.

Because there is something about this wannabe nanny that makes me want to lose my mind.

I don't even think that Angelina made me feel this way.

Fuck. That's not something that should have been a thought.

Shaking my head, I try to stop thinking about my dead wife in that capacity.

I think of her, of course I do, but I will not disrespect her in any way, even if it was just a random thought.

Forgetting about it, I pull on a T-shirt and jeans, before

heading out of my bedroom and heading downstairs to find the kids.

It's Sunday, and I usually work on Sunday mornings. I either head to the club or deal with whatever Rosetti *famiglia* business that needs taking care of.

Today, it's one of those rare Sundays that I have nothing pressing, so I decided to stay home this morning. Maybe even take the kids somewhere, what with the weather still being somewhat nice and all.

When I hit the first floor, I stop for a second and just listen.

It's quiet. A little too quiet for it being a home with two small children.

For a second, I start to panic and feel anger start to boil in me, all with thoughts that my children are gone.

Did Arianna take them?

Is this the moment that I've been waiting for, ever since I hired her?

I'm ready to yell for my security team when I hear a baby laughing.

The anger and the panic quickly dissipate and with a deep breath, I follow the laugh until I find the three of them in the kitchen.

Angel is sitting in his high chair, cereal all over the place and what looks like a banana smashed all over his face.

His sister is sitting on the counter, with Arianna next to her, tossing what looks like blueberries into a bowl to be mixed.

There is flour all over the counter and Arianna is

looking down at my daughter with the biggest smile on her face.

"Do you want to mix, Allie?" she asks the little girl, holding out the whisk. "Can you say mix?"

Alessandra ignores her last question and gladly takes it and starts to whisk, what I'm assuming is pancake batter, like it's the most important job in the world.

I bask in watching the three of them as I think about the nickname that Arianna just used.

Allie.

A nickname that I've heard her use more and more since she moved in. The first time I heard her use it, I was floored. It was a name that Angelina always used.

The name Alessandra came about because both Angelina and I liked it, but she thought it was too much of a mouthful for a kid, so she called her Allie.

When she died, I stopped using the nickname because it reminded me of her. Hearing it now, I should be angry, but I'm not.

I like that this woman is calling my daughter Allie and I know I shouldn't.

"Good morning," I announce to the room.

I guess that it wasn't known that I was standing at the kitchen entrance because at the sound of my voice, Arianna jumps, meeting my gaze with scared eyes. The bowl releasing from her hands in the process and batter going everywhere.

Even on Allie's face.

"Oh my god," Arianna mutters, looking away from me and over at the mess, a bit flustered.

I approach the kitchen island, smirking a bit at how Arianna can't seem to even form a word as she looks around the kitchen for the paper towels to clean up the mess.

Grabbing the roll for where it sits next to Alessandra, I hand it to her, and her eyes go slightly wider.

"Thank you," she mumbles, taking it.

I give her a nod. "Pancakes, huh?" I ask as I wipe some of the batter from Allie's cheek.

My daughter gives me a big smile when I swipe the batter and place my finger into my mouth.

"Yeah," Arianna says as if she's in another world.

Looking up, I see that she's looking at me and Allie, as if she has never seen me interact with my daughter before.

She looks between the two of us for a few seconds before she shakes her head and goes back to cleaning the counter.

"It's Sunday, why not have pancakes on Sunday?" Arianna says, not looking up at me as she continues cleaning.

Alessandra grabs a blueberry and holds it out for me to take. I lean down and let her pop it into my mouth, batter in all.

"Would be better if there were chocolate chip pancakes, but blueberries will do." I grab another blueberry and hand it to my daughter to take it.

"I thought that you were already at work," Arianna says, taking me out of the back-and-forth with my daughter.

I shrug. "Nothing pressing had to be done, so I decided to stay home. Maybe take these two somewhere."

Looking up, I find that she is looking at me again, this time with curiosity.

"Oh, okay."

"You can have the rest of the day off. Do something for yourself today," I tell her.

Usually, I try to give Arianna Saturdays and any other day during the week she wants off. Sometimes it works out but other times, most of the time, I'm calling her back because one of my soldiers decided to do something stupid and I have to take care of it.

She gives me a nod. "Okay, then I will clean up and get them dressed for you and I will be on my way."

"Or we can both clean up, eat breakfast together and then you can go."

The room goes silent.

Arianna stops cleaning and even the kids stop moving like they are surprised by the words that just left my mouth.

Frankly, I am too.

Since when did I care about the nanny joining us for a meal? I usually excuse her to fend for herself, yet I just told her to share a meal with us.

"Um, are you sure?"

No, I'm not. Especially given the fantasy I jerked off to in the shower.

"Yes, I'm sure." Having her for breakfast will be good for the kids.

I mean, having her *here* for breakfast, definitely not

having her for breakfast. Even if my cock wants to stand up at the thought.

"Okay." She gives me a small smile but still looks over at me questioningly before looking at my daughter. "Do you want to help me clean up?"

Alessandra looks at her before giving her a nod.

"Can you say yes?" Arianna asks her, optimistic.

This has been going on since she started, trying to get Alessandra to speak. Every time Arianna asks her a question, she asks if she can say a specific word. One hundred percent of the time, Alessandra looks at her nanny with a look of indifference.

Just like right now.

I want to tell Arianna to give up, that Alessandra isn't going to speak, but a part of me wants to be optimistic with her and believe that it will happen.

Arianna lets out a sigh and reaches for Alessandra, who gladly goes into her arms.

While the girls clean, I grab Angel from the highchair and clean up the mashed banana as best I can. The kid has it all over his hair so if we are going to go anywhere, he's going to need a bath.

Soon the flour and pancake batter are cleaned up and I'm flipping pancakes while Arianna reads the kids a book at the table.

As I plate two pancakes, an odd sensation flows through me.

Normality.

Nothing in this house has felt normal in almost eight

months, yet here I am flipping fucking pancakes for the nanny.

I'm a mob boss for fuck's sake, I should be planning which head I'm going to chop off next. Not having quiet Sundays wanting to know if the nanny's pussy tastes like blueberries or not.

She's twenty-four, Dante, and she's lying about who she is.

For some reason, I keep forgetting that small detail. On top of the fact that I know she's Joseph's daughter.

I really need to get my shit together.

Finishing up the rest of the pancakes, I grab the plates and take them over to the table.

After cutting up the kids' food into little pieces, the four of us eat, mostly in silence with a few giggles and baby talk from Angel.

"I have—"

"What are you—"

We both start and stop at the same time.

Blush creeps up her cheeks before she waves at me to speak. "Go ahead."

"I was going to say that I have a meeting tomorrow. It's in the morning and I don't know how long it will take, so I might be back late."

The meeting with the king of Chicago is finally happening and I'm trying not to roll my eyes at the thought.

"Oh, okay," she says as if she was expecting me to say something else.

"What were you going to say?" I ask.

The blush comes back before she answers. "I was just about to ask what you guys were going to do today?"

I give her a shrug. "I was thinking about taking them to the park. Let them play a bit."

She gives me a nod before she turns to Allie and gives her a bright smile.

"Do you want to play at the park, Allie? I bet it's going to be so much fun."

Alessandra nods before going back to her food.

We finish up our food and once Angel's pancake starts landing mostly on the floor rather than in his mouth, I grab the plates and start doing the dishes.

"It's just going to be you guys and *Papi* today, okay? I will see you guys tomorrow and I will put your hair in pigtails just how you like it," Arianna tells the kids.

Turning slightly, I catch Arianna giving each child a kiss on the head and smoothing their hair back.

My heart constricts a bit at the sight.

In a short time, she has gotten close to them. Has started to care about them and from the looks of it, deeply.

"Have fun at the park, okay?" Arianna says before throwing them a smile and starting to make her way out of the kitchen.

I turn back to finish up the dishes when a faint sound has me dropping the dish in my hand, causing it to shatter.

"Bye."

It's faint. So faint that I think that I imagined it. I turn around, forgetting about the broken dish, trying to figure out that I really heard what I thought I did.

Did...?

From the looks of things, I wasn't the only one that heard the faint sound, because Arianna is standing in the kitchen entryway with a shocked expression.

"Did...?" she starts, looking at me and then to the little girl sitting at the kitchen table. "Did she just say 'bye?'"

I nod, not knowing if *I'm* able to say anything.

We both heard it so it must have happened, right?

I walk over to the table and crouch down next to Alessandra, taking her small hands in mine.

"*Gioia mia,* did you just say bye to Arianna?" I ask her, hoping, fucking praying that my ears aren't playing tricks on me.

Alessandra looks at me and then she looks over at Arianna before turning back to me and giving me a nod.

A nod yes.

She said bye.

For the first time in almost eight months, my daughter has said a word.

"Can you repeat it?" Arianna asks, now crouched down next to me, an encouraging smile on her face.

Alessandra looks at her and for a long minute, I think that she isn't. That she isn't going to repeat it. That she is just going to shake her head and I will never hear her beautiful voice again, but just like her mother, she surprises me with every turn.

"Bye."

One simple word.

Just a simple whisper and everything in me wants to crumble to the ground just hearing it.

Forget being a mob boss, forget being the most feared man in Chicago and every bad thing that I have done.

All of that is forgotten because right now, I'm just a father. A father that just heard his daughter speak a word for the first time in so long and he wants to hear the simple word again and again.

"Bye," Arianna echoes, a grin on her face.

"She said bye," I say, not taking my eyes off Alessandra.

"She said bye," Arianna repeats.

I turn to face her and that smile she has on her face is so fucking intoxicating. She's excited just as much as I am about this, and I can feel my smile grow to mirror hers.

We stare at each other for a few seconds, smiling like two fucking loons because a four-year-old said a word. Until Arianna breaks the stare and starts to jump up and down, giving Alessandra a hug and a kiss on the head in the process.

I stand and watch her, marveling at her excitement before she turns back to face me. Without warning, she jumps into my arms and places her lips against mine.

Something that I don't digest is happening until my arms wrap around her body, and my tongue is fighting its way into her mouth.

She tastes fucking delicious and like fucking blueberries and syrup.

It's a moan that escapes her that brings us back to reality.

Just as fast as it happened, it ends with Arianna frantically pulling away from me and setting herself back on the ground.

The look on her face tells me that she can't believe what just happened.

What did just happen?

We were so fucking happy about Alessandra speaking that we basically started to maul at each other.

Fuck.

I should regret it, but I don't. All I want is her mouth back on mine.

"I have to go," Arianna says, turning away quickly and leaving the room.

Just as quickly as the kiss happened, she's gone.

And I'm left standing here wondering if I should chase after her because whether I liked it or not, I was starting to like the nanny in more ways than what I can comprehend. That kiss solidified that.

I'm royally fucked.

16

ARIANNA

Oh my god. Oh my god. Oh my *god*.

What is wrong with me?

Who the hell lets excitement go to their head so much that they jump into their boss's arms and kiss them?

Apparently, I do because that's exactly what I did. I let the excitement of hearing Alessandra speak for the first time, get the best of me and I didn't think about it.

I didn't think about jumping into his arms and placing my lips against his. I didn't think about sliding my hands into his hair and holding myself to him and melting into his hold.

God, I kissed my boss.

Not only did I kiss my boss, but I kissed Dante Rosetti, the man that possibly has ties to my father's murder and I fucking liked it.

I liked that he was kissing me back.

I liked that I forgot that the children were in the room

and the fact that Evelyn had gone to visit family and wasn't going to walk in on us

I liked it so much that I let him slide his tongue into my mouth. So much that I moaned because it felt so good.

The stupid moan that made me realize what I was doing and took me out of the damn lust-filled cloud that I was in.

I got out of that cloud and quickly got out of there.

I needed to get out of there before anything else happened, like me telling the man to take me upstairs and fuck me until I was left begging.

And trust me, I wanted to beg.

So much.

After I ran out, I ran straight to my room and didn't leave until I heard car doors closing outside an hour later.

Dante, the kids and a few of the guards were gone and I was able to let out a deep breath.

Then all the emotions came rolling back in. My mind was replaying what I had done and had come to the conclusion that I needed a reminder as to why I was there, more than ever.

I needed a reminder as to why I wanted to work with Rosetti in the first place and why I wanted to insert myself in his life.

I was supposed to go visit my dad's grave a few days ago for his birthday, to clear my head. To remind myself why I was doing this in the first place, but I didn't.

Not because I had to work, or because I had something pressing to do, but because I couldn't.

I was all set and ready to go, but I couldn't leave the

house. It felt too painful to even head to the cemetery. So, I stayed and mourned my father in my room, wishing someone was there to give me a tight hug.

Now, because I didn't take that outlet to clear my head, I'm as confused as ever.

Because I heard Alessandra speak. Because I felt how good it was to be in Dante's arms and have his lips pressed against mine.

I need to be reminded as to why I'm here.

And what better way to do that than do some laundry.

When Dante told me I had the day off, I thought of maybe going to visit Cora and Jimmy at the bar and maybe even Tommy. Instead of doing that, I'm in a taxi heading to Little Italy.

Could I have used the burner phone to talk to Gallo and get my head back in the game? Yes, yes, I could have, but there were still guards on the property.

I can't have someone overhearing how I want to take down the boss.

And I had some laundry to do anyway, so I took the opportunity.

The taxi ride takes close to an hour, since the Rosetti manor is on the outskirts of the city, so by the time I get there it's midmorning.

When I arrive, I notice the Laundromat is a lot more packed than the last time that I was here. Fortunately, though, I'm able to find an open machine and get situated before using the burner phone to send the number I have saved under Gallo, a text.

· · ·

ARIANNA: I'm at the Laundromat and need to talk.

THE MESSAGE GOES THROUGH, and I look at the screen, waiting for something to pop up.

A response comes in two minutes later.

GALLO: Come to the door and knock six times.

WHAT'S with the overly specific knocks?

Pocketing the phone, I discreetly make my way over to the door that is hidden in plain sight. As I knock, I look around casually to see if anyone is noticing me. Thankfully everyone is just going about their business.

Six knocks later, and a minute of waiting, the door opens slightly, and I'm being pulled in by Gallo's man. The same one that was a little too handsy the last time I was here.

"Against the wall, back turned. I need to search you." A smirk comes across the man's face, knowing that he is going to feel me up again.

I do as he says and the whole time, he's touching me, I want to let out a scream and push him away. There is uneasiness running through me and I hate it.

In the time that I've worked with Dante, I've never felt this way, not around him or around his men. I wonder why I would feel this way around this man and Gallo. I shouldn't, since they are the ones that are helping with this.

The search takes longer than needed and when the bastard finally lets up, he asks for my phone and guides me to Gallo's office.

Much like last time, Gallo is sitting behind his desk, looking disheveled and his suit is wrinkled beyond help.

I wonder if he sleeps in it. It's a possibility, but either way, he still doesn't look like the Mafia boss that he wants to be. Dude needs to take a serious lesson from Dante Rosetti, because that man is a mob boss and more.

Focus, Arianna.

"Ms. Vitale, to what do I owe this visit? I haven't heard from you."

He's right, he hasn't.

After I sent out the message that I had an in with Rosetti and needed fake documents, communication has been nonexistent once I got what I needed.

I blame it on the fact that I've been spending time with the kids and developing a crush on their father, because that's what that is. A crush.

A stupid, silly crush that needs to go away.

"Yeah, I've been a little busy, but I wanted to talk to you about something," I state.

Gallo looks at me and then gives me a nod, waves me to take a seat in the chair in front of him.

"What did you want to talk about?"

"I need help finding information that will help us bring down Rosetti. I don't know where to look or what to even look for and everything is so guarded. I need direction."

I'm not lying. I have no idea what to do. Once I was able to get inside the house, I thought it would be easy, that information would come flowing out. That all I would have to do, was grab a small snippet of information and Gallo would do the rest.

But that has become more difficult than I thought it would.

Dante, being the mob boss that he is, doesn't do or say things without thinking about them first. If a phone call comes through, he either leaves the house altogether or just ignores it. If someone comes into the house wanting to talk to him, they go outside or into his office, which by the way, is soundproof.

His office and bedroom are always locked and the one time I tried to go to the basement my first week living in the house, I was stopped by Dante himself.

Finding anything to bring him down is becoming hard and I'm sure it's only going to get harder from here.

"Does he trust you?" Gallo asks, looking bored.

"I take care of his children," I answer.

"Not with his demon spawns. Does he trust you being in his house without supervision? Does he trust you enough to leave you alone without any eyes on you for hours on end? Have you given him reason to doubt why you're there?"

The words Dante spewed at me on my first day working for him come back to me.

I haven't trusted you from the second you stepped foot into my club. You may be the nanny, but you are here for a reason.

From the very beginning, Dante has told me that he

didn't trust me. He told me that he knew that I was there for a reason, and he was going to find out what it was.

I don't know why, but I thought that since I was spending more time with the kids, taking care of the most important people in his life, even picking up Allie from school every other day, he trusted me.

But now that Gallo is asking the hard questions, I know that Dante Rosetti doesn't trust me. He may let me watch his kids but there is always someone there looking over us when I'm at the house alone. Either his bodyguards are by the entrance and checking in every few minutes or Evelyn is working from her office at the house.

I don't have his full trust and that's why I'm not able to find anything on the man. If I don't have that, then I won't be getting revenge for my father.

Fuck, I'm screwed.

"Make him trust you," Gallo says after I take long too respond. The answers to his questions must be written all over my facial expression. "Make him think that you aren't there for information. Let him see you for something else than the nanny that was a little too eager to take the job. And once you do that, he will let you in and then you will get what we need. Once he trusts you, will destroy the fucker. You just have to do the work."

Make him trust you.

I can do that, I think.

But how?

How the fuck do I make Dante Rosetti trust me enough for me to destroy him?

17

DANTE

I didn't know how much I needed to just spend a day with my kids and not worry about all the little things going on in life.

To just go to the park and watch them play and not worry about which cop was on my tail or which one of my men was stealing money from the family.

For a few short hours, I wasn't one of the elite members of society. I wasn't a Mafia man that everyone is afraid of. For a few hours, I was just a dad and it was fucking amazing.

After taking the kids to the park, I was able to call in a favor at the children's museum and took them to see the dinosaur exhibit.

Both Alessandra and Angel smiled and laughed the whole time and it made me realize that I needed to spend time more with them.

Yes, I spend time with them every day. I take Alessandra to school, and I still get up with Angel at five in the morning, but I need to do more. I need to be more of a father and less of a club owner and a mob boss. I needed to take days off and solely concentrate on my kids or I will miss everything.

Or if I'm ever killed, they won't have those times to remember.

I have to try better.

After the museum, I took them to eat and grab some ice cream and now we are driving through the gates at the estate, both of them fast asleep.

When we pull to the front of the house, Evelyn is out front waiting for us.

"I thought that you weren't coming back until tomorrow," I say to her instead of a greeting when I open the door and slide out.

"I was but my parents wanted to start their Hawaii trip early, so I came back," she answers, giving me a nod.

Evelyn is a valuable employee, so when she asked me for a week off, I gave it to her. I would have given her a whole month off if she asked, but she knows that I would be lost without her.

I give her a nod back and start taking the kids out of the car. Evelyn takes Angel and I take Alessandra, carrying them upstairs so they can finish up their nap before I wake them up for dinner.

Once each of the kids is settled in their rooms and I have the baby monitors, Evelyn and I make our way back downstairs.

"Alessandra spoke today," I say as I walk over to the fridge and grab a bottle of water.

The fridge is stocked up, something that I'm sure Evelyn had taken care of as soon as she got in.

My assistant looks at me with surprise. "Really?" she asks, excitement coating her voice.

I nod. "I had given Arianna the rest of the day off this morning, and she had said bye to the kids and Alessandra repeated it. It was small, but just hearing it was like a wave of relief going through me."

What I don't tell her is that wave of relief led to me kissing the nanny and wanting to take it further.

If Evelyn found out, she would scold me to the point that it would make even me run for cover.

"That makes me so happy." Evelyn comes over to me and gives me a hug of excitement. A hug that feels like a big sister being happy for little brother.

Completely different from the embrace that I experienced with Arianna.

I really need to forget about that, or I'm going to need to take another shower today.

Besides, nothing can come from it.

Arianna is my employee and that is all she will ever be. Especially given the fact that I have still not found out why she is here in the first place. Something that I need to hasten the pace on before she does something that will have me living with the consequences.

"I'm happy about it too," I tell Evelyn after returning the hug.

"And you told me not to hire the girl. I knew it was going to be a good thing for Alessandra."

I shake my head. "I'm still on the fence on it but if she

continues to speak, then I will admit it then that you are right."

Evelyn just rolls her eyes.

Because it's Sunday, and my chef doesn't work on Sundays, I decide to make dinner.

Yes, I have a chef. Just like I have a gardener and I have a housekeeper. They have been the people that helped me survive these last eight months without Angelina, I'm never getting rid of them.

I make spaghetti and meatballs while Evelyn gives me all the information of the day. Everything from which of the dancers didn't show up at the club today to which high profile athletes did, to what some of my men got their asses into.

Evelyn not only helps me with personal shit and club stuff but also with some of the things that have to do with the *famiglia*.

She isn't involved in the nitty-gritty, I have men for that, but she is involved in helping keep my men in check.

If one of my capos wants to meet with me when they can't get to Lorenzo, they call her to set up a meeting.

Speaking of Lorenzo, he's going to the meeting with me tomorrow. I got a text from the king asking for my second-in-command to be a part of it.

So Lorenzo and I will be going to downtown Chicago bright and early.

As I finish up the spaghetti sauce and am about to make my way upstairs to wake the kids from their naps, I hear the front door open.

A part of me thinks that it's Arianna coming home,

since I know she left a bit after me and the kids left. But it isn't Arianna that walks into the kitchen, it's my head bodyguard, Bruno.

"What's up?" I ask, on high alert since he doesn't seek me out unless it's important.

"I just got something sent to me that I thought that you should see," he says, his whole body saying that he means business.

I feel my jaw tic and my shoulder tightening, the knots from this morning coming back. I nod for him to come farther into the kitchen and shows me whatever it is.

Bruno pulls out his phone and he hands it over to me.

As I take it, I can see Evelyn step closer, curious as to what I'm looking at.

I look at the screen, and for a second, I'm confused as to why there's a picture of Arianna getting out of a cab staring back at me. From the looks of it, the picture is from today, but why does Bruno have it?

Bruno must see my look of confusion because he clears his throat, calling for my attention.

"That's a picture of Ms. Amato getting out of a cab in Little Italy. One of our men was stationed at the train station as ordered. He reported that Ms. Amato went into a Laundromat nearby," Bruno tells me.

"Okay, so she went to do laundry. Why does that warrant a picture?"

I know why it warrants a picture.

I know why we had a man stationed a block away and why it matters if Arianna went into a Laundromat. I know, but I need confirmation of it before I react.

Because I will react.

"It was Roberto Gallo's Laundromat, sir, and according to our man, she walked in and disappeared for about half an hour before appearing once again. She didn't walk out, she stayed in the building."

And there was the confirmation that I needed.

I know what that Laundromat is like in my sleep, and if she disappeared without being seen, I know exactly where she went.

There is one person that is always there and that is Roberto Gallo.

I know without a doubt that Arianna went to meet with him.

But why?

It's time I have a serious conversation with my nanny and find out once and for all why she's here.

Nobody messes with me.

Even the twenty-four-year-old with the doe eyes.

18

———

ARIANNA

I t's close to ten at night when I make it back to the house.

After my meeting with Gallo, where he told me what to do, I finished my small batch of laundry and went about my day.

The day I had planned all along.

My first stop was the bar.

When I got the job with Dante, I called Jimmy and told him that an opportunity had come up and that I was going to take it. He told me that he hated to see me leave but that he understood and wished me luck.

The bar and everyone working there was my family at one point, so I wanted to go and catch up for a bit. But going to the bar was just a diversion, just like my second stop.

My second stop was Tommy's. When I knocked at his door, he was a little surprised because in the time since my father's funeral, I hadn't called or stopped by once. He gave me a big hug and invited me in for a late lunch.

Tommy and I talked a bit, I even told him that I had gotten a new job, I just didn't tell him with whom. Like Jimmy, Tommy was excited for me and even told me that he was glad that I left the bar because it wasn't the place for me.

I bet if I had told him who I was working for, he wouldn't be saying the same thing.

After lunch, he took me to the garage to show me the progress on the car. The same car that my dad was trying to rebuild before he passed.

A few days after the funeral, I asked Tommy if he wanted it. I told him that I was trying to figure out what to do with the house but that the car should go to someone who would finish it. So, he took it, and in the time since then, he has made a lot of progress on it. It doesn't look like piece of junk that it did when my dad had it.

I left after that, wanting to give him time to work on the piece of metal before the darkness came.

Then I was on to my last stop. The stop that I had been avoiding all day. The stop I have been avoiding for weeks.

The cemetery.

The plot still looked fresh, the only difference was installation of the simple gravestone that I had bought for him. It was small and simple and the only thing that I could afford.

Maybe now with the paycheck I'm getting from Dante and the money I have from the donation; I can replace it and give him something better.

It hurt to be there, but I had to do it. I had to visit him, visit them because if I didn't, I was never going to have the courage to do it in the future.

I cried the second I saw his gravestone next to my mom's. I cried until my eyes hurt and tears were no longer forming.

I sat there in front of their graves for a lot longer than I thought I would, until well past sundown.

For most of the time there, I stayed quiet, but eventually I started talking about nothing, the small plates with their names on it.

I talked about what I was doing and who I was going after and why. I told the headstone just how I needed to clear my head because it was being clouded by two young children that I was starting to love more than anything. How it was also being clouded by the children's father and I didn't know how I was going to finish the job.

The question wasn't if I was going to do it, but how, because I was going to finish what I started. I was going to bring down my father's killer one way or another.

Because they needed to pay for their actions.

It was just the how that was stopping me, but I was going to figure it out.

I was also going to figure out how to make Dante trust me.

I told all of this to my parents and the only reason that I left was because the night guard came by and told me that I had to go.

Much like my father's funeral, he called me a car and I was on my way home.

It was in the car that I realized that my head was no longer crowded, and I had a clear picture of what I wanted to do.

At least I think I do.

Now it's almost ten and I'm trying to walk through the house and stay as quiet as possible, so that I don't wake up the kids.

Tomorrow morning, I start on gaining Dante's trust in any way I can.

I'm able to walk up the stairs and make it into my room without too much fuzz. I even go as far as letting out a sigh of relief when I close the door and turn on the light.

I start to take off my shoes and head to the actual bedroom, when I notice something or more so, someone, sitting in the living room area.

I don't need to ask who it is; I already know.

Much like the time in his office, a shiver crawls down my spine as I feel his murderous gaze on me.

It's daunting and very full of power.

"Mr. Rosetti," I say, my voice shaking in the process. "What are you doing here? Sitting in the dark?"

Not once has Dante stepped foot in my living quarters, so him being here now is making me go on high alert.

"How was your day, Ms. Amato?" Dante asks, his voice hard and nothing like it was this morning.

Caring and kind.

"Um, it was fine," I say, the words coming out a bit confused.

Was it the kiss? Did the kiss change something?

"Just fine?" he asks, giving me a look of indifference. I give him a nod. "You didn't go to any interesting places?"

A bead of sweat rolls down my temple. Why would he ask me that?

"No, just ran a few errands, went to do some laundry." I shrug as if it's something I do every Sunday, but given the look he is giving me, he doesn't believe me.

"You could have done laundry here," he says, with the same indifference in his voice as before.

"I could have," I say, standing as still as possible. Maybe if I don't move, he won't see that I'm lying to him.

I watch the man in front of me, very much the mob boss that he is. The way he is sitting, with his back straight, his left ankle placed on his right foot, his arms on the armrest unmoving. Everything about the man screams out danger.

Yet, I wish I was closer to him, so that I can feel all the danger that he exudes all over my body.

"Yet," Dante says, breaking my concentration of him. "Yet you decided to go to Little Italy and go do laundry at a place owned by Roberto Gallo."

His face goes from one of indifference to one of anger. Fuck. Fuck. *Fuck.*

How does he know? How does he know where I was?

"I-I don't know who that is. And h-how do you know where I went?" Not only is my voice shaking, but it feels like my whole body is too.

He knows everything. I know he does.

I was stupid to think that it would take him longer than a month to find out that I'm a fraud. There is no doubt in my mind that by next week, I'm going to be buried next to my parents.

"I don't believe that you don't know who that fucker is. Roberto Gallo is a piece of shit that has things coming his way," Dante starts. "That man has wanted me dead for years. Do you really think I'm stupid enough to not have a man always watch that Laundromat? I have someone telling me every single person that walks through those doors. So, imagine my surprise when I get told that my nanny walked in there today and it wasn't her first time."

I feel the tears forming at the back of my eyes again and my mind is working overtime trying to find a lie that will stick. A lie that he will believe.

"I was just doing laundry," I say, my voice so small that I'm surprised he heard it.

"Why there? Of all the fucking Laundromats that this damn city has to offer, why that one?" His voice rises a bit, his anger is starting to seep out.

I feel my lips tremble as I start to form words. "I don't know. It was just a place that my dad used to go to."

The lie flows off easily. So easily that it causes Dante to stand up from his seat and stride over to me.

"I don't believe you," he says through his teeth, his face hard and his eyes filled with so much anger that I have to take a step away from him. In all my time being here under his roof, I have never seen so much anger swimming in his light brown orbs.

Make him believe you, Arianna.

"It's the truth. I swear to you, I only went there because my dad used to go there occasionally. His birthday was a few days ago, and I wanted to feel close to him, so I did things that he would do on Sundays."

Not a complete lie but its still hurts to use my dad's death like that. As far as I know, Dante doesn't know about my dad and how died, so by me bringing it up, it could open up a bigger can of worms.

Dante scoffs and rolls his eyes at my statement. He looks like he's about to say something but then he stops himself before speaking again.

"Pack your shit. You're fucking fired," he spits out before shoving past me toward the door.

Instantly I react. "What? No. You can't fire me, especially not over where I went to do laundry. I need this job!" I yell, letting the tears that were brewing fall.

"Give me one fucking reason why the fuck not. Give me one good fucking reason as to why you need this job!" he yells back, a vein in his neck popping out. "I know you're here for something, so you might as well come out and say it. That way firing you would be worth it."

Make him believe you, Arianna. Make him believe you. This is your chance. This is your chance to gain his trust.

"Okay! I will give you the truth," I say through the tears, trying to calm myself down as much as I possibly can. "My dad died almost three months ago, and when it came to his funeral, I had to pay for everything. He wasn't retired, so there was no pension yet and the life insurance isn't going to come in until next year sometime. I used all the money that I had and took out loans to pay for the funeral and I've been trying to pay them off."

The truth, it's stretched and lies are sprinkled everywhere but it's still the truth. And I'm about to give him more of it. All to gain this man's trust.

"My dad was a police officer, a detective, and because of that, I use my mother's maiden name as my last name. I didn't want my father's enemies, if he had any, to come after me. My name is Arianna, but my name at birth last is Vitale. I'm Arianna Vitale."

His eyes go wide when I tell him my real name, like he wasn't expecting me to reveal that detail. I wasn't either, but if I want to gain this man's trust, if I want him to let me in so I can get information, I need to give him everything, even if everything is sandwiched between lies.

When he doesn't say anything, I continue. More lies coming out.

"I'm here because I needed money. I'd heard how much you were paying your dancer and about the tips they earn, so I thought I'd give it a shot and interview. We both know that went to shit. That's why I took this job, because I knew you were rich and that you could help me get out of the hole I dug for myself financially. I was here just for the money. As for the Laundromat, yes, I've been there a few times. To be close to my dad, like I said. I didn't even know it was owned by whoever Roberto Gallo is. I never even heard that name. But if he's who you say he is then maybe that's why the washing machine at dad's house always broken. I never interact with anyone while I'm there. I go in, do my laundry and get out. That's it. That's the truth. Please believe me. Please believe me, and please don't fire me. I love working for you and I really love working with the kids. Please, I need this job."

I beg.

I let the tears continue to stream down my face and I beg this big, bad man to believe my words and to let me keep this job.

If he doesn't, then me even taking this job would be for nothing.

Dante doesn't say anything. He just continues to stand there, looking more pissed off than before.

He's going to tell me to get out. He doesn't believe me, and he's going to fire me and tell me to get out. And he has every right to.

But even with his stance, and how unapproachable he looks, I step closer to him, just one step closer.

"Please, believe me," I beg again, trying to meet his eyes as best as I can, but he won't budge. So, I step even closer.

"Please, Dante," I say, making a bold move and stepping closing the distance between us.

This time he meets my pleading gaze with a hard stare of his own. His eyes don't convey any of the emotions that were swinging in them before.

This man is an enigma, a beautiful enigma that I wish I could crack. A beautiful man that I wish I had met under different circumstances, because maybe then I wouldn't feel guilty about closing the last bit of distance between us and placing my hand against his chest.

"I promise you, Dante, you can trust me. I will never betray you." My hand starts to move as I say the words, rubbing methodical circles against his shirt.

I wish I was doing this under different circumstances.

I wish my words were true. I wish that I was telling him the truth and that he could really trust whatever was coming out of my mouth. That he could wholeheartedly believe that I would never betray him.

But the words are just lies that I'm making up, all because I'm a bitch and feel the need for revenge.

I'm about to pull back when I feel that I've crossed the line a little too far, when he stops me.

Dante's hand lands on mine and he holds me to him, not letting me pull away.

"That's the truth?" he asks, his voice rough, a slight touch of an Italian accent poking through.

"That's the truth." I say, trying to convey confidence in those three words and I hope to God that it's working.

"Continue begging then."

"Excuse me?"

Dante shifts, shifting his hand from mine and moving it down to my elbow, pulling me even closer to him, if that was even possible.

He looks down at me, his eyes hooding a bit, before he shifts us, and my back meets the bedroom door.

"Continue to beg."

19

DANTE

Arianna's eyes go wide at my words.

Her breathing hitches and if I wasn't holding her like I was, I would have missed the shiver that ran through her.

Ever since I saw the picture of her at the Laundromat, frustration has been brewing in me. At the time that frustration was anger filled, but now that frustration is more of the sexual manner.

I was going to kick her out, I was going to fire her, but then she spoke.

She told me the truth.

She told me her real name, told me about her father, and something in me shifted.

It shifted even more when I saw her tears and I felt her hand on my chest.

Now all I want to do is fuck her against the door, all so that I can continue hearing her beg.

"Are you going to do as I ask, *amate*?" I say, leaning forward and placing my lips against her neck.

Another shiver releases through her body in the process.

"What do you want me to beg for?" she asks, her body melting into mine.

"Beg to keep your job." I press my hardening cock into her body.

"Beg for my trust." I move my lips to her jaw, and she lets out a whimper.

"Dante, please," Arianna pants out, her body moving against mine but not pushing me away.

She's wants this just as much as I do.

"Beg for it, *amate*. Beg and maybe I will give you what you want."

I pull my mouth away from her skin and look down at her small frame against my bigger one. This girl fits perfectly against me.

Her eyes are filled with questions but there's also lust trying to shine through.

"Tell me what you want, *amate*," I say through my teeth, my hand going to her neck, wrapping around it slightly.

Arianna lets out a small gasp but still doesn't push me away. I would almost say she likes my hand around her throat.

"I want to keep my job," she pants, my grip growing a bit tighter.

"What else do you want?" I say, leaning in a bit closer to her mouth.

"I want you to believe me, because I am telling the truth. Everything I said was the truth," she says, never taking her eyes off mine.

The truth.

She told me the truth. She told me about her dad dying and she told me why she used a fake name. Told me about Joseph's routine trips to Little Italy, something that I knew already. She told me things that I never thought I would ever hear come out of her mouth.

Was I shocked? Yes, but her honesty only had me wanting her more. The admission made me want to grab her by the waist and slam my lips against hers.

"Dante," Arianna says when I don't have an immediate answer.

I look at the girl, the woman that is in my hold.

I look at everything from her eyes to her mouth to how her eyebrows and jaw are set. Nothing in her facial expression is telling me that she is lying to me. Hell, even every single background check that I have done on her has come back clean. I've only doubted her because the timing between her father's death and when she walked into my club was alarming. Because of the name she used.

There is one thing I need to know before I can give her the words that she so desperately desires.

My grip on her throat tightens, cutting her airway slightly. I need the truth, and this is the only way I'm going to get it.

"When you walked into my club that day, did you know who I was?"

The second the question leaves my lips, I see the answer in her eyes.

She knew.

Of course, she fucking knew, her father was one of Chicago's finest after all. A friend.

Joseph never said anything, but he must have told her to keep away from me. I know I would have.

"And who I am doesn't make you fearful?"

It should. Knowing who I am and what I do, should have been enough for her not to want to even step foot into my club, let alone my house.

Yet here she is, acting as the nanny.

Arianna, even with my hold on her neck, shakes her head.

Such a brave girl.

"And what if I told you that I wanted to fuck you from the second you walked into my office that day, would you be scared then?"

I feel her throat constrict a bit at my words. Letting my hold on her neck relax a bit, I place my lips on hers, tasting her slightly.

"Answer the question, Arianna. Would you be scared if I had told you that I wanted to fuck you?"

A whimper escaped her lips and I swallow it down as my lips circle hers.

"Answer," I order, pulling not only my lips away from hers but putting a few inches between us, so I can get a good look at her.

"No, I wouldn't be scared." Her voice is shaky but the way she is standing is projecting power and it's sexy as hell.

"And what would you have done?" I ask. I move my hands off her body and place them on either side of her head.

"I would have let you do anything you wanted to me."

My lips meet hers before the last syllable is said and it's nothing like how our lips met this morning. This time is more aggressive, more hungry, more sensual.

My tongue swipes along her lips and when she opens up, it swipes against hers, causing the sweetest moan to release from her mouth.

This kiss is not something that I expected to come from a girl like Arianna, but I'm grasping every single aspect of it.

Every moan.

Every whimper.

Every movement of her body.

I grasp everything she is giving, and I want more of it.

Without breaking our lips apart, I slide my hands from the wall back to her body. Moving them down until I'm cupping her ass and lifting until her feet are off the ground and her legs going around my waist.

I dig my fingers into the fabric of her yoga pants, pulling her closer against my body until I feel her grinding against me.

Wanting more, I move us over to the bedroom. It's when I sit on the mattress with her on my lap, that she pulls her lips away from mine.

She looks at me with those doe eyes, that I feel like I can crumble below her. It's a feeling that I have only felt with one other person, my wife.

Her hands move along my hair as she speaks. "Do you really believe me?"

It's a simple five-word question, but I know my answer means something to her.

Do I?

For all I know, she could be lying through her teeth, and I wouldn't know it.

I look at her, and when I look into her eyes, I know my answer.

She gave me the truth, it's time I give her mine.

"I believe you."

The smile she gives me is one that she hasn't granted me before. It's beautiful, just like her.

"Good. Now fuck me."

It's as if my words made her a bit lighter.

I can't help but smirk at her use of colorful language.

"*Amate*, I will not only fuck you, but, I'll fuck you until you no longer know how to use your legs."

She looks like she's about to say something, but I stop her before a sound can leave her.

I stand us up and without thinking I throw her on the made bed and strip her of all her clothing.

Not a word is said between us as I slide her bottoms off her, followed by her shirt. It's as she lies there with just a small triangle covering her pussy and a bra that just covers her nipples, when thoughts start to creep in.

Is fucking the nanny the right thing?

It takes a second for me to realize that I don't give a fuck if it's the right thing or not, that covered pussy is calling for me and I'm going to fuck the nanny into tomorrow.

With my mouth salivating, I lean forward and rip away the remainder articles of clothing covering Arianna's body.

She lets out a yelp and gives me a fake glare.

"Did you have to do that? They were my good set."

"You liked it," I growl out, leaning forward and sliding a finger along her folds that are already wet.

So, fucking wet.

"Dante," she whispers, enjoying what I'm doing to her even if it's minimal.

"What do you want, Arianna? Tell me," I order her, my fingers moving along her pussy without stopping.

"Keep touching me," she lets out, her eyes closing in the process.

"Keep your eyes open, or I won't," I say as I pull my hand away from her and start to undress myself.

Arianna's eyes fly open and when she sees what I'm doing, she leans up on her elbows and watches me undress.

"Has anyone ever told you that you look really good for being thirty-seven?"

I give her a shrug as I slide off my shirt. I don't tell her that someone has, and she died almost ten months ago.

A minute later, we are both fully naked and my fingers are back to stroking her pussy.

Arianna moans every few seconds and keeps her eyes on all my movements.

I circle her clit and slide my fingers along her pussy lips before teasing her entrance.

I don't slide my fingers into her. I don't lean down and replace my fingers with my tongue. I just continue doing what I'm doing no matter how much more questioning Arianna's expression grows.

Tonight, I'm not going to taste her. I'm not going to take her clit in my mouth and suck on her pussy until she explodes on my tongue. I'm also not going to mark her tits like I'd wanted to that day in my office.

No, tonight will only be raw, fast fucking.

We both have a thirst that we need to quench and tonight we will do just that.

I continue to stroke her until she is a writhing mess under my touch, and she comes without any penetration.

Such a pretty sight, if I do say so myself.

With her now all ready for my throbbing cock, I reach for my wallet and grab one of the two condoms that I have.

I wasn't planning this, not with Arianna, but here I am.

Arianna keeps her eyes on me as I sheath myself.

"Get on all fours. No more foreplay, just fucking," I say to her and she listens.

Now it's my turn to watch as she turns on the bed and does as she's told. The view of her ass asking for attention is perfect.

I give in to temptation and give one of her ass cheeks a slap before settling behind her.

"Such a pretty sight. Are you going to be a good girl and let me fuck you?" I say, smoothing where my hand met her skin.

"Yes," she whimpers.

"Good," I say before I open her entrance and slam into her.

Moans and gasps fill the room and after giving her a minute to adjust to my size, I start to move and everything fucking changes.

Everything becomes more raw and more animalistic. I've only been in her pussy for not even a minute and I'm already wanting more.

"Dante." Arianna moans, her head plastered against the mattress.

"So tight, *amate*. So fucking tight. I bet no man has ever filled you up like me." My hands grip her hips, holding her steady, as I slam into her with more force, trying to make a point.

"Just you." She groans, and hearing it just makes me feel wilder.

I grab her hair, glad that she let it down, and wrap my fist around it, pulling it until her back is bowed and my lips are mere inches from her temple.

"Nobody has fucked you like I'm fucking you, have they? Nobody has ever made you feel this good, have they?"

Arianna shakes her head, trying to gasp for air.

"Nobody."

"Are you a dirty girl, Arianna? Do you like your hair being pulled while your pussy is being filled with a cock?" I take her earlobe between my teeth and if I wasn't hard already, wanting to explode, I would be with the gasp she lets out.

"Yes. Yes." She answers completely breathless, her pussy tightening around me.

"That's it, be a good girl and come all over my cock."

My fingers dig deeper into her hips, probably bruising her, but I don't give a shit. I need to get her there. I need her to come.

"Dante. Fuck, Dante. More. Please, don't stop." Arianna begs, and I can't help but smirk into her neck and comply with every order that she throws my way.

"Whatever you want, *amate*. Whatever you want."

And I give it to her. I fuck her until her body is shaking in my hold. I fuck her until she throws herself forward, not being able to hold herself up anymore. I fuck her until she is convulsing and coming around my cock, my name nothing more than a pant that is filling the room.

Sweat runs down my body as I continue my motions of sliding into her entrance.

I slap her ass more than a few times until there's a hint of red coating it.

A moan escapes me as I feel my balls tightening and when Arianna starts to rock her ass against me, I can't hold back anymore.

I come into the condom, my grunts the only noise that I can register.

It takes me a minute to catch my breath and when I slide out of Arianna, I instantly miss being inside of her.

Too tired to do anything, I fall onto the bed next to her. I should get up and get rid of the condom. I should go into the bathroom and grab a wet towel and clean her up, but I don't. I just continue to lie here next to her, not even reaching out to touch her, basking in how good it felt.

Because it did feel good and I'm not even going to deny it.

The bed shifts slightly and Arianna cuddles into my side, my arm automatically opening for her and letting her head cradle into my chest.

And that's how we stay until I turn over about twenty minutes later and fuck her until we both fall asleep.

The consequences of tonight I will think about tomorrow.

20

ARIANNA

A groan escapes me as I turn over in my bed, my alarm goes off in the background.

No way it's already six thirty. I feel like I just fell asleep fifteen minutes ago.

Letting out another groan at the soreness my body is feeling, I grab my phone off the nightstand. It's as I push the stop button on the screen that I remember why I feel so damn tired and why my body is so sore.

I let Dante Rosetti fuck me, and it wasn't just once, but twice.

After catching our breath and sleeping for about an hour, we quickly jumped into round two with me straddling him and making all the cowboys in the world proud.

After my inner cowgirl made in an appearance, we made out like we were in high school until our eyes could no longer stay open.

The last thing I remember was looking at his sleeping form and thinking that he looked like a different person.

When he sleeps, Dante Rosetti doesn't look like the deadliest man in Chicago or even the mafioso that sits at the head of the table. He just looks like a normal man that had just ruined me for every other guy.

It was a strange sight, but still one that I liked.

How I also liked having him inside of me. How I also liked having his arms around my body as I fell asleep.

Dante must have gotten up a while ago because the side of the bed he was lying on is cold and the bunched-up sheets act as a reminder of what happened last night.

Where not only did we have crazy hot animalistic sex, but where he also told me that he believed me. He believed the words that I told him.

Does him believing what I told him mean that he trusts me? Definitely not but it's a step in the right direction.

Something deep in me, though, tells me that I went about it the wrong way. I shouldn't have opened my leg for him, no matter how much I wanted to. He should believe me because his gut tells him to, not because his cock was cozy inside of me.

But it did happen that way and there is nothing that I can do to change it. I just have to make sure that it never happens again.

I have to stay away from anything sexual that involves Dante. Staying away from him will be the only way that I will be able to follow through and bring him down for my father's death.

I just have to. One night doesn't change anything.

Even if that part deep in me says it does.

Sighing, I throw the covers off my body and start getting ready for my day. I ignore the soreness between my legs as I shower and get dressed. I also ignore all the memories that come running in as I walk over to the kids' rooms.

If I keep thinking about Dante and his magical dick, I won't be able to get through the day. Let alone my plans.

Angel is awake when I walk into his room and after giving him a bottle and changing his diaper, we are on our way to Alessandra's room.

Thankfully, she's already up and greets me with a smile. We get her dressed and do her hair and are all ready to go before seven-thirty.

One month in and I'm really getting the hang of this nanny stuff.

When we make it downstairs, I half expect Dante to be gone already, given that he said that he had a meeting in the morning. But to my surprise, he's sitting at the dining room table, reading the morning newspaper.

"Good morning," I say as if I didn't have his cock in me just a few hours ago.

Dante looks up and catches my gaze. His eyes look like they have a bit of surprise in them, but he quickly recovers.

"Good morning," he says just as he opens his arms for Alessandra to run into.

I watch as the little girl goes to her dad, and a small smile forms on my lips when I see how much he loves her. It's a sweet father-daughter moment.

Strapping Angel into the high chair, I drag him over to Dante's other side before taking a seat at the other end.

"Why are you sitting all the way over there?" Dante asks, but I just ignore his question and start filling my plate.

There is a chef that comes and cooks meals every weekday, so I definitely take advantage of it.

I eat in silence, with Dante speaking the occasional word to his daughter.

"Did she say anything else yesterday?" I ask before stuffing a huge bite of pancakes into my mouth.

Unfortunately, I don't chew fast enough because when Dante looks up, my cheeks are puffed up like a chipmunk's and I try my hardest to swallow down the food.

A smirk gets thrown in my direction before he answers. "No. I tried at the park and at the museum, but she didn't say anything else."

"It will happen. We just have to give it time," I tell him after swallowing down my food. I am a little disappointed that she didn't say more, but Alessandra will speak when she wants to speak.

Dante gives me a nod before finishing up his food and standing from the table.

"Can you take her to school? My meeting starts in half an hour, and I can't be late," he says, grabbing his suit jacket from behind his chair and sliding it on.

The second his jacket is on and buttoned, I swear my mouth starts to water.

There is something absolutely sexy when a man wears a suit, especially a well-tailored one, but with Dante Rosetti, it's as if that sexiness is on a different level.

Everything about it, about him, is perfect and now that

I know what is under the suit, I just want to peel it off him and lick him all over.

Okay, not thoughts I should be having with the kids around.

I try to rein in the tingling that is happening between my legs and watch as Dante says bye to the kids before grabbing his phone and walking over to me.

His eyes are on me the whole time as he closes the distance between us, and the whole time I have to keep my nerves at bay.

When he reaches me, he leans down, placing one hand on the table and the other at the back of my chair, his lips to my ear.

"When I get back, you and I are going to talk about what happened last night." He says, before pulling away and walking out of the room.

All the while, leaving me a big puddle of mush right where I'm sitting.

What there is to talk about, I'm not sure.

I just know whatever it is, I sure as hell won't be prepared for it.

21

DANTE

"Who the fuck calls a meeting so damn early in the day?" Lorenzo groans from the seat next to me as we make our way downtown.

Lorenzo Romano may be my second in command and the underboss that likes to get his hands overly dirty, but he sure as hell doesn't like mornings. Anything before noon is too early for him.

Which is why I usually start my days around four in the morning, because the asshole leaves the mess from the night before for me to clean up.

I'm honestly surprised that he's even awake.

"People that actually want to get shit done," I mutter out, not even looking up from my phone to do it.

"I get shit done. If I didn't, you would have killed me a long time ago."

I should kill him now, but what would be the fun in that if I would have to take over all his work?

A grunt releases from my mouth in agreement and for a while, I think he went back to sleep, until he speaks again.

"What's this meeting about anyway?" he asks.

"I have no idea. All I was told was that he was calling a meeting and for you to come."

The last time I was called into a meeting like this was about three months after Angelina died. At the time it was about the *famiglia* because it was getting out of control, and I wasn't doing a thing about it.

Nothing like that I currently going on, so I'm stumped.

"Did you get the info that I asked for?" I say, changing the subject.

Right away, Lorenzo is on high alert, completely forgetting his dislike for mornings.

He gives me a nod. "From the looks of things, Gallo is trying to lie low, hardly leaving the building where the Laundromat is. As for his bank account, my guy tells me that it's been stale, the only activity coming a few weeks ago. A wire transfer of five thousand dollars. He's working on getting me the information of the account that sent it. The way I see it, the guy is trying to turn into a ghost."

Ever since I took over the Falcone *famiglia* and made it my own, Gallo has been a thorn in my side that won't die. The fucker wants my seat at the table and will try anything to get it.

Him not leaving the sole building he owns in the city could be nothing, but I don't know that for sure. For all I know, Gallo and his small number of men could be thinking up ways to poison me.

"Anybody suspicious showing up to do laundry?"

Lorenzo shakes his head. "Other than your girl? No. But I got more eyes on the building and at his house. Someone comes over, we'll know."

After Bruno showed me the picture of Arianna, I got a call from Lorenzo. I guess news traveled fast as to where my nanny was spotted.

He chewed my ass out about hiring untrustworthy people. I didn't argue with him.

"Did you take care of that?" he asks me, for sure an eyebrow rising in the process.

"Yes." I grunt out.

"Really? That's odd, because I was sure I would have gotten a call to get rid of the body."

This fucker.

I sigh because a few years ago, I would have done just that. I would have taken care of Arianna by killing her and calling Lorenzo to get rid of her, leaving no trace.

But now, now that thought didn't even cross my mind.

Was I pissed? Abso-fucking-lutely, but when I heard her explanation, the anger decreased.

"You're fucking her, aren't you?" Lorenzo muses.

I hate this man sometimes.

I face my second-in-command. "I took care of it. I don't have to fucking tell you how, you nosy fucker."

"Touchy," he says, giving me a smirk, before turning away to face the window. I think the subject is dropped when he turns to face me again. "Her pussy was good, wasn't it?"

"I'm going to fucking kill you when we get out of this car."

"I would like to see you try." The fucker winks at me before letting out a chuckle and leaning his head back and trying to sleep for the remainder of the car ride.

Twenty minutes later, we're arriving at an address in the financial district.

The streets are filled with people in business suits hustling to get to work, so our presence goes unnoticed.

Lorenzo and I walk into the building that has the word Lane on all the glass windows.

The lobby is surprisingly empty besides a few security guards

The guards at the front desk look up and are about to stand up as we approach it, when they are stopped by a female voice.

"They are cleared to come up," the voice announces.

From the corner of my eye, I see the figure approaching and when I turn, I'm greeted by a beautiful smile.

"Ella," I say, greeting the beautiful woman by placing a small kiss on her cheek. "I'm surprised that he let you come down here to greet me instead of one of his assistants. I must be special."

Ella gives me a smile, one that I'm sure has one man falling to his feet constantly. How Ella Vincent settled for a man like that, I have no idea. She's way above his pay grade.

"I volunteered, I didn't want you brawling with one of them and staining my new floors with blood."

I look around the lobby and it looks like it was remodeled recently.

"Well, I'm happy it was your pretty face to greet me." I tell her.

Ella lets out a laugh before turning to Lorenzo and greeting him. Not much time passes before the three of us make our way to the elevator and head up to the thirtieth floor.

I guess it pays to have a bunch of money laying around, then you can buy buildings that are a part of the Chicago skyline.

Once we arrive on the floor, which is completely furnished and overlooks the Chicago River,

Ella guides us through until we reach the back office.

The first thing that I notice are the windows that covered with a dark tint that have a perfect view of the city.

The next thing I see is Bennett Lane, the one and only king of Chicago. A name given by the people of the city.

The so-called king is standing by a long wooden conference table in a three-piece suit. The bastard looks very much like the young billionaire CEO that he is. He's currently trying to look at me as if he hates me, but both of us know that is definitely not the case.

"Dante, so happy that you could show up somewhat on time," Bennett says, not moving from his spot.

"Bennett. Did Ella dress you this morning? You look like a corporate puppet." I throw back at him.

The man raises his eyebrow at me, challenging me, before he looks over at where his wife stands and gives her a smile.

"Well, I am her puppet. So I guess she can do with me what she wants." He voices, throwing a wink in her direction.

They're cutesy. I don't do cutesy.

Bennett greets Lorenzo before the three of us go ahead and take a seat at the conference table, Ella leaving us to do business.

"Why are we here, Lane?" I ask him, getting straight to the point.

Bennett Lane and I go back years.

We first met when we were teenagers and we were both attending the Chicago Academy for boys, the school where all the rich parents send their kids in the hope that they become politicians one day.

I was only there because Alberto wanted to keep up an image and somehow convinced my mom that it was a good place for me. It wasn't. I was surrounded by preppy assholes that would most likely end up in jail for stealing money from their families' companies.

The only person that I was okay with was Bennett Lane. He was still a preppy asshole, but the way he saw the world was slightly different. To this day, he sees the world differently.

Bennett may be the richest person not only in Chicago, but in the country, yet he views his wealth as a tool for others. He would rather help every single poor individual he encounters, than make his board of rich men richer. He's also not against breaking the law to make that happen, even more so when nobody knows about it.

He's the total contradiction of what he's supposed to be and that's why we developed a friendship.

I have respect for him and reach out to him when I'm in a bind. And when he needs something taken care of, within reason of course, he calls me.

Bennett looks between me and Lorenzo before speaking.

"A business opportunity." He states.

"A business opportunity?" The two of us have done countless business deals together, that isn't anything out of the ordinary. What is out of the ordinary is doing this with Lorenzo right next to me.

"What kind of business?" I ask, feeling my eyebrows bunch up in the process.

Instead of answering, Bennett checks his watch and when he looks back up with his mouth open to say something, he gets interrupted by footsteps entering the room.

"This kind of business," Bennett answers my question, standing up to greet our new guests.

Turning slightly, I see exactly who this meeting is with and when I see the three individuals, I'm not even the least bit surprised.

Standing by the doorway is Bennett's nephew Elliot with two other gentlemen dressed in suits similar to mine. Two gentlemen that I know well.

Leonardo Morales, the head of the Muertos Cartel and Santos Reyes, his right-hand man.

My dealings with the cartel have been sparse. Alberto used to deal with them before he died, especially since they had ties in Canada or something. When I took over, that relationship dissipated almost out of existence. But just because the relationship ended, doesn't mean that I haven't kept up with their dealings.

I have to be in my line of business.

I know that the founder of the cartel, Ronaldo Morales, Leo's father, was killed by the Drug Enforcement Agency nine months ago. I also know that Leo and Santos escaped charges and Leo is now holds the title of his father.

Everyone in this business knows who these two men are. Knows how deadly the cartel can be, but they aren't as deadly as me.

Which is why Lorenzo snorts a bit and doesn't reach for his gun as he sees the two men.

I can also take Leo Morales anytime he fucking wants.

"Dante, Lorenzo, you know my nephew, Elliot," Bennett tells us, waving over to the slightly younger version of him. If I didn't know he was his nephew, I would say it was his brother since there is only a ten-year age difference between them.

"It's good to see you again, Dante. How are the kids?" Elliot asks, extending his hand for me to shake.

With a nod, I shake his hand and answer. "They're good. Growing like two little weeds."

"I'm sure in no time they will be old enough to be running your business," he states.

Never, I don't voice.

My kids will never be involved in this business. I will burn this family to the ground, before my kids are involved in this type of life.

But I just give him a nod and turn to the two men, standing a few feet away.

"Should I address you as Mr. Morales, or is Leo still okay?"

Leo gives me a smirk before holding out a hand for me to shake.

"Leo is still fine," he says as I take his hand. "I'm still wrapping my head around the fact that I'm sitting at the head of the table."

I nod, understanding. "I was in your position not too long ago; I know what it's like. My condolences to you and your family."

Leo gives me a nod before the two of us both turn to the other's right hand and greet them.

Within seconds of our greeting ending, the six of us are sitting around the conference table.

When nobody says a word and is just looking at each other like a bunch of school kids doing a group project, I speak.

"I have my theories, but does someone want to tell me why we are here? I have shit to do."

The two men that look alike don't say anything or move, so my stare turns over to the two Mexicans. They only have to give each other one look for me to know that they called this meeting.

Eventually, Santos clears his throat and meets my stare straight on.

"We wanted to see if you would be interested in a few business opportunities."

Again, with the cryptic business opportunity bullshit.

"What kind of business opportunities?" I ask, wary of where this is going.

Santos gives me a smirk. "The kind that involves you letting the Muertos Cartel use your streets to move product."

22

———

DANTE

When I took over this business, I told myself that I wouldn't touch one thing, and that was drugs.

I could launder money, murder whatever fucker owed me money, hell I could even distribute military-grade weapons. Yet out of all the things I could do with my new title and new resources, I decided to never get near drugs. Marijuana, Cocaine, anything, I wasn't going to touch it.

Things change though. People grow older, opinions change, and business gets tougher and tougher.

That's why when Santos told me their proposal, an enticing one at that, I found myself agreeing.

About two years ago, Elliot came to me with an offer from the Muertos. They wanted to move product in through the Canadian border. Much like today, I had agreed to let them, since it would have meant money in my pocket. I wouldn't have a direct hand in it. But that never happened.

Now it is happening and this time around I do have a direct hand in letting the deadliest cartel in the world into my streets.

With a stipulation of course. They sell their cocaine to whoever they fuck they won't, but kids.

Surprisingly, they agreed.

Now nearly six hours later, all the details are settled and now only me and Bennett are left in the conference room.

"I can't believe that you, of all people, are letting the cartel step foot into the city limits." I muse to him, sipping the scotch that he handed me about ten minutes ago.

Bennett is silent for a moment, looking out at the view of the city before letting out a sigh.

"Someone has to do what's right for this city. The politicians aren't doing anything, and you know my board members would rather make money than help the people they employ, the people that are struggling. Me knowing that the cartel is within city limits gives me a bit more control and if the city politicians want the cartel out, then they need to get off their asses and do something about it."

For as long as I've known him, this man has always tried to make the city that we call home a better place.

Something that he learned from his father he told me once.

Being the owner and CEO of the most influential company in the world helps him achieve that, but from what he tells me, the board members only care about themselves. They care about getting richer, not caring about how they go about it or who suffers.

I'm sure if he really wanted to, Bennett Lane would give away every penny he had to help the people that really needed it.

The city needs more people like him, and not murderous individuals like me.

"A CEO that is using corruption to take down corruption."

Bennett lets out a snort at my comment. "Drake calls me the real-life batman."

I can't help but laugh at thinking that Elliot's youngest brother sees his uncle that way.

He's halfway there. Billionaire CEO that helps the city in every way he can, loves to buy fast and expensive toys, I definitely see it.

"The kid might be onto something. You should have a suit made," I say, which causes Bennett to let out a laugh that I don't think I've heard since we were teenagers.

"I'm going to take a wild guess that you finally found a nanny," he says, changing the subject.

I just wish the subject wasn't the nanny.

The same nanny that I left speechless when I left this morning. The one that I fucked last night until she was breathless.

"Yes, I hired a nanny. She just finished her first month," I voice.

"And why don't you look happy about this nanny?" Bennett asks, throwing me a raised eyebrow.

I throw a shrug in his direction. "She's young."

Young, beautiful and filled with my cock less than fifteen hours ago.

"And that's a bad thing?" he asks and before I can even answer his question, he speaks again as if he realized something. "Ah I get it. It's a bad thing because you find her attractive and want to fuck her."

I let out a grunt confirming his assumption because there is no reason to deny it now.

"So fuck her," he muses, finishing up his scotch.

"She's my employee and watches over my kids."

"And? I slept with my employee look how well that worked out." He shrugs.

This fucker. "If I remember correctly, you kept playing with Ella's heart because you thought it was what was best for the company. The only reason you two are even together is because you got your head out of your ass when you almost lost her."

Besides, what Bennett and Ella went through is completely different from what is going on with me and Arianna. The biggest difference being that besides the sex, there is nothing going on between me and Arianna.

Fleeting looks.

Urge to talk and to hear her voice.

I ignore those thoughts and finish up my drink.

"Okay, fine. Me and Ella are the exception. But you sleeping with the nanny wouldn't hurt. It's not like you've been celibate since Angelina died. From what you've told me, you've enjoyed a night or two with the women from the club."

I should tell him who she is. I should tell my friend that my new nanny is Joseph Vitale's daughter. The daughter of the man that the Chicago Police Department suspecting I killed.

I may have been involved with the man, but that doesn't mean that I called the kill. They don't believe me, no matter how much I tell them. The only reason they haven't arrested me is because they haven't found evidence to pin it on me, and they never will.

"Honor was different, that was a distraction from my dead wife and life. With the nanny, it feels as if I'm cheating on Angelina every time that I look at her."

That is something that I realized this morning when I woke up with her wrapped up in my arms.

I looked at the woman and for the first time in months, I didn't miss Angelina the way I should have. Nothing in my mind was telling me that what I had done was wrong. It felt as if Arianna belonged in my arms, and I shouldn't let her go.

When that thought came crashing in, I got out of that bed as fast as I could.

In those moments, I was going to put what had happened between us behind me and move the fuck on. But then I saw her with the kids, and I wanted her all over again.

Now all I'm feeling is guilt because I shouldn't be forgetting about my wife so quickly.

"Angelina would want you to be happy. She would want you to get out of this life, raise the kids the best you could and be happy."

"Pretty sure she wouldn't want that to happen with the twenty-four-year-old nanny," I grunt out.

"Does she care about your kids?"

I don't even have to think about the answer before I'm nodding yes. Arianna really does care about the kids.

"Then what's the big deal? No reason to get your feelings involved. I say just sleep with her and see what happens. Nothing wrong with that."

Nothing wrong with that.

Those words are so simple to say, but yet even I know there are so many things wrong with this situation.

So many fucking things.

23

ARIANNA

Dante wasn't lying when he said that he would be coming home late from his meeting.

It's currently eight at night and I'm in Alessandra's room reading her a story. It's as she's about to fall asleep, that I hear the front door open.

Knowing that the security guards don't come into the house unless their boss is home, and Evelyn being at the club tonight, I know it's Dante.

"Your *papi* is home," I tell Alessandra, giving her sleepy gaze a smile.

I continue to read her the story as I listen to the footsteps moving through the mega mansion.

It's crazy how big the house is, yet I'm able to hear him walking through the first floor.

After a few minutes, as I'm reading how the cat was able to get rescued from the tree, I hear the footsteps coming up the stairs.

I'm close to finishing up the book when Dante finally

appears at the door. When I look up, he gives me a small smile and then nods for me to finish.

When I do, Alessandra is fast asleep against my arm, her little snores filling the room.

"I tried to keep them up so that you could see them when you got home, but I didn't know how late that would be." I explain as I close the book and place it on the small nightstand.

"It's okay," he says, his voice sounding delicate and soft, not something that I'm used to hearing from him.

"I'll leave you to say good night to her then," I tell him as I slowly move Allie's head off my arm to her pillow.

As I make my way out of the room, I think that Dante is going to stop me. That he's going to grab me by the elbow and pull me close to him and tell me in my ear to remember that we still need to talk, but he doesn't. He doesn't even look at me as I walk past him and head downstairs.

Once I'm downstairs, I clean up the living room of the mess that the kids and I made after dinner. I try to keep my mind occupied and not try to think about the man that is upstairs.

To my surprise, Dante comes downstairs as I fluff the decorative couch pillows for the fourth time.

He doesn't approach the living room. Much like he was upstairs, he stands by the entryway of the room, leaning against the wall.

I try not to look up at him as I finish the fluffing. He looks too delicious standing there like that. What with his shirtsleeves rolled up to his forearms, the two top buttons popped open, his hands in his pockets.

The man is so damn sexy, he doesn't even know it. My eyes keep betraying me by looking up at him every chance they get.

"You know you don't have to clean, right?" he says as I move to the pillows on the love seat.

Am I overdoing it? Yes, yes, I am.

But I have to do something to keep busy because otherwise, I'm going to close the distance between us and climb him like a monkey.

And I can't do that, because I'm pretty sure that "we are going to talk about what happened last night" is code for you're fired.

He may not have fired me last night, but he definitely can today.

"I know, but I don't like leaving a mess for your maid. She cleans enough, she doesn't need me adding to it."

"Is that why you lock your room when she's here?" he asks, and the question has me straightening up, finally looking at him.

"How do you know I do that?" I ask, a bit confused.

He gives me a shrug. "She told me the other day. I guess she's tried it a few times but hasn't been able to get in."

"Does she need to clean my room?"

Why does my voice sound shaky? It's not like I'm hiding something I don't want her to find. The burner phone, sure, but that's deep in my clothes, so there's no way that will ever be found. I also haven't found anything that I had to take and keep in there.

Dante shakes his head. "Not if you don't want to. That's your space. Do what you want with it."

Sometimes this man surprises me. He may come off as someone that you should be fearful of, but then he says things that are so normal, and it throws me off.

I give him a nod and go back to fluffing pillows.

Fluff. Fluff.

Fluff until they are all sitting perfectly and there is no more fluffing to do.

Crap, maybe I should have done this a bit slower. Now I have no reason to not look up at Dante.

Nervously, I straighten up and turn to Dante again.

He's watching me with curiosity instead of the indifference that I'm used to as he continues to stand there as if his presence isn't affecting me.

"I'm going to head to my room." I say, my voice revealing my nervousness.

Dante doesn't say anything, he just stands there, his eyes never leaving me.

Unlike when we were upstairs in Allie's room, this time when I walk past him, he does stop me. His rough hand catches my arm, holding me in place.

I let out a gasp as he grips my arm tightly before letting go just a bit. Just enough to let his hand travel down to my fingertips and back up.

Like a caress.

"I think I told you this morning that we're going to talk

about what happened last night," he says, his eyes looking down at his hand movements.

I swallow the lump that I have in my throat. "Are you going to fire me this time?"

My question stops his movements and causes his dark eyes to look up at mine.

"Why would I fire you?"

Another swallow. "Because we slept together. Doesn't that go against some code or something?"

Dante looks at me for a few seconds before he speaks. "Did you not want what happened to happen?"

His question has no malice in it, just a bit of curiosity.

I shake my head. "No. I mean, no, I did want it to happen but you're still my boss. It doesn't matter how much I wanted it to happen, you can still fire me because of it."

A smirk forms on his face and I want to lean in and kiss it off so badly, but I don't. I don't know what's happening between us and whatever it is, I don't want to complicate it even more.

"You did hear me last night when I told you that I've wanted to fuck you since you walked into my office, right?" He asks, his smirk deepening.

"Yes." The word comes out almost in a whisper.

"And did you hear every single word I said to you last night as I slid my cock into your pussy?" His words are rough and low and travel down to my sex, making things a bit uncomfortable.

"Yes, I heard them."

A growl escapes him as he leans even closer, his fingers slipping into mine. "And did I give you any indication that I didn't want anything to do with what happened last night?"

I shake my head, not trusting my voice to speak.

Dante moves closer to me, dropping my hand altogether and moving his to my hip.

His touch is simple, but even through my clothes, I can feel it. It's as if it's burning through the material and I want more of it. A whole lot more of it.

"And what if I tell you that I want to do it again? That the reason why I wanted to talk was not to fire you, but to come up with a plan to fuck you over, and over again. Would you hear that?"

I can't breathe. All the oxygen has left my lungs and my body, and I have to really think about not melting at his words.

He wants to fuck me again.

Dante Rosetti wants to have sex with me again and I can't breathe. I can't even comprehend his words. All I'm focusing on is the fact that he's touching me and that he wants me under him again.

"Answer the question, *amate*. Would you hear those words?"

I breathe in his cologne and nod. "Yes. Yes, I would hear."

He lets out a chuckle, before forcefully pulling my body against his. He pulls back slightly to look down at me, with a gaze that has me holding my legs tighter together.

Dante is leaning in, but I stop him before his lips make contact with my skin.

"Why?" I breathe out, hating myself for not letting his lips meet mine first.

"Why what?" he asks, not pulling back from his position.

"Why do you want to fuck me again? There is nothing special about me."

I watch Dante as he takes in my words. He has yet to pull away from me and his cologne is still enveloping me.

After a few seconds of us just staring at each other, Dante moves. One of the hands on my hip, travels up my body, grazing my breast along the way before it settles on my cheek.

"But there is. There is something special to you. I just don't know the full capacity of it just yet, but something in me is telling me to figure it out. That I will regret it if I don't."

Those are words that I've wanted to hear from a man since I was eighteen. Now here they are, being spoken and from a mob boss of all people.

"There's something special about you too," I say.

And it's not a lie that I have to say to get him to trust me. It's the honest truth.

There is something special about this man, maybe it's the power, maybe it's something else, but like him I want to figure it out.

I want to figure out why I'm attracted to this killer. I want to know why I'm so entranced with him that I'm forgetting why I'm actually here.

"So, what should we do about this attraction that we are both feeling then?" His words caress against my lips, while his fingers caress the skin along my jaw and neck.

I don't even think about my next few words. "We should have sex. No emotions, just sex." Because that's the only way I will make it out of this without a broken heart.

"Sex, no emotions.?" He asks, and I nod. "One condition."

"What?" I look at him curiously.

The hand that is still on my hip moves but not to my ass or to my thigh like I had hoped, but to cup me at my core.

"This pussy is mine and only mine for however long this arrangement is."

I should be offended that he's claiming me, but all that is doing is making me wetter.

I nod, not even fighting him on it.

"It's yours," I say, and he starts to lean in to kiss me, but I stop him. "But that goes both ways. If I'm yours, then you're mine too."

Did I just say that? Did I really just tell this man that he was mine? What the hell has gotten into me?

"I think we can work with that," he says and before I am able to say anything else, his lips meet mine and I'm completely encapsulated in everything that this man is doing to me.

While the hand on my pussy starts to stroke me, his other moves from my face to my hair, pulling my face even closer to his.

My own hands grab at his shirt with hunger.

When his tongue slides along the seam of my lip and then enters my mouth, I let out a moan.

This man knows how to play my body like it was a piece of music and I'm loving every single second of it.

"Dante," I say when he moves his mouth to my neck.

I feel his tongue slide along my vein, and I wonder what his tongue would feel like along my pussy.

"What?" he growls against my skin, his own body grinding against mine. I can feel every hard inch of him, including what is going on under his slacks.

"I want..." I pant out, not able to form coherent words.

The way his fingers are working against me and the way his tongue, lips and teeth are attacking my neck, is making me needy.

"What do you want, *amate*?" Dante moves his mouth attack from my neck to my chest, sucking on my breast through my shirt.

"I want you to..." Again I'm rendered speechless. Why can't I think while he is touching me?

"You have to tell me, Arianna. Tell me what you want," he says, his fingers moving faster.

"I want you to lick me. I want you to lick my pussy." I can feel the lust flowing through me as I say the words.

Dante must be feeling it too because he stops stroking my heat and stops his attack on my chest. He looks down at me with so much hunger that I have no idea how I'm not bent over the couch yet.

"That's what you want?" he asks, almost sounding a bit nervous.

Why would he have any reason to be nervous?

It's not anything different than what he did to me last night.

I give him a nod. "That's what I want."

Dante gives me a grin, one that actually reaches his eyes before he leans down and places his mouth back on mine.

I let out a moan when not only my tongue meets his, but when his hands move until they are cupping me again.

With my body pressed against his, I can feel how hard his dick is, so with the leverage of his hands, I lift myself enough to rub my clothed center against him.

Dante gets the hint and lifts me up so that I can wrap my legs around his waist.

As we kiss and I grind myself against his hardness, Dante starts to walk.

At first, I think he's taking us to the couch, but that isn't the case when my ass lands on something hard.

The kitchen counter.

Before I can say anything, Dante goes to the freezer and grabs a pint of ice cream. Moose tracks.

I'm about to say something snarky, but he's back to me, pint in hand. is pushing me until my back meets the marble. I watch his every move as he drags me to edge of the counter, pulling off my pants in the process. My panties quickly following.

A smirk gets thrown my way as he opens the ice cream container. "I'm going to feast on you, sweet Arianna. I'm going to eat this pussy raw until the only thing that you call out is my name."

I have the word yes on the tip of my tongue, but the

second that Dante spreads my legs, covers my pussy in the ice cream, it's forgotten.

And when his mouth meets my core, I'm transported to a different world.

Feast on me, he does.

24

———

DANTE

My eyes pop open and I don't have to even look at the time on my phone to know it's a bit past four in the morning.

Over the years, my body has gotten so used to waking up at this early hour, that I no longer need an alarm to go off.

Usually as soon as my eyes pop open, I start getting ready for my day. I would push the covers off and not waste a minute. But for some reason, today, as my eyes pop open, I want to spend just a few more minutes between the sheets.

Maybe it's my body telling me that I need to slow down more. Or maybe it's the woman that's currently lying next to me that's making me want to stay longer.

As I look over at her, I know it's the latter. It's the latter because the more the days go by, the less I want to leave bed every morning.

It's been three weeks since our agreement in the living

room. Three weeks since we decided to let this attraction that is going on between us move forward and see what happens.

Sex with no emotions, she said, and I agreed.

Because I told myself that after I lost my wife, I would never go through that again. I won't do anything that even resembles a relationship because losing my wife fucked me in more ways than I can comprehend. I told myself that I would never bring another woman into my children's life, for them to love her and then lose her.

Yet here I am, lying in bed next to a woman that my children love already, contemplating if I should get up or not.

After a long minute of staring at the back of Arianna's head, her dark hair all over the place, I decided to get up.

If not for anything but my own sanity.

That decision goes to the trash, though, when my bed partner shifts and turns to look at me with sleep-filled eyes.

"You get up too early," she says through a yawn, her eyes closing again.

"It's easier to get things done," I voice, laying my head back down against the pillow.

Arianna hums and scoots closer to me until I feel her breath against my arm and her legs interlacing with mine.

Shifting, I throw an arm around her shoulders, bringing her naked body closer to mine. The action alone should put me on high alert to stop what we're doing, but it doesn't.

And that right should be concerning enough.

"You should at least sleep until four thirty," she says, her eyes still closed but her arm moves to lie across my stomach.

"Then I won't have time to work out," I muse into her hair.

This is one of the things that has been keeping me in bed these last three weeks. The normal conversation, the normal banter that happens between us.

Fuck. Are emotions starting to form?

No, they haven't started to form, they're already there.

Double fuck.

"Hmm. I do like your abs," she says running a hand against my stomach.

"Why are you awake?"

"Because you're awake. It's like my body knows it, so it wants to be awake when you are." She cuddles deeper into my hold, her hand drawing circles against my stomach, sliding closer to where my dick lies.

"Does it now?" I ask, feeling myself wanting to push her hand farther down until it's wrapped around my dick.

"Uh-huh, and it's definitely awake now. So maybe you should skip your workout and let me give you a workout of my own."

"You won't hear me say no to that."

"Good," she says, before sliding her hand down to my cock and starting to stroke me.

I shift the covers and the sheets so that I can watch her hand move up and down my length.

She gives me a few more strokes before moving from next to me to lie between my legs.

A sexy grin and a lust-filled eyes get thrown in my direction before she licks me from tip to base.

I let out a groan when she takes me in her mouth and I'm surrounded by the warmth of it.

"Fuck," I moan out, my hand going to her hair and giving her a hard pull.

Arianna hums around me and makes me harder than I was a few seconds ago. She definitely knows how to use that mouth of hers, but her slow rhythmic movements aren't cutting it.

Placing both my hands on either side of her head, I pull just enough to make her look up at me. Her eyes are asking a silent question but she still doesn't relent in her movements. She continues to take me until I reach the back of her throat and then she slides me back out.

"I need to fuck your mouth. Think you can do that, *amate*?"

Her eyes go wide for a second before they go back to looking hooded and ready for whatever I want to do to her.

She gives me a nod and I can't help but grin.

I pull at her hair and hold her head steady a few inches from my body before I shift my hips and start pumping into her mouth.

It's slow at first, as I pump my cock into her mouth but when I pull myself out to let her breathe, she gives me a seductive smile. One I can't ignore so when she takes me again, I don't hold back.

I fuck her mouth just like I told her I would.

Moans, and gags fill the room. Arianna's spit along

with my precum that is leaking out, coats my dick and when I see her eyes get watery, I can feel how close I am.

"I'm close, baby. Tap on my thigh and I won't come in this pretty mouth of yours." I let out a groan, feeling the pressure ready to release.

Arianna doesn't do as I say, instead she moves the one hand that lies on my thigh to my balls and gives them a hard squeeze.

That's what pushes me over the edge and I fill her mouth with everything that I have.

My cock pulses as I drop my hold from her hair and once she swallows my load, Arianna is able to catch her breath.

Not wasting any time, I drag her body up mine and help her wipe away the tears that had escaped from my attack of her mouth. In the process, I also wipe some of the spit and cum from the corner of my lips with my own tongue.

Without thinking, I pull her face to mine and explore every crevice of her mouth until I'm ready to go again.

"I think I owe you a workout of your own." I say against her plump lips.

She gives me a smile before shifting to straddle my thighs.

And I give her a workout. I work her body out until I hear the cries of my son right at five seventeen in the morning.

∼

"HAS Helen Baker said anything else to you?" I ask Arianna as I finish up going through the menu for thanksgiving with the chef.

I wasn't planning on making a big deal of the holiday, since that was Angelina's job, but somehow Evelyn convinced me.

If not for me, but because the kids should be able to look back at pictures of how life went on without their mom.

Even though I hated the idea.

So, I conceded to a small dinner for me, the kids and Arianna, if she wants to join. Maybe she has friends or distant relatives that she wants to spend the holiday with.

Arianna shakes her head as she gives Angel, who sits in his high chair, a little car to play with.

"Not since that day. I guess my words really hit her because she can't even look at me whenever I do pickups."

I don't tell her that it was actually my words that made her go silent.

"That's good." And it better stay that way, I don't say.

Actually, I wouldn't mind paying Helen and her husband a little visit, so maybe she should run her mouth.

"Are you going to the club today?" Arianna asks, taking my mind off how I want to torture Mr. and Mrs. Baker if the time ever comes.

"Yeah, just going to do some paperwork and make sure everything is going smoothly."

All lies.

The club is doing just fine and doesn't need me to stop by every chance that I get. If something does go wrong, one of my guys or Evelyn will call me if they need me.

Telling Arianna that I'm going to the club is easier than clueing her into what I'm actually doing. Mafia business.

"While you're gone, do you think that you can get me a computer charger? I'll give you the money for it. I can't find mine and I need to do a few things regarding my dad's house and accounts."

"Just use the computer in the office," I say, plucking a strawberry from the bowl at the center of the kitchen island.

Mario, the chef, leaves fruit out for the kids throughout the day just in case they need a snack.

"Which office?" Arianna asks, turning to me and giving me a confused look.

"The one on the second floor. It's not like I'm going to use it today, " I give her a shrug.

"But that's your space."

"And? You live here. You need to use it, use it." I tell her, like it's not a big deal.

Which it isn't. I know when she was first hired, Evelyn told her that she wasn't allowed to go in there. I mostly set that rule because I didn't trust the woman and didn't want her to go snooping around and finding things she shouldn't.

But now, weeks later, I trust her maybe not one hundred percent, but I trust her. Besides, if she does snoop, she won't find a single thing.

"Are you sure?"

"I'm sure." I give her a curt nod.

"Thank you." She says, giving me a small smile that tells me that she appreciates the gesture. It's a beautiful smile, one that I didn't like to see at first but have grown to like.

"I should get going," I say to the room. Grabbing one more strawberry, I head over to the table and give the kids each a kiss on the cheek.

I then turn to Arianna and place a kiss on her lips and get awarded with a bright smile before walking out of the kitchen and heading out.

It's as I walk to the car that I realize what I just did. That I just kissed her not only in front of the kids but in a relationship type of way.

In the way that I used to kiss my wife every single time I left for the day.

The kiss wasn't something that I planned but I guess subconsciously I wanted to do it.

Can't change it now. What's done is done.

Ignoring all thought of the kiss, I get in the car with Bruno in the driver's seat and we make our way over to the Lower West Side.

I got a call from one of my capos, Andrea, last night and he told me that he had gotten into a little bit of trouble.

Apparently that trouble meant that I had to be the one to take care of it and not him or even Lorenzo, for that matter.

The drive to the Lower West Side is unadventurous but the second that we arrive at the address that Andrea sent over, I know that I will be going home with blood on my shirt.

As I get out of the car, I make sure that my suit jacket covers the holster that I'm sporting. Nobody needs to know that I have two guns and three knives on me.

Being armed at all times is what a man like me has to do, especially when you sit at the head of the table.

Bruno and I walk into the building that has seen better days and head to the third floor as instructed.

Once we hit the third floor, I see exactly why I had to be the one to clean up this fucking mess.

In the middle of the abandoned area, tied to a metal chair, is City Supervisor Mitchell Clarkson.

Clarkson is the supervisor for the Lower West Side and I can only guess why he's fucking tied to a chair right now.

"Mr. Rosetti," Clarkson cries out as soon as he sees me. "I'm sorry. I didn't mean to, I swear."

I ignore the grown man's cries and turn to my capo for answers.

"Our supervisor friend here thought it would be a good idea to take some of the Mexican product for himself and keep the profit."

I knew something like this was going to happen sooner or later. I just didn't expect it in the first month.

It's been a few weeks since I met with the Muertos Cartel and agreed to let them deal on my streets.

My men were excited about this because it meant more money in their pockets

But someone was bound to get greedy and it so happened to be the supervisor.

Letting out a frustrated sigh, I approached the thief.

"How much?" I ask him, my hands sliding into the pockets of my slacks.

Clarkson whimpers but he doesn't answer. His bottom lip just trembles.

For fuck's sake.

Not giving a shit, I backhand the bastard across the face and repeat the question.

"How fucking much did you take?"

A whine that sounds like a cat in heat escapes him, as the pain of the slap finally registers. "Two kilos."

Two kilos, which means that this fucker took nearly sixty grand from the cartel. This is why city supervisors are destroying it, they are shitty when it comes to money.

"Where's the money?" I crouch down to eye level with him, so he can see exactly what his actions will lead to.

"I spent it," Clarkson says, tears streaming down his face. "I bought a new car."

Another hard slap sounds through the floor, this time with some blood splatter.

I'm pissed off, so I think time to really take care of this bastard.

"Sell the car. Get as much money as you can from it," I say to Andrea, who gives me a nod and leaves to do what I just ordered.

I nod to Bruno, and he gives me a nod back, leaving the room and leaving me and Clarkson alone.

Without taking my eyes off of the bastard, I slide my jacket off, leaving my holster on full display.

Clarkson lets out a whimper and a full-on sob as he

watches me. He knows what's coming and there is no way to stop it.

No words are spoken as I grab one of my knives and slide it against his fingers.

A scream escapes Clarkson as he feels the blade but that scream is nothing compared to the one that he releases as I slice through the skin.

I slice until the blade hits bone. I slice until blood covers the floor. I slice until Clarkson's cries are completely silent and his fingers hanging by just a thread.

When I'm done, I study the handiwork. For now, Clarkson will stay alive, but this will be a lesson for him. Mess with me and my deals and you will pay.

It doesn't matter who you are.

I will find out and I will destroy every single inch of you.

25

ARIANNA

"Oh my god. Oh my god. OH MY GOD!" I yell out as I run from the living room to the kitchen to grab my phone.

As soon as I have the phone in my hand, I run back, relieved that I didn't miss it.

Angel is taking his first steps.

He's been standing up on everything more and more for the last two weeks or so and he's tried to take a step but every time he just falls.

This time though, this time he looks like he's got it.

"Angel, come here. Walk over to me," I say to the baby boy as I crouch down and wave him over.

I start up the video and prop the phone up on the coffee table so that I can capture it.

Angel has a big smile on his face and a look of determination that tells me that this is it.

"Allie, come here. Help me get your brother to walk," I tell the little girl that is currently coloring on the floor.

She looks up and gives me a nod before abandoning the coloring book and coming over to me, copying my stance.

"C'mon, baby, walk over to us. Walk over," I say as I wiggle my fingers at Angel with the biggest smile on my face.

He lets out a laugh that comes from deep in his belly and he takes a step and then two.

"That's it. You can do it." I encourage him, as Allie claps her hands for him. Angel lets out another laugh and takes a few more steps.

Both Allie and I clap for him. "Yes, my sweet boy. You can do it. Just a few more steps."

Angel stops about three feet away from me and Allie and claps at our enthusiasm.

Without thinking, I leave my spot and grab my phone, end the video and start dialing Dante through video call.

He has to see this.

After the fourth ring, Dante's face appears on the screen.

"Arianna?" he says, sounding a bit confused. That may be because in the time I've been here and worked for him, I have never called him. Everything has been strictly through text or in person. Even with our arrangement.

I ignore his questioning look.

"Look!" I say turning the screen over so he can see his son walk toward his daughter.

"He's walking?" Dante asks, a bit of joy and laughter coating his voice.

"Yes!" I yell out, a big smile on my face.

I go back to where Allie is and crouch down so that Dante can see Angel close the last couple of steps toward us.

The room fills with cheers as Angel come closer and throws himself into Allie's arms.

I can't help but smile as both kids laugh and fall to the ground, celebrating this big accomplishment.

"I can't believe I missed seeing it in person." Dante's voice takes me away from the kids.

"I recorded the beginning of it, so you can see it when you get home," I say, turning the screen back to me.

For the first time since I started the video call, I see Dante's face. More importantly, I see the specs of red that cover his cheeks.

Blood.

And from the looks of it, it's fresh.

"Arianna." Dante's voice comes through, again with a confused tone to it.

"What?" I ask, not being able to take my eyes off the red dots.

"You look a bit off," he states and that's when I finally move my eyes away from the blood to his eyes.

They are filled with curiosity, his face a bit stoic.

"You, um, you have blood on your cheek," I say, no reason to lie to him.

Dante's eyes go slightly wide at my comment, and I watch him swipe at his face and the small specs spread on his olive skin.

"I must have nicked myself or something," he says with a nervous chuckle.

Or something, because a nick to the face wouldn't splatter like that.

He didn't go to the club like he said he was. He went to deal with something Mafia related.

I don't say anything though, I just give him a closed-mouth smile and nod.

"I'll leave you to finish out your day, I just wanted to show you Angel walking."

"Thank you."

"No problem." Another tight smile from me.

"I'll talk to you when I get home," he says, before ending the call and I'm left staring at my screensaver.

I don't know why, but the fact that I saw blood on Dante's face stays with me, more so than the kiss he gave me before he left.

Did the kiss surprise me? Absolutely. Since we started this whole arrangement, he has not once kissed me before he left the house. Better yet, he has not even kissed me in front of the kids.

We've kept strictly it to either my wing or the living room and kitchen when both kids are asleep.

So yes, it surprised me.

But the kiss was still not enough to keep me distracted and not overthinking about why Dante had blood on his face.

That little fact stays with me as I get the kids their afternoon snack and put Angel down for a nap.

Why was he covered in blood?

Because he was probably off killing someone, just like he killed your dad.

I try to push that thought away as I get Alessandra settled in the living room with some schoolwork she has for the holiday break.

The more I let the thought circle in my head, the more I feel the need to do some digging.

"I'll be right back, okay? I just have to grab something from your *papi's* office. I will be gone for only five minutes," I tell Allie.

She gives me a nod, and starts to work on her turkey drawing.

When she's set, I quickly make my way upstairs and head directly to the office.

Another surprising thing that Dante did this morning was to give me permission to use his office.

I really had no reason to ask, but Gallo has been sending so many messages to the burner phone asking if I've found something that I just took the chance.

I don't know what is making Gallo so persistent all of a sudden, but it was enough to build up the courage to ask this of Dante.

He didn't even think about it, he just said yes. And now as I approach the door, I feel like I'm going to puke.

Am I really doing this? Am I really going to walk into his office and snoop around until I find something incriminating to either put him in jail or six feet in the ground?

After all the time that he has spent in my bed these last few weeks, do I still want to do this?

No, it has nothing to do with what I *want*. It's what I *need* to do. For me. For my dad, and for every other person that has suffered because of something the media has done.

So that's why I place my hand on the doorknob and twist it open even with nerves running through my body.

When I push the door back, I'm instantly hit with everything that is Dante.

His scent. His personality. Everything that makes him the man that he is, the man that make me melts every time I'm in the same room as him, everything is in this room.

Taking a deep breath, I walk, leaving the door open slightly just in case one of the kids needs me.

I ignore the picture frames of the kids that adorn the room. I ignore the massive collection of books that seem to reach all the way to the ceiling. I ignore it all and head straight to the computer.

Dante texted me the password when he left this morning, so I type it in and a second later, I'm in.

I just logged into the computer that belongs to the boss of the Chicago Mafia. Now I really want to puke.

Quickly, I find the document hub and start looking through all the file names waiting for something to pop out.

The only thing that stands out to me though, is the fact that every single file on this computer is labeled by a set of numbers.

Numbers that mean absolutely nothing to me but might mean everything to Dante.

I click on a random file and instantly get asked for a password. Of course, they are password encrypted and knowing Dante and what he does, each file has a different password.

Giving up on the documents, I look at the internet history and again that gives me nothing.

Why I thought someone like Dante Rosetti would keep his most important documents and internet searches ready for me to find is beyond me.

Logging out of the computer and shutting it off, I start to look around the office from where I sit in his chair.

Everything looks a little bit too clean to be an office, especially one that is used frequently. There has to be something that was left out by accident or at the very least, put somewhere so it can be worked on later.

I start pulling at the desk drawers, checking to see if they are locked, and by some miracle they aren't.

The top drawer is filled with office supplies. Pens, pencils, crayons that I'm sure belong to the kids, staples. Nothing useful.

I move to the second drawer, and I instantly regret opening it. There are picture frames in this drawer but it's the one that lies on top that has me regretting everything.

The frame contains a picture of a woman with a beautiful smile and dark hair that is styled perfectly in waves that frame her face beautifully. She looks absolutely gorgeous and as I look into her eyes, I know who she is.

Dante's wife.

Her eyes are the same as her children's. They are bright and a blue-grayish color that I will never forget. The eye color is a complete contrast to her skin tone, but it makes her unique and even more beautiful.

From what Evelyn has told me, she died less than a year ago, so why are her photos in the drawer? They should be around the house so that her kids can see her every single day. So they can live life and still see her beautiful smile as they go about their day.

Maybe I should bring it up to Dante.

As I continue to look at her picture, more guilt starts to form inside of me.

Not only am I looking for something to bring her husband, the father of her children, down, but I'm also sleeping with the man. Not even a whole year since she passed.

She has to be looking down at me right now and thinking of ways to burn me alive from the grave for doing what I'm doing.

I'm such a horrible person.

Putting my feelings to the side, the picture frame goes back into the drawer, and I shut it just as quickly as I opened it before moving to the third and final drawer.

This drawer is filled with green hanging files and each one has a manila folder in them. I brush through the labels on each file, looking to see if one of them catches my eye.

Unlike the computer files, one of them does.

The one with the label, D J V.

Cryptic, but those three letters wouldn't stand for Detective Joseph Vitale, would they?

One way to find out.

I pull out the file and open it right away.

D J V does indeed stand for Detective Joseph Vitale

because the file is filled with pictures of him. Everything from him in his car during a stakeout, to him walking into the brownstone one random day.

There are so many pictures of him that just looking at them is making me teary-eyed.

Dante was keeping track of my dad and all his movements, but why?

I continue to shift through the pictures until I reach the end of the file and find a note.

Taking it in my hand, I see that the note is written not in Dante's handwriting but in my dad's.

My breathing hitches when I see his familiar scrawl, one that I didn't think I would ever see again.

I push down all the emotions forming in the back of my throat and try to read what the note says.

My dad didn't have the neatest handwriting, so it takes me two tries to comprehend what words are what.

G Mafia.
Drug smuggling.
Trafficking.
Will kill me.

There are more words to the piece of paper but those are the only ones that I'm able to make out.

Trafficking? Like sex trafficking?

Could Dante be involved in sex trafficking? The drug smuggling is something that I expected to come from the Mafia, but sex trafficking? That never crossed my mind.

And G Mafia? What does that even mean?

So many questions are running through my head right now that I can't even comprehend what I'm reading.

But the biggest question that I have is. *If* my dad wrote this note, why does Dante have it? Did my dad have it on him when he was killed and Dante took it? If that were the case, wouldn't there be blood on it?

Nothing is making sense to me.

Knowing that I'm running out of time before Allie comes looking for me, I quickly take out my phone and take pictures of everything that's in the file. Including the note.

Once I have everything that I need, I put the file back in its place and close the drawer. Looking around, I check to see if I missed anything and when I find that I'm in the clear, I leave the office.

The second I close the door behind me, I let all the air out of my lungs.

I stand there, catching my breath for a quick minute.

I found information. It may not be information that tells me that Dante killed my father, but it's enough to tell me that Dante was watching him.

Even though what I just did makes me feel like I've betrayed Dante in some way, I make a plan to send all the pictures to Gallo later tonight.

I will send them to him, and he can do what he wants with them.

I did my part, now I just have to see if I will succeed in this. In taking Dante Rosetti down.

And hopefully it's soon.

Because as I stand here outside of his office, I realize one thing, my feelings for Dante are starting to grow.

But that's not what scares me the most. My feelings for Dante Rosetti, I can deal with. What I can't deal with is the amount of guilt that grows within me every passing second.

Guilt for putting myself in this man's life.

Guilt because I've come to love the kids and I want to take their dad away from them.

Guilt because I should be thinking about my dad and getting revenge for what was done to him, but in reality, I haven't given it much thought.

Guilt because I've come to know Dante and see that he really isn't the man that people think he is.

There is so much guilt that when I send the pictures to Gallo later that night, I cry.

I cry because I realize I don't want do this anymore.

I just don't know what I mean by this.

Taking Dante down? Or continue to fall for a man that might kill me for my actions.

26

DANTE

Arianna has been quiet. A little too quiet, and after experiencing it for almost five days, I've realized that I don't like it.

The fact that I don't like it is a red flag all on its own.

Look, I'm a man of very few words and can definitely do without all the chatter that surrounds me half the time, but I hate this. I hate not having Arianna speak more than two words to me when I address her.

And the fact that I'm thinking about her as Arianna and not the nanny, is another red fucking flag.

She hasn't said a full sentence to me since the day she video called me to show me Angel walking.

Everything that comes out of her mouth is either clipped or a simple yes or no. Hell, she's even gone back to addressing me as Mr. Rosetti instead of Dante and I hate that too.

But the thing that I hate the most, and this may make

me the most pussy-whipped bastard around, is not being able to touch her. I haven't been able to hold her body against mine as I slide into her. I haven't been able to feel her pussy tightening around my cock.

And fuck me, I really am pussy whipped and I'm not even in a relationship with this woman.

And yes, I'm fucking pissed she won't talk to me. If this was any other woman, any other nanny, I would say fuck it and would have no problem calling up Honor and

letting her take care of my needs.

But she's not any other woman or a nanny and she has me in a fucking trance.

Now I'm at a point where I can't take it anymore.

So tonight, I'm going to find out what is going through the beautiful nanny's head.

First things first, I need Evelyn to finish giving me the rundown of the numbers for the club this week and as soon as she heads to her own place, I will go through with my plan.

Evelyn lives here on the property in a small cottage that can easily house ten people because there are times that I need her for pressing matters.

She has lived here for years now, even becoming best friends with Angelina in the beginning, and as far as I know, she likes it. It can also be that I don't question the men that she brings into her home.

Whatever she does in her free time is not something I want to be privy to.

But right now, she needs to go.

"I have a few new men and women auditioning in the next two weeks that look very promising, so come the new year we should grow in dancers and clientele," Evelyn tells me, shutting her laptop.

Finally.

I give her a nod. "Send me the schedule for the auditions and I will join you."

"Will do. There is one more thing," she says, biting her lip.

"What?"

"We got a new high-profile client this week."

"We get high-profile clients all the time. What's the big deal?" I throw back at her.

It's not unknown that Perversa is a sought-after place, especially in a city that is filled with billionaires and professional athletes.

High-profile clients are our norm.

"It's Maddox Bauer," Evelyn states.

"Fucking hell." I groan.

Maddox Bauer was one of the best pitchers that major league baseball has ever seen, and I say "was" because this last season, everything has gone downhill for him.

Word has it, the money has gone to his head as he spent the majority of this season in clubs and saw more cocaine than the pitching mound. He was suspended sometime in August for substance use and there are talks of him being cut from the majors altogether.

He's one of Chicago's own, so seeing him go downhill so quickly has been hard on the baseball fans in the city.

I've met him, shit I know his mother, and I know that Maddox is capable of a lot, he just has to see that.

Having him become a client of Perversa can be a very bad thing, especially if he hasn't gotten clean.

Or a good thing if I can keep him in check.

"Let him join but keep a close eye on him. If he does anything, anything at all, even looks at a bartender weird, have whoever is working, call me. I'll take care of him."

Evelyn nods. "I will pass it along and let Maddox know he is welcome at Perversa anytime."

With that, Evelyn gathers her things and heads out.

After she leaves, I ignore the files that are on my desk and go find where Arianna and the kids ended up.

Since we started exploring our sexual attraction with each other, because that's what it was and definitely not a relationship, I've noticed Arianna has taken on a role here as more than just a nanny.

Every day, I see how much she cares for the kids, how she doesn't mind when I tell her I have to work late. I see that she enjoys eating meals with us and interacting with them outside of a professional capacity.

I also see just how much the kids love her.

To them, this woman is what most people would consider a mother figure and as I see more and more of it, I would agree.

Arianna looks at Alessandra and Angel as her own and not a job.

That pains me to even think, but it's true.

I find the three of them in the living room watching some cartoon movie on the big screen. Angel is fast asleep on the couch and Alessandra is snuggled into Arianna's side.

To an outsider, this would be just any ordinary family enjoying a night in.

There is nothing ordinary about this situation.

Alessandra must feel my presence because her little head pops up and a smile forms on her face. She dislodges herself from Arianna before getting off the couch and coming over to me. Her little hand grabs mine and drags me over to the couch and pushes me down where she was just sitting. Right next to Arianna.

There's a good six inches between us.

Happy with where I am, Allie climbs up onto my lap and situates herself between me and her nanny before moving to lie down. She lays her head on Arianna's lap and extends the rest of her body over mine.

Arianna looks at me with wide eyes before turning her attention to my daughter.

"I think maybe I should let you have a movie night with just you and your dad," she says to Allie, brushing her hair back.

Allie shakes her head and situates herself deeper into Arianna.

I guess she's staying.

"Don't want to spend time with me?" I say jokingly, an instant blush covering her cheeks.

"What? No, that's not—" She stops to collect herself. "I just thought you would want to spend some time with just your kids."

"I was joking."

"Oh, right. Yeah, I knew that," she says, before turning back to watch the movie.

Wanting to see how much deeper I can make that blush of hers go, I decide to play with her some more.

"I mean, it's okay if you don't want to spend time with me. You didn't want to spend time with me all week, why would tonight be any different?" I shrug, throwing an arm on the back of the couch, letting my fingers fall inches away from her hair.

She turns back to me and I see it

Deep red. Her blush gets to a deep red.

"I-I..." she stutters, before turning back to the TV. "I'm just trying to put distance between us, Mr. Rosetti."

There she goes with the mister crap again. And distance? If I remember correctly, she was enjoying what we were doing. Why the fuck would she want distance?

Instead of giving her a response, I follow her lead and turn to watch the movie.

For a good twenty minutes, I watch something I'm sure Alessandra picked out, trying my best to ignore the woman next to me.

But as much as I want to ignore her, I can't. What happened between the morning when I kissed her goodbye and when I got home? What happened that she would want to distance herself from me and go back to acting as just my employee?

Maybe it was the kiss that shifted things. Maybe my doing that triggered something within her that made her realize that we were moving on a different course. One that she may not be completely comfortable with.

Is that it?

"She fell asleep," Arianna says, her voice almost at a whisper.

I look over to her and watch as she looks down at the little girl adoringly, pushing the dark hair away from her little face.

"Good," I say, not even stopping to think about my words. "Now me and you, sweet Arianna, can have a conversation."

Her eyes leave Alessandra and meet mine. The blush from earlier is still there and I can't help but think that she looks beautiful like this.

Eyes slightly wide, color on her cheeks, hair down in an untamed fashion and lips slightly parted.

I'm concentrating on taking in every detail of her face, so that her question takes me by surprise.

"Why do you call me Arianna?"

A bit confused by the question, I answer, "Because that's your name."

She shakes her head. "Everyone calls me Ari. Evelyn, your bodyguards, everyone that walks into this house daily calls me Ari. You don't, why?"

"Because it's your name." I reiterate once again.

Why is this conversation even happening?

"So is Ari."

"Why is it so important what I call you? Maybe I like your full name better than a three-letter word that doesn't suit you. Calling you Ari makes it seem to me that you're a little girl and not the grown woman you are. Are you seriously putting distance between us because I won't use a childish nickname for you?"

"What? No," Arianna answers, shaking her head in the process.

"Then why?" My voice rises a bit but when I remember that the kids are in the room sleeping, I tone it down. "Why the fuck are we having this discussion?"

"Because I'm trying to avoid having any other type of discussion with you." She says a little too loudly, so she looks down at the kids to make sure she didn't wake them.

"You mean the discussion where I call you out for ultimately ending our agreement without speaking to me?"

I'm being childish with this, I know I am. I'm not a man that would argue with a woman over this type of shit, but I've come to realize something.

I've come to realize that since I lost my wife, I want to go after things that I want, and one thing I want is Arianna.

Yes, I want this woman. In whatever capacity I can get, I want this woman. So, I will continue with these arguments that are a little childish for a thirty-seven-year- old man.

"Yes. That discussion," she says taking her lower lip between her teeth.

"We're having it, so have at it. Tell me why you decided there needed to be distance between you and me. Was I making things uncomfortable?"

She shakes her head no.

"Was it our age difference? Is being thirteen years apart too much or too icky for you?"

Another shake.

"Then what the fuck is it?" I say quietly through my teeth.

"I felt guilty, okay!" she says a little too quickly that even her eyes go wide when it registers what she said.

"Guilty over what?" I say, my voice coming out hard as if I was speaking to one of my men. As if it were Clarkson in front of me again and not Arianna.

My mind automatically goes to the worst-case scenario as to what might come out of her mouth.

Stole money.

Found something and gave it to the cops.

So many things.

Arianna is silent for a few seconds before she lets out a sigh and answers my question.

"So many things. One of them being that day you let me use your office, I accidentally opened the drawer that had your wife's pictures. I wasn't snooping, I swear, I was looking for paper clips for some things I printed out. I just opened the drawer and I saw them. The second I saw her face, it was like this big wave of guilt swallowed me whole. Guilt because I was sleeping with her husband not even a year after she died. Guilt because while we weren't sleeping in the bed you shared with her, we were still doing it under her roof, in her house. It was guilt because I was supposed to be watching over her children, not making sure her husband's needs were being met. I felt like she was judging me over my actions when it came to you. Then, of course, there was guilt over—" She stops abruptly like she was about to say something that she wasn't meant to.

"Guilt over what?" I press, not letting this conversation end.

Arianna looks at me, a bit of sadness in her eyes but the more I look, the more I see that there is also fear swimming in them.

"Guilt over what, Arianna?" I press some more. After another long minute, she lets out a sigh.

She keeps my stare as she speaks. "Guilt over knowing who you really are and not even caring. You had blood on your face and that should have been the moment where I told I was quitting and wasn't going to look back. I know who you are, Dante, I know you're a part of the Mafia. I know people fear you, and yet here I am, sitting next to you, not feeling an ounce of fear toward you. I feel guilty, because I should. I should be fearful of you, but I know that I would rather get to know you in a way not many people have, than run away from you."

Her voice flutters at the end. It's as if the words she just said were the hardest thing to speak.

I don't say anything. I don't tell her that she has nothing to be guilty for. That, yes, Angelina died nearly ten months ago, but she would want me to move on. She would want me and the kids to be happy.

Maybe not this quickly, but she would want it.

I should tell her that her guilt was well placed and that she should walk away from this job, from the kids, from me, and live the life that every twenty-four-year-old is supposed to live.

There are a lot of things that I should tell her, but I keep each and every one at bay. Instead, I turn to face her completely, shifting Alessandra as I do, and let my fingers wrap around her strands of hair.

"You should fear me. Every inch of you should be scared of even being within ten feet of me. Because I'm not just a part of the Mafia, *amate*. I am the fucking Mafia. Everyone answers to me and only me."

I watch as she stiffens at my words, but I don't address it as I continue speaking.

"That being said, I'm not going to force you to stay here if you don't want to. I also won't force you to continue with whatever was happening between us. You have every right to want to put distance between us and to feel guilt. I feel guilty too. Every time I look at you, every time I feel the need to be near you, I feel so much guilt that I fear that I will drown in it. Yet, that guilt is not enough to stop me from wanting you. Wanting you in ways that I can't even comprehend."

A small gasp leaves her lips at my confession. A gasp that I wish I was able to swallow down as I pressed my lips against hers.

"You want to be with me?" she asks, her voice barely a whisper.

I can't tell if it's because the kids are asleep or because she has lost her voice to the point she can't speak.

I give her a nod. "I shouldn't, but I do. Just like you want to get to know me in different ways, I want the same with you."

We both go silent for a minute, her most likely marveling at my words and me trying not to let the ghost of my dead wife fill me with even more guilt.

"Then where do we go from here?" she asks, again in the same whisper.

There isn't an ounce of hesitation in my voice when I answer. "We go upstairs, put the kids to bed and figure things out some more."

27

ARIANNA

I sink my body into the tub, instantly being surrounded by warm water and a lavender scent. The second I take in the lavender, every inch of me relaxes and I sink deeper into the water.

Letting my eyes close, I let my head lean against the edge of the tub and enjoy the moment of silence.

Never have I been much of a bath person. Maybe because I stopped taking baths when I was around five and my studio only had a standing shower. I never understood why taking a bath would appeal to people, but now I can see how relaxing it could be.

Especially when you have a man that is shirtless, barefoot and only wearing slacks in the same room, looking down at you.

This night has definitely taken a different turn than what I expected.

I thought that I was going to watch the movie with the kids and then once they went to sleep, I would be spending the rest of the night ignoring Dante. Just like I've been doing this whole week.

But then he popped into the living room and Alessandra made him sit next to me and my plan of ignoring the man went out the window.

Then everything continued to go to shit when he called me out for ignoring him and asked the big question. Why?

Why, indeed.

It was his persistence that made the words spill out in an uncontrollable way. So much so that I almost told him everything. I almost told him about Gallo and why I was really in his office. I almost let it spill out about what my intentions really were when I accepted the job as his nanny.

What I told him was the absolute truth and I wanted to tell him even more of it. I wanted to tell him that my guilt ran so deep that after two days of thinking, I did something that I never thought I would do at the beginning of all this.

I wanted to say that I texted Gallo a few days ago and told him that I no longer wanted to be a part of whatever we had set up. That I called a stop to the takedown of Dante Rosetti.

But I didn't let those words spill. I kept that inside, no matter how much I wanted to say them.

And when he told me how he also felt guilty and the way he felt, it took everything I had not to climb over his daughter and kiss him. Never did I think I would see this man be so vulnerable, yet I did, and I loved it.

And not in the "wanting to see this man suffer" type of way.

Now I'm in his bathroom in his room, enjoying the sight of him half undressed.

When he said we'd put the kids to bed, he really meant he was. I was directed to his bathroom and told me to take a shower or whatever, his words not mine, and he would join me shortly so we could talk some more.

Was I scared to walk into the master bedroom? Yes, yes, I was. It's one of the two rooms in this mega house that I had yet to step foot in. In our first few weeks of exploring each other's bodies, not once did we venture into his bedroom and now that I was walking in, it felt off.

As much as I wanted to look around the room and snoop a bit, I didn't.

It felt like I would be invading his privacy. Which is rich considering what I've been doing since I started this job.

So I went straight to the bathroom and when I saw the Jacuzzi-sized tub, I decided on a bath.

Now I'm just sitting, marveling at how relaxing it feels, waiting to see if he's going to join me.

"Are you really okay with me being here?" I ask, breaking the silence of the room.

Dante leans against the bathroom counter and gives me a nod. "I'm sure."

"Then maybe you can join me?" I say, using the most seductive voice that I have.

This man has fucked me every which way, I have no idea why I'm acting like a shy schoolgirl around him now.

Dante throws me a small grin before pushing off the counter and taking off the remainder of his clothing.

I watch as he slides his slacks and boxers off as if it's Christmas morning.

Everything about this man is perfect. The olive complexion, the toned muscles all over and I've never been a body hair person, but Dante definitely makes me one.

Once he's undressed, he makes his way over to the tub, waving for me to slide forward so he can get in.

I do as I'm told, and the water moves around as he settles behind me.

Without hesitation, I slide back until my back meets his chest and his hands move from the edge of the tub to settling on my thighs.

I was relaxed earlier, but now that I'm enveloped in everything Dante, I feel contentment

Contentment is not something that I would have thought I would have wanted from Dante, but here I am.

That contentment grows even more when I feel Dante's face press against my neck and a small kiss lands on my skin.

It feels good. It feels...

"This feels very relationship-like," I say out loud.

I don't think about what I said until I feel Dante stiffen a bit behind me.

I'm already working out an apology in my head when he speaks.

"It does feel that way." He voices before placing another kiss against my skin, not pulling away in the slightest.

"Are you okay with it feeling that way?" I ask.

A lot of things were said downstairs. Shit, a lot of

things were said when we started sleeping together, but just because those things were said doesn't mean that we are ready to call whatever we are doing a relationship.

This time when he answers, he does pull away from me.

"Yeah, yeah I think it's definitely okay for it to feel that way," he says.

"You don't sound all that convinced," I say, turning slightly so that I can see him.

He looks down at me for a second before he lets out a sigh and turns his line of vision to the wall in front of us.

"When Angelina died, I decided that I was never going to put myself in that type of situation again. I lost my parents, I lost her, and bringing someone else into my life and losing them would have been too much. Did I want to move on? In all honesty, no. I was going to put all that behind me and just concentrate on what I had. The club, the kids, the business, but things happen in strange ways. Like nannies walking into your life and making you over-think every decision you made for yourself."

I watch him as he speaks. His eyes may not be on me, and I may not be able to see the kind of emotion that is swimming in them, but I can tell he's a little lost.

Lost in thought.

Lost in his past.

He continues to talk, and I take in every single word as if it's my very own bedtime story.

"Since I'm being honest here, I should tell you that I haven't been celibate since Angelina died. I slept with someone else five months after her funeral. I needed an out, needed to feel something that wasn't sorrow or anger and that's what I used to get it. It wasn't anything serious, never did it feel I was betraying Angelina and her memory. It was just an out for me, but then you came along. You came along and after that first night together, I knew you were different. You were different because you made it feel as if I was cheating. It felt as if I was cheating on my wife, and she had been gone for months. And as time keeps moving, I'm becoming more okay with it, no matter how much I tell myself that I shouldn't be."

I shift even more so that I can take his face between my hands and make him look down at me.

"I don't want you to feel like you're cheating. You're not. I don't want you to ever think that you are, but I also don't want you to regret anything we do."

His dark eyes spark a bit at my touch. "I don't regret it, and I never will. It will just take a little more time for me to get through the fact that I met someone that I really want to be with so soon after my wife died. It doesn't seem fair. It's like she's gone, and I just have to forget about her."

Now when I move, I straddle his thighs, bringing me even closer to him. All to drive a point across.

"She was your wife. The mother of your kids. The woman you loved. She will always be a part of you. She will always be the woman that you loved, and you will never forget her."

"How do you know that?" he asks, his eyebrows bunching up a bit.

"Because if you wanted to forget her, you would have

destroyed every picture of her, not put them in a drawer for safekeeping."

If Dante and I go through with this, if we label what we are doing as a relationship, then I will make it my mission to put her pictures up again. The kids need to experience their mom and she doesn't deserve to spend the rest of their lives in a drawer.

Frankly, neither does Dante.

"If I say that I am okay with this feeling like a relationship or even calling it one, would you be okay with me still taking the time to mourn my wife?"

"Yes. I will be absolutely okay with that. Why? Because she's a big part of three people that I've come to care very deeply about. She deserves a lifetime of memories and stories to be told about her." I say, leaning in slightly and placing a kiss against his lips.

He doesn't kiss me back. Dante just looks at me with wonder as if he can't comprehend who I really am.

The same way I've been feeling since my dad's funeral.

"So where does that leave the two of us?" he asks, his hand shifting slightly and moving to my hips, his fingers digging into my skin.

"Back to the original question, are you okay with this feeling like a relationship?"

With no hesitation, he answers. "Yes. I'm okay with it, I'm even okay with calling it one if that's what you want. I want it. I want you. Now the question is, do you want me just as much?"

This time, I'm the one that doesn't hesitate. "I want

you. Just as much, if not more. I want all the emotion, not just the sex anymore."

The second I say the last word, the both of us make our move.

Lips meet lips and the both of us are fighting to get more of each other.

As my tongue slides into his mouth and explores every inch of it, I feel his hands move to my ass and feel them grip me.

Dante brings my body closer to his, as if we weren't close enough, and starts to move me to grind against him.

The water and bubbles start to spill over the edges of the tub as I continue to move, and Dante continues to explore my body with his hands.

Our kisses are filled with bites, tongues and moans, and I love every second of it.

When I pull away to catch my breath, Dante's mouth falls to my neck. He explores the skin for a second before he moves his face down farther, to my breasts and gives them all his attention.

A moan escapes me when I feel his teeth sinking into my right nipple.

Never have I been into pain mixing with pleasure when it came to sex but being with Dante, it makes me want to explore it. He makes me like the pain and makes me want to explore every side of it.

"You keep making those noises and we will flood the bathroom." He says before giving me another bite.

I can't help but giggle, actually liking the sound of that happening. "I don't see the downside of that."

For emphasis, I slide myself along his hardness, letting out another moan when I feel his tip enter me.

"*Amate*." He growls out, still not wavering from my chest.

Amate.

He's been calling me that since our first night together and as much as I want to ask what it means or even look it up, I haven't. Being Italian, I should know what the word means, but since my parents wanted to shy away from their roots, I don't.

I haven't asked or looked it up because I don't want to get my hopes up over a little word.

Embracing the nickname he has for me; I continue to slide against him until more than just the tip enters me.

"You're asking for trouble, Arianna." Another bite follows his words. He's marking me and I fucking love it.

"I want it. I want trouble. I want everything you can give me. Please, Dante." I let out another moan, wanting to feel more of him.

Dante gives my tits one more bite before moving his lips back up my neck until they are hovering just over mine.

His eyes are dark but are filled with lust. He looks hungry and ready to eat everything that's in front of him. If we weren't in a tub surrounded by water, I'm sure he would be able to feel my slickness against him from that look alone.

"Everything that I can give you?" He pants out, his eyes closing a bit as I slide him in me once more.

"Yes," I say in a breathy tone.

One simple word and that is all that it takes for Dante to slam his lips against mine and to use his grip on my ass to lift me up and slam into me.

The sensation feels so good that I have to pull my lips away from his to let out a moan. "Oh fuck."

"You ignored me for five days, so it's time you received the repercussions of that," he growls out, not giving me the chance to get used to his size.

No, Dante continues to lift me up and slam into me repeatedly until all I see are black spots in my line of vision and I have to grab onto the tub to keep me up.

"Dante. I—" I stop speaking the second I feel his mouth back on my chest and his finger seeking entrance into my puckered hole.

"It feels good, doesn't it, baby? It feels good to have my cock fill your pussy and my finger teasing your asshole. Maybe if you learn to be a good girl and stop ignoring me, I will fuck this ass of yours and mark it as mine. Ruin you for every single man that comes after me. Do you want that, *amate*?"

All I can do is nod.

"I need words, Arianna. Do you want me to ruin you for other men?"

A groan escapes. "Yes."

"Do you want me to claim your ass as mine?"

A moan. "Yes."

"What about the rest of you? Do you want me to claim that as mine too?"

A whimper. "Yes."

"Then hold on tight, *amate*, because I'm about to fuck you raw and claim every inch of you as mine."

"Yes."

It's as if a switch was flipped and the animalistic side of Dante comes out.

He fucks me hard and raw just like he promised, hitting the right spot repeatedly.

It doesn't take long until I'm seeing black spots again and my legs are shaking against his body and I'm reaching the biggest high that I've ever experienced.

"That's it, Arianna. Let this cunt of yours tighten around my cock. It feels so good," he moans out and I completely lose it even more.

This man has fucked me on numerous occasions but never like this. Never with this much emotion.

As I come down from my release, Dante continues to fuck me hard and fast, until he lets out a groan that fills the room and gives into his own release.

It's as he is coming down from his own release that I realize something. The man that just fucked me was not Dante Rosetti.

No, the man that just fucked me was The Devil and I loved every single second of it.

And I want more.

28

DANTE

"I don't give a fuck how you take care of it, Lorenzo, just fucking do it. The asshole is stealing my money, so take care of it. If you don't, it will be me putting a bullet in the fucker's head and you will be the one to clean up the mess."

The call ends without another word coming from my right-hand and I slam the phone against the seat next to me.

If I was anywhere besides the back of a car, the phone would be meeting a wall and shattering into pieces.

Sometimes having the title of the boss means fucking babysitting grown men more often than not.

I would be a happier man if I didn't deal with morons every fucking day of the week.

I would be even happier if said morons wouldn't steal from me.

You would think when you pay each of your men each

thousands of dollars every month, they would be fucking loyal to you.

Yet there is always one greedy bastard that wants more and instead of coming to you for it, he steals it.

"Should I get the body bag ready?" Evelyn jokes from the seat next to me.

I look over at her with narrowed eyes and the woman has the audacity to give me a smirk.

"I like you better when you don't speak," I say through gritted teeth.

Her smirk just deepens and she turns to look back down at her phone.

Evelyn and I are on our way back to the house after a long day of auditions at Perversa.

There have been auditions going on since the start of December. But given that the holidays just came and went and the fact that some dancers only work when they are really strapped for cash, we had a few open spots.

Today was the last of it and from the looks of it, we have a solid lineup.

"Just so you know, I blocked February third completely off on your calendar."

It's with those words that all thoughts of my men stealing from me and the auditions, go out the fucking window.

"I also wrote a note for Alessandra's school to excuse her that day." Evelyn continues when I don't respond.

February third.

The one-year anniversary of Angelina's death.

In only a few weeks' time, I have to live with the fact

that my wife, the mother of my children, has been dead for a year, and there's nothing I can do about it.

"I think you should take the day and just spend it with the kids, maybe even go to the cemetery and visit her," Evelyn voices, trying her hardest to get me out of the spiral that my head is going through.

The only thing I can think of doing to acknowledge her comment is to nod.

Just nod.

One year. One year without the woman that I thought I was going to spend the rest of my life with. I knew very early on in our relationship that I wasn't going to need anything else if I had her in my life. Now I was able to live a whole year without her a few feet away from me.

I was able to make it a whole year without hearing her laugh or seeing her smile. A whole year without seeing her with our children. A whole year of birthdays and holidays that she didn't get to experience.

A whole damn year.

"Maybe you can even bring Arianna with you."

It's at that comment that I'm able to find my voice and it sounds angry. "You want me to bring the nanny, the one that I'm fucking not even a year after my wife's death, to said wife's grave?

I look over at my assistant with astonishment that she would even suggest something like that, but all I get is a look of indifference in return.

"It's just a suggestion. To make the day easier for you. Because even if you don't want to admit it to me, that girl is way more than just the nanny. I see it, security sees it, hell,

I'm sure your kids see it, no reason to keep hiding it, especially from yourself."

I let out a sigh. "I'm not going to take her to the cemetery with me on the anniversary of my wife's death."

Because Evelyn is right, Arianna is more than just the nanny, she has been for close to two months now, and it wouldn't be fair to her or Angelina if I took her there.

"Again, it was just a suggestion," Evelyn voices, reaching over and giving my arm a squeeze.

I just nod and look out the window.

For the remainder of the drive, as much as I want to forget about my ever-growing relationship with Arianna and Angelina's death, I can't. Even if two months have passed since me and Arianna became a thing and twelve since Angelina died, I still feel guilty for not waiting longer to move on.

I'm a goddamn jackass and I know it.

After fifteen more minutes, the SUV pulls into the estate and heads straight to the main house.

When I walk in, Evelyn heading to her cottage, I'm immediately surrounded by the sound of music and children giggling.

A smile instantly forms on my face as head to the living room.

Arianna and Alessandra are in the middle of the living room, jumping up and down with the kids' music video playing on the screen. All with Angel watching them and giggling from his jumper in the corner.

This is a visual that I've been coming home to a lot more often since Arianna started working here. Some lighthearted scenes where the kids are laughing, smiling, playing or dancing. Something that they didn't really do for a few months. Having Arianna here has really been a bright spot, not only with the kids but also in the house. It feels lighter, happier.

And it's all because of her.

Arianna catches sight of me in the entryway of the living room and gives me a bright smile that I can't help but return.

When she stops moving, Alessandra notices and turns to see what has gotten her nanny's attention. When my little girl sees me, she also gives me a smile before she runs over to me with her arms open wide.

I crouch down to catch her and as soon as she's in my arms, my smile grows even more.

The little girl that I thought I was never going to see smile and happy again is coming back. Slowly, but it's happening.

"Hi, *gioia mia*," I say into her hair.

"*Papi*," she says and everything around me just stops.

Did she just...

"What did you say?" I ask my daughter, pulling away from her slightly so I can see her little face.

"*Papi*," she repeats, her little brows bunching up a bit in confusion as if she wants to ask me why I'm making her repeat herself.

I give her a smile and bring her little body back to mine and hold her a bit tighter.

Looking over Alessandra's shoulder, I catch sight of

Arianna looking over at us, a smile on her lips while a tear rolls down her cheek.

I let Alessandra go when she starts to squirm in my arms and as soon as she is preoccupied by her brother, I turn to Arianna.

"She just said *papi*." I say, still astonished by what I heard.

She walks over to me, giving me a nod. "She did. I'm sure she will be saying full sentences again in no time."

"Yeah, maybe she will," I state, watching her as she watches the kids.

I don't know if it's the joy of hearing Allie say another word, or it's the joy that this woman brings me and my children, but I grab her chin and bring her face closer to mine and place a chaste kiss on her lips.

When it comes to our relationship, we are not very affectionate toward each other when the kids are around. But I think this is a solid exception.

"What was that for?" Arianna asks, a shy smile forming on her lips.

"If you weren't here, she would probably still not have said a word. In the time you've been here, she's said two. So, thank you. Thank you for being here and thank you for bringing her out of the shell she was in."

"I had nothing to do with it. It was all her."

Arianna leans up to place a kiss on my lips before she pulls back, giving me a smile and heading to where the kids are.

That felt normal.

The kiss, the interaction, it all feels normal and there isn't an ounce of guilt flowing through me.

No guilt as I smile as I watch her interact with my kids.

I broke the vow to myself to never be involved with someone in this capacity again, and there is no guilt at all.

29

———

ARIANNA

There's a happiness in my chest that I haven't felt in a very long time.

I'm sure if I thought about it, thought about the last time I was this happy, I would be taken back to a time when my dad was still alive.

Years. I haven't felt this way in years and I don't want it to go away.

I should want it to go away, considering who is the root cause of the smile on my face, but even knowing that I'm sleeping with The Devil of Chicago isn't enough to take my joy away.

That's what I realized as I watched Allie run to her dad and say something for the first time in weeks. And I realized it even more when Dante placed a chaste kiss on my lips as if that was our new normal.

In a way it was.

As I fold some of the kids' laundry, a smile spreads on my face. I did the right thing by telling Gallo that I was done with our plan. If I really want to see where my relationship with Dante is going to go and still be a part of the kids' lives, I had to do it. And I'm happy I did.

I'm done trying to be a vigilante and done with trying to bring down the bad and powerful that Chicago has to offer. It's not my place.

Do I still think that the person that killed my father has to be brought down? Yes, yes, I do, but I will leave that to the cops. I no longer want any part in finding his killer, even if I do still want to torture the bastard in the same matter.

Do I think it was Dante that did it? I don't know anymore. Yes, I saw the picture that he has hidden in his desk. I saw the note, but what if he has those things for another reason besides wanting my dad killed?

There could be so many reasons why he has those things and maybe none of them are because he called the hit.

If he did though, if Dante did have a hand in my father's murder, and the truth comes out, I will deal with it accordingly.

How? I have no idea, but for right now, I don't want to think about it.

For right now, I want to live life as if I'm not sleeping with my father's killer. I want to live life happy and content with the man and kids that bring a smile to my face every time I think about them.

Because I've fallen for the three of them and fallen so hard it will kill me not to have them in my life.

Not letting that last thought bring me down, I continue

to fold the clothes with a smile on my face before finishing up and heading downstairs.

Dante got home a few hours ago and after spending some time with him and the kids and having dinner, I decided to give them some time together.

As I make my way downstairs and I hear nothing but silence, I suspect that Dante must have put the kids to bed already.

My suspicion is right when I walk into the large kitchen and find Dante by himself, riffling through what looks like mail.

"The kids go down okay?" I ask, announcing my presence.

Dante turns and gives me the small grin that I love seeing so much. "Yeah, you seem to tire them out so much that they fall right to sleep."

"That's good. I hope that Allie is tired enough not to have any nightmares."

Since about the middle of December, she has been waking up in the middle of the night with nightmares.

According to Dante, the nightmares aren't anything new, she's been having them since her mother died. He just stated that they had been far and few in between, but from the looks of it, they are back and in full force.

I've become more aware of their occurrence because I'm practically sharing a bed with Dante. I still have my own room, but since I told him I wanted more emotion and not just sex, I've been sleeping there less and less. So I experienced Allie climbing into bed with us after a nightmare.

"I think it's going to continue to happen for the next few weeks. Her mind must remember what happened this time last year." Dante responds, his face going a bit stoic.

"Angelina died this time last year?" I ask and as soon as I do I regret doing so.

Dante went from looking happy to stoic to angry and sad all within two minutes.

He looks at me as if he's angry at my question but also as if he's sad at the thought of giving me an answer.

I'm about to tell him to forget it, that I didn't mean for the question to come out, when he speaks.

"On February third."

That is only two weeks away. Alessandra must have remembered and triggered the nightmares.

"How did she die?" I ask, emotion starting to form on my throat.

Dante lets out a sigh. "A car accident. She hit a patch of ice and swerved into a utility pole. She died on impact."

Oh my god.

"She was stubborn, that woman, didn't want to take security with her, said she wanted some independence. So, she got into the car with the kids, and she didn't make it back."

When I hear his voice crack a bit when he mentions the kids, it makes the lump in my throat even bigger.

I try to push it down as much as I can so I can speak. "The kids were in the car?"

Tears are burning behind my eyes, trying to escape at the thought of Angel and Alessandra no longer being alive. Of them being taken away like their mother was.

Dante nods. "Angel had his two-month checkup, so she was taking him to it. Alessandra never wanted to leave her mother's side and with a new baby around, she always wanted to be with them, so she went too. When I got to the hospital, they had told me that one of them didn't make it, and it wasn't until an hour later that they told me it was Angelina. Angel came out with only a few scratches, his car seat saving him. As for Alessandra, a piece of metal somehow got loose and hit her face. That's where the scar came from. She also had a broken leg and had surgery to repair it."

Alessandra got her scar from the car accident that killed her mother. I've wondered from day one how a beautiful little girl with blueish gray eyes could have something so ugly be done to her, and now I know.

"That's the day she stopped talking, wasn't it?" I ask, my voice small, barely audible.

Dante gives me another nod. "She was always a happy little girl, always talking and curious about the sounds leaving her mouth. Her laugh would always fill the house, but after that day, it all stopped. I tried to get words out of her. I tried so hard but she never spoke. For months, all I heard from her were grunts and closed-mouth screams. Never words. I took her to so many specialists and therapists thinking something happened during the accident that they didn't see, the first time around, but they all said nothing was wrong. She just didn't want to talk. I was told to give her time. When she said bye in the kitchen, it was the first time I had heard her voice in months. I didn't know how much I missed it until that moment."

I can hear the love he has for his daughter in his voice and see it in his eyes. Hearing him speak like this, finally causes the tears that I've been holding back to escape.

Not knowing what to say, I give him the piece of me that relates to his precious daughter.

"My mom died when I was twelve. Also in a car accident and like Angel and Allie, I was also in the car. We were heading to Wrigley, going to meet my dad at the game, when we got T-boned. The car hit the driver's side and according to the paramedics that arrived a few minutes after, she died on impact too. My only saving grace was that I was in the back, behind the passenger side. A few cuts, but I was fine, physically at least. Mentally, it has stayed with me through the years, but it gets better."

He watches me as I speak, and I can see a bit of sympathy in his eyes for me. Without wanting any more room between us, I go to him, breaking the space and wrapping my arms around him.

I relax when I feel him shift and feel his hands move to hold me to him. We stand like that, wrapped in each other's arms for a long minute or two.

"It won't be long before she is talking in full sentences again. It will happen." I say against his chest.

"I hope you're right." He mutters into my hair.

I hope I'm right too, because I don't think that I can keep seeing him so beat down over something that he has no control over.

"Hopefully the nightmares will be kept at bay soon." Dante voices, more to himself than anything, when he pulls away and walks over to the fridge.

"Hopefully they will," I say back.

Moving my eyes away from him, I look down at the mail that he was looking through when I walked in.

It's mostly junk, except for a cream-colored envelope that is addressed to Dante. Curious, I flip it over to see who it's from and instantly feel my eyebrows shoot up.

"You know the Lane family?" I ask, not taking my eyes off the pretty embossed envelope.

"Doesn't everyone in Chicago?" he voices.

He's right, to an extent. Hell, up until a few months ago I could say I had no connection to them. Then the pretty lady showed up at my door with a check, and boom, instant connection.

I wonder what Ella Vincent would say if she found out that not only did I not heed her warning, but I'm sleeping with the man.

Bet she would be so proud.

"I don't know, but it looks like they invited you to something," I say, sliding the envelope over to him.

He takes it and rips it open to look it over. It's not even a second before the fancy piece of paper is back on the counter.

"It's just an invitation to the Lane Foundation Gala. It's on the first," he tells me without a care.

My eyes go wide. I may not know the Lane family personally, but I do know that the Lane Foundation Gala is the biggest party in Chicago. Only donors and the almighty elite get invited.

"You donate to the foundation?" I ask, a little stunned

that he was invited. I've always wanted to go to one of those parties.

Dante shrugs. "They help a lot of people that are struggling."

Like me, they help people like me, I want to say.

For a second, my thoughts go back to the check I received. Was there another reason for me getting that check besides the kindness of Bennett Lane's heart? Like possibly him getting a phone call from my father's killer asking to make a charitable donation in his name to me so that I don't struggle?

Could that be possible?

Yes, it really could.

But would Dante do that? Would he kill my father and then make sure I was taken care of with someone else's money? I really don't know.

I try to shake that thought out of my head and try to remind myself that there could have been a million reasons why Mr. Lane felt incline to make that donation to me.

"Are you going to go?" I ask, continuing with the subject.

He shrugs again. "A gala of that nature is not my cup of tea."

"You should go, I bet it would be fun. I've always dreamed of going to one, just to act like a princess for one night."

The hair. The makeup. The shoes. The dress. The handsome guy to dance with, preferably one that some- times has an Italian accent sneaking out for the night, would be perfect.

"I think the question is if *you* want to go."

"I mean, if I was the one getting the invitation, I would RSVP in a second. Every girl wants to dress like a princess at least once in their life." I can feel a blush creeping up my cheeks.

I sound like a little girl and definitely not someone who is dating an older man.

"Then I guess you'll get to act like a princess for one night," Dante says, taking me out of my inner thoughts.

"Wait, what?" Did he just say what I think he did?

"You're going to the gala. Well, that is if you want to be my date for the night."

"Really?" I say, a smile growing on my face.

He nods. "Really. We'll get you the princess dress and everything."

"Yes! Thank you!" I let out a shriek before I run over to him and literally throw myself at him.

He lets out a laugh as he wraps his arms around me to keep me steady. I lean up and place kisses along his neck and jaw before placing a kiss on his lips.

It was supposed to be just a chaste kiss filled with excitement, but within seconds of our lips meeting, things get heated.

So heated that I feel his hands slide beneath the waistband of my linen pants and grab at my ass.

I start to grind against him when I feel something vibrate against my thigh.

No way this man has a vibrator in his pants pocket.

I pull my face away from his and look down at where the vibrations are coming from.

"It's my phone," Dante says, his voice raspy and a bit annoyed.

Understanding, I untangle myself from him and place my feet back on the ground, not putting any distance between us.

As he reaches for the device, I lean up on my tiptoes and continue my attack on his neck.

His hand lands back on my ass as he answers the call.

"What?" he answers, a bit annoyed. If I wasn't kissing him or had his hand on me, I would be too.

"What do you mean he's not following the rules?" Dante growls into the phone, causing his nails to dig into my bare skin.

I continue with my kisses, not even flinching at the new inflicted pain my ass is getting.

"Lock him in a room with a guard. I will be right there," he says, hanging up the phone.

That statement right there is what makes me pull away and give him a pout.

"Where are you going?"

He drags a frustrated hand across his face. "To the club. I have a client that isn't behaving."

Dante leans in to give me a kiss before pushing himself away from me and starts to walk out of the kitchen.

"Can I go with you?"

30

DANTE

This is not how I expected my night to go.

I thought after the emotional conversation Arianna and I had in the kitchen, I would spend the rest of the night with her squirming under me.

That I would be pounding into her without any interruptions, but it only took one phone call to turn all that to shit.

A stupid fucking phone call that now has me heading to Perversa at eleven at night all because a high-profile client is fucking spiraling.

At least I have Arianna sitting in the passenger seat.

After she asked if she could come with me, I wanted to tell her no, but there wasn't any real reason for her to stay behind. So, after I called Evelyn to stay with the kids and Arianna changed into a little black dress, we are heading to the club.

"You didn't have to change," I say to her, as I maneuver the car through late night traffic.

"Um yeah, I did. I can't walk into your club, in yoga pants that have seen better days and a shirt that I've had since high school," she says as she closes the visor mirror.

I could tell her that I don't give a shit if she wore a sack as clothing, that she would still look beautiful, but I know it will go in one ear and out the other. So instead, I place a hand on her bare thigh and let my fingers draw small circles on her skin as I drive.

Arianna is wearing the smallest article of clothing that I have ever seen her wear. Nothing like the dress she wore to the interview all those months ago. It's short, formfitting and fucking makes me want to stop the car and fuck her.

And don't get me started on her shoes.

Definitely not how I expected my night to go.

Her hand lands on mine and I try my hardest to not move it farther up her thigh and explore her pussy with my fingers.

But before I get the chance, we are pulling into the parking lot of Perversa.

As soon as the car is parked, I get out and make my way over to Arianna's door.

With her hand in mine, we make our way into the club. Not the first official date I would have wanted us to be on but nothing I could do about it now.

When we approach the door, my lead guard gives me a nod and lets us in. We make our way through the club, everyone going about their business, not one person caring that the boss just walked in. Or notice that he just walked in with a woman that is thirteen years his junior.

As we approach the second-floor stairs, I hear a small gasp coming from Arianna.

"There's a second floor?" she asks. I don't know if it's directed at me, or she was just thinking out loud but I answer it anyway.

"It actually has four," I say, guiding her up the stairs and making sure she doesn't trip and fall with those heels she's wearing.

As we make it to the second floor, we are greeted by my club manager and the head of security.

"Jesus fuck," I grumble, not liking this already.

"Sir. Evelyn said to call you if he got in any trouble," Austin, my club manager, says, approaching me. His eyes go to the girl next to me quickly, before turning them back to me.

"What did he do?"

"He got a private room and decided that it would be a good idea to mix cocaine and alcohol while one of our girls was dancing. She told me that she was going to ignore it, but then he started having a spastic episode. She thought that he was overdosing."

Motherfucker. I knew getting the bastard as a client was going to be a pain in my ass. I should have told Evelyn no when she brought it up to me.

Letting out a growl, I grab Arianna's hand and bring her to stand in front of me.

"Take her to my suite. I'll take care of our guest," I grunt out, already feeling pissed about the situation.

"Yes, sir," Austin answers, nodding at Arianna to follow him.

She gives me questioning eyes, and when I give her a reassuring nod, she follows Austin down the hall.

"Let's get this shit show over with," I mutter as soon as Arianna is out of sight.

I make my way over to the room where the client is and the second I walk in, all I can do is shake my head.

Britney, one of our top female dancers, stands up from where she's sitting on the couch and makes her way over to me. I would say she is relieved to see me.

"I think he's fighting some demons or something," Britney tells me, looking over at the man face down on the couch.

"Did he hurt you?" I ask. It's one thing to do drugs in my club, but a whole different one to hurt one of my dancers.

Britney shakes her head. "He was too out of it to do anything. He threw a wad of cash at me and then one glass of scotch later, he started shaking. I was able to get him to tell me that he did a few lines before coming here. I checked his vitals, there was no need to take him to the hospital and cause a scene."

I give her a nod. "I guess it's a good thing that I pay you enough to go to nursing school."

She lets out a small giggle. "You're just lucky that it was me in here and not someone else."

She's completely right. "Thank you. I'll take it from here."

She gives me a nod and soon she is out of the room and it's just me and the passed-out baseball player.

I walk over to the couch and the second that I can, I kick his leg to wake him.

It takes a few kicks but eventually, Maddox Bauer stirs awake.

He jumps up as if the place were under attack, but when he sees it's only me and him in the room, he relaxes. Well, relaxes however much a person high as a kite can relax.

"Fuck," Maddox groans, sitting back down on the couch.

"Is there a reason why you are pulling this shit in my club?" I ask, not bothering to sit down as I do it.

"Dante, I'm sorry," he lets out, letting his arms fall to his knees and bowing his head.

"You're lucky my people called me and not the press or worse, the fucking cops."

"I know," is his response.

The kid looks distraught. At twenty-seven years old, he shouldn't look like this. He should be living life, not throwing it down the drain.

"You want to tell me why the fuck you're doing this shit and throwing your career down the fucking toilet?"

Maddox has the potential to be the best pitcher that the league has ever seen. He should be getting ready for spring training, yet he's here, in my club, coming off a near overdose.

"I'm suspended. I don't have a career anymore," he response, defeated.

"Your suspension only goes until May. You have four months to get your shit together," I tell him.

I have better shit to do than to be here trying to have a fatherly pep talk with Maddox. Like sliding into Arianna's tight pussy.

"Not if my ma is dead by then."

Jesus. "She's sick?"

He nods. "Brain cancer. Found out last year."

That explains the spiral.

"How bad is it?"

"Stage three. When they found it, it was already at stage two."

"Is that why you're killing yourself? And destroying your career?"

"I'm going to lose her, man. She's all that I got. I might as well go with her."

Fucking hell. The kid is worse than I thought.

"A solid plan you got here, then. Overdose and have her plan your funeral before hers. Can't see that backfiring." I scoff. I'm being an asshole, but if it gets Maddox to see straight, I'll put a gun to his head if I have to.

"What would you do if you were me, huh? You don't know how hard it is to see your parents die before your eyes." He finally looks up, anger in his eyes.

I ignore the parent comment and try to set him straight. "I would get fucking clean and spend every single moment I could with her. I wouldn't let myself get suspended and I would put in the work to support her. You want her to plan your funeral instead of you planning hers? Fucking go for it but know one thing, you're breaking her heart."

The anger from the kid's eyes disappears and it's

replaced with sadness. His body slouches over and it looks like he's going to cry.

Good job, Dante. You made a grown man that didn't have a gun pointed at him or was being threatened with death cry.

Maddox looks at me for a solid minute before he bows his head once again, this time letting out a sob. A sob that I'm sure he's been holding on to since his mother's diagnosis.

"What do I do now? How do I get myself out of this hole? God, what the fuck am I doing?"

Letting out a sigh, I finally concede and sit next to him. A hand landing on his back for reassurance.

"You are mourning a person that is still here. You get out of this hole by getting clean. Get clean for your mom, for your sport and for you."

Maddox wipes his nose on the sleeve of his suit jacket. "I don't even know how to get clean."

"It's a good thing I do. Go get some sleep but come back tomorrow and we will talk about starting the process," I offer.

There are people in this world that see me as a cold-hearted, murderous monster, and at times that title is true, but it's times like this where it's nowhere near close.

I feel for the kid, I really do, so if I could help him, why not do it?

"What about my mom?" He sobs once more.

I give his shoulder a reassuring squeeze. "I'll take care of her until you can take over."

Maddox turns to look at me and stares at me with admiration before giving me a nod.

"Thank you, Dante." He gives me a hand to shake and within a few seconds we are both making our way out of the room.

Maddox promises me that he will be here tomorrow and I hope that he keeps that promise. If not for him, then for his mother.

Once he's out of sight, I make my way to my suite. Hopefully Arianna was able to find something to entertain herself with while I was gone.

I nod at the guard standing in front of the door and knock against the door before opening it.

When the door opens and I walk in, I find Arianna standing at the floor-to-ceiling glass, looking out into the club at tonight's customers.

"Are you enjoying yourself?" I ask, closing the suite door behind me and locking it.

Arianna turns to look at me with surprise, which quickly turns to this sexy, lust-filled look that I know so much.

She gives me a nod. "Got everything handled?"

"I did."

"Good," she says turning back to the window. "I wouldn't be able to do half the things that these women do."

I chuckle. "If I remember correctly, you wanted to be one of those girls. Isn't that why you came that first day?"

"I needed the money, and if I remember correctly, I also offered to be a bartender." She gives me a shrug before she continues. "Besides, I like the job that I actually got. Way better than dancing in my opinion."

"Is that so?" I ask and I make my way over to her.

"Oh, definitely. Angel and Alessandra are my life now. Best decision I made was saying yes to Evelyn when she called."

Angel and Alessandra are her life now.

It's a simple sentence that I'm sure she wasn't aware was coming out of her mouth, but I hold on to it.

I've known for a while that Arianna cared for my children; I see it every single day with how she interacts with them. I see it more so in the way that she treats them as if they were her own and she wasn't their nanny.

Seeing it and hearing confirmation of it being true feel like two different things.

Hearing her say that the kids are her life now makes it feel like a switch was flipped and I'm looking at this from a new perspective.

Like not wanting what's going on between me and Arianna to end.

"Which by the way, I think you should fire me," she states, taking me out of my headspace.

She wants me to fire her?

"Why would I do that?" I can feel a bit of anger boiling inside of me as I wait for her to answer the question.

"Because you shouldn't be paying me to watch your kids. Especially when we're, um, you know." Even through some light makeup, I can see a blush creep up her cheeks.

I take a step closer to her. "Fucking?" The blush grows

a bit. "Sharing a bed? In a relationship? Because we're a couple?"

Her bottom lip goes between her teeth as she mulls over my words.

After a minute is or so, she speaks. "Are we... are we those things?"

"Do you care about my kids?" I ask.

"I love them with everything that I am."

I smile. "Do you care about me?"

"I—" She starts, but quickly stops and starts over. "Yes, I care about you. A lot."

She was about to say the same word she said for the kids, love. I can see it in her face and how she gnaws at her lip. She shouldn't love me, yet there's a possibility she does, and I'm more than okay with that.

Fuck.

I think I've really fallen for this girl.

"I care about you too," I say, closing the distance between us and wrapping my arms around her body. "So I would say yes, we are those things. You okay with that?"

Her bottom lip is released from between her teeth and she gives me a bright smile. "I'm more than okay with that."

"Good, but I'm still not going to fire you." I tell her.

Her eyes narrow at my words, and I give her a smirk.

Me not firing her has nothing to do with liking the boss/employee kink. It's all about having some stability if we don't work out. I don't want her to be put out on the streets because our relationship ended.

But I don't tell her that.

Instead, my smirk grows deeper and I bend down and place my lips against hers.

Every part of her mouth is sweet, as my tongue mingles with hers and I swallow every single moan that she releases.

I bring her body closer to mine and dig my fingers into the fabric of the dress, wishing she wasn't wearing it.

My fingers travel to the hem and drag it up until her ass is exposed.

Before I can order for Arianna to get on her knees and let me fuck her mouth, she pulls away.

"Want to know a secret?" she asks, her voice having a hint of mischief in it.

"Not really," I say, digging my fingers deeper into her flesh to drive the point. "But tell me your damn secret."

The mischief grows as she reaches up until her lips are almost touching my ear.

Her voice is almost a whisper and if my suite wasn't soundproof, I wouldn't be able to hear it.

"The day of the interview, I went home, stripped and danced as if you were still in the room. Then as I swayed my hips with no clothes on, just my boots, I played with my pussy. Thinking about you and only you."

Her words are a purr and they quickly travel all the way to my cock, making me rock hard.

My hands are still on her body, still digging into her skin, possibly marking her, but I don't care. I will mark her however she will let me. Because she's mine. Mine to claim. Mine to fuck anywhere I want. All fucking mine.

With my cock still pulsing at her words, I let go of her

ass and take a step back. Instantly her eyes go wide as if she thinks I'm walking away from her.

I'm not, but I do have a plan. Letting my hands drop from her body, I step away from her fully, keeping her gaze as I move to the leather couch.

Arianna's brows bunch up in confusion as I take a seat and get comfortable. When she opens her mouth, about to speak, I stop her.

"Show me." I order, my arms going to the back of the couch.

"Excuse me?" she asks, her bottom lip going between her teeth again.

"Show me. Show me how you danced for me that night. Show me how you touched that sweet cunt. Show me."

My dick is getting harder the more I think about her naked and dancing to music. I'm almost leaking out precum when I picture her hips swaying and her fingers sliding against her folds.

Hopefully, that image will become a reality.

"Here?" she says, looking toward the glass window that overlooks everything.

"They can't see up here. And what better place to strip than in a strip club? So, show me."

Arianna comes closer but doesn't move to take off her dress. "There's no music."

Without saying a word or taking my eyes off her, I reach for the remote sitting next to me. Pushing a few of the buttons, music comes flowing through, surrounding us.

A small smile forms on her lips and without another order, she starts to sway her hips.

I watch every one of her movements. I watch as she closes her eyes and lets the music take over her body.

I watch as her hand lands on the tiny strap of her dress and she slides it down.

I watch as she pushes the strap down until her tits are out in the open, much like our first meeting.

Arianna continues to push down her dress until she is only in her heels, her hips never missing a beat.

She shows me. She shows me everything she did to her pretty pussy that night.

And when she's done showing me, I give her the pearl necklace that I wanted to give her that day.

31

ARIANNA

I can still feel it.

The glass window against my body. The way his fingers dug into my skin and marked me everywhere he could.

It's been almost two weeks and I can still feel him pounding into me against the glass. As if he was telling people below us that I was his, even though they couldn't see us.

He was claiming me, and I loved every single second of it.

I loved everything about the night and every night that followed.

I loved it, just like I love him.

That was a revelation I came to that night, when he asked me if I cared for him. The three little words almost slipped out.

The thing that shocked me the most though, was the fact that I was okay with saying the words. I was okay with telling this man, the man that is a killer and represents everything evil, that I am in love with him.

I loved him because of who he was and not because of the man people pictured him to be.

As much as I wanted to let the words slip out, I held them in. It was the best decision. I didn't want him to think that I was being a clingy little girl that couldn't get her feelings in check.

But after these last two weeks, I get the feeling that he might feel the same way.

Since our night at the club, things have shifted drastically. We are a lot more open with our relationship, not just leaving things for when we are behind the doors of our bedrooms. There's a lot more touching and kissing and just being a couple, than there was before.

Not only have there been more displays of affection, Dante seems happier. It's as if he is lighter on his feet and everything I notice and it brings a smile to my face.

And the sex, oh my god, the sex. If I thought it was good before, I was fucking wrong.

It's as if when we finally admitted that we were indeed a couple, the sex went up ten levels.

I thought Dante was animalistic before, but nothing and I do mean nothing, compares to this. It's hot, sexy, and fucking amazing.

It's as if Dante craves hot, rough, amazing sex and I'm all for it.

Now that I think about it, I think we should make a trip to Perversa at least once a month.

I'll bring it up to him, but for now, I have to finish getting ready.

Because tonight is the Lane Gala and I'm a little bit too excited for a night out with my man.

Dante Rosetti is my man.

Shit, never did I think those words would make me so happy to even think.

It's also a statement that I feel my dad wouldn't like.

Even if I decided to drop my mission of destroying Dante from the inside out, I still think about the fact that my dad and Dante were connected. As much as I want to know the answers to all the questions, I don't have the courage to ask Dante.

I've told him my last name. I told him my dad was a cop and he was killed, I've told him almost everything.

So why can't I find the courage to tell him that I know he knew who my father was. To ask him how he knew my father? If he knew who I was when we first met? Why can't I be straight up with him and ask if he was the one that killed him? We're in a relationship, a couple, these are questions I have a right to ask, so why can't I?

Because you're afraid of him telling you that he did it.

But it can be the opposite. He could tell me that it wasn't him and we could move on. I could move on.

He could lie and just tell you what you want to hear. Take yourself as an example.

I think that's what's holding me back. As much as I've been truthful, I've lied a lot more to Dante throughout our relationship. From the second I stepped foot into his office at Perversa, it has been lie after lie. He only knows the truths that I've wanted to tell him.

So what is keeping him from not doing the same to me? For all I know, he's lied just as much as I have.

That's why I don't have the courage to ask, because I'm scared to fall for a bald-face lie.

I shake my head. No, I can't think like that. Our relationship is new, and eventually I'll find it in myself to ask the questions and get answers.

For now, I'm going to continue marveling at the fact that we're together and happy and enjoy tonight.

Since the gala is tonight, I took the day off and went to get my hair and makeup done. All because I didn't want to look like I was running around all day.

Angel finally got the hang of walking and has moved on to running and climbing things that he shouldn't. You would think that one-year-olds would be mellow and chill but nope. Now that the kid can get around on his own, he finds any little thing to climb.

Yesterday, I found him in the pantry trying to climb the shelves. It also doesn't help that he has a big sister that encourages the madness and sometimes gives him a boost to reach whatever snack they want.

Cookies, fruit snacks, a chocolate bar I had hidden, they find everything.

So I took the day off, left the kids with Evelyn and went to get pampered.

As I look in the mirror as I slide on my dress, I'm happy with my choice.

"Arianna." Dante's voice travels to the en suite bathroom.

Since the club, I have only gone into my room to get clothes that haven't made their way to the master just yet.

"In here," I say back, struggling to zip up my dress.

Why must they put zippers in the back?

"Need help?" Dante's voice echoes through the room.

I look up and see through the mirror that he is smirking at my struggle.

"Yes, please." I let out a huff, turning my back to him, defeated I couldn't do it myself.

A small chuckle rumbles out of him as he walks deeper into the bathroom. I move my hair out of the way and watch through the mirror as he comes to stand behind me.

His eyes hold mine as he places a hand on my hip and the other on the small metal tab of the zipper. The whole time he pulls it up, his eyes do not move.

This man can make something so minimal, like pulling up a zipper, so sensual.

A small gasp leaves my lips as he leans down and places a kiss on the back of my neck when I'm all closed up.

"Thank you."

"Anything for you, *amate*," he says, wrapping an arm around my waist, bringing me closer to him. "Is this the dress you're wearing to the gala?"

His question throws me off and suddenly I'm freaking out.

"Am I breaking dress code?" I look down in panic at my burgundy satin dress. "Is it too revealing?" I ask, turning to the cutout on my side. Oh my god, it's too much. Fuck. "Crap, I really should have gone for the black dress."

I'm reaching for the zipper again to take off the dress when Dante stops me.

"Relax. The dress is fucking perfect." He leans down once more and places another kiss against my neck. "The only reason I asked is that I don't think I can wait all night to rip it off you."

If I were wearing panties, they would be soaking wet right now.

I can't even think of anything coherent to say.

This is what this man does to me, he leaves me an incoherent mess.

"So the dress is okay?" Is the dress okay? Really? I could have told him to rip the dress right here and now, but instead I ask if the dress is okay?

I guess my brain is also oxygen deprived around him.

"The dress is okay," he says, turning me and placing a kiss on my lips. One that he cuts a little too short.

Dante lets out a small laugh when I give him a pout and he rewards me with another kiss.

"Are you ready to go?"

I give him a nod. "Yes, I just need my shoes."

We walk out of the bathroom and I beeline it to Dante's closet.

The master bedroom has two massive walk-in closets, one of them Dante's and one of them Angelina's.

When my stuff slowly started to make its way into the room, Dante offered me the other closet. But I saw it in his eyes, how much it hurt to even make the offer. He tried to hide it, but I was still able to catch it.

It hurt me too. Angelina was only gone one year and I was invading her space. I was sleeping in her bed, in her room with her husband, and taking over her closet didn't feel right. It didn't feel right for Dante to move her stuff out, all so I could move in.

He was still married to her, she was still his wife and she will be for as long as he lives.

If he wasn't ready to get rid of her things just yet, I wasn't going to push him. So I declined and took over a small section of his.

He looked relieved when I did it.

Grabbing the shoes that I picked up last week, I head back to the room and find Dante sitting on the bed, putting on his watch.

The way his arm flexes doing that small thing, makes me wish he would rip off my dress.

As I walk over to him, I get an idea.

Instead of taking a seat next to my boyfriend, I stay standing, holding out the shoes to him and placing a foot on his lap.

Dante looks up at me questioningly, a hand going directly to my calf.

"Help me put them on?" I ask, trying my hardest to give him a seductive smile.

I dangle the shoes on the tips of my fingers, and I start to think my plan is about to fail when Dante takes one of them

His hand drops from my calf and he goes to unclasp

the strap, so I take the opportunity to steady myself. I stand on my left foot and let my right foot travel from his hip up his body.

This boldness is making me feel sexy as hell.

As the strap of the shoe comes loose, I slide my foot along the buttons of his shirt. Dante grabs my foot and slides on the shoe, keeping my gaze like he did in the bathroom as he does the clasp.

Once the heel is secure, I make sure to move it slowly down his body, applying small amounts of pressure along the way.

A groan slips out when the heel grazes his crotch, a little harder than expected.

Oops.

Once my foot safely makes it to the ground, I steady myself and lift up my left foot and do the same thing.

My gaze keeps his and my foot moves up his body and I almost combust completely after the shoe is on.

As the strap of my left heel is fastened, I'm starting to remove my foot from his chest when a hand lands on my exposed thigh.

My dress not only has a cutout but also has a full-on slit that stops halfway up my thigh.

And because of the position that I'm in, what with my foot still on his chest, Dante has a full view of what I'm wearing under my dress.

Or should I say, what I'm not wearing.

I thought he had noticed in the bathroom when he was zipping me up, but the look in his eyes tells me otherwise.

Dante slides the fabric of my dress to the side, the

movement causing him to come face to face with my freshly shaved pussy.

His grip on my thigh loosens and his hand moves upward until his knuckles are grazing my inner thigh and his fingers are touching my folds.

"Sweet Arianna, you're going to make me lose my mind tonight," he taunts, his thumb gently sliding over my clit.

My heel involuntarily presses into his chest. "Maybe that's what I want."

A growl comes out of his mouth as he slides his fingers into my folds again and spreads my wetness all around.

I thought placing my heel on his chest, causing him a slight discomfort, was erotic, but the way he's touching me in this position takes it up a level.

One of Dante's fingers slides into me and I have to remind myself that I'm standing on one leg. I try to keep as steady as I can as he slides his finger in and out of me, but the more he does it, the harder it gets.

"Dante," I moan out, wanting more than just his methodical thrusts.

"You were planning on teasing me, weren't you, *amate*?" One of his hands grips my calf to keep me steady as the other one continues to work my pussy.

I shake my head. "Panties didn't really go with the dress."

Dante lets out a hum, but he continues to move his finger in and out of me.

I'm about to yell at him to go faster and to use one more finger when he slides his finger out and drops his hand completely.

He grabs my heel and glides it down the remainder of his body until it's firmly on the ground and my dress is covering me again.

"What are you doing?" I ask, the sexual frustration evident in my voice.

"We're going to be late," He says, sliding his finger into his mouth to wipe it clean.

Dante stands up from the bed, places a kiss on my lips and goes to grab his tuxedo jacket from the small couch he has in the corner.

"Dante," I whine as he slides the jacket on.

I'm worked up and if we leave now, having sex with him is all I will be able to think about. Especially with the visual of how goddamn sexy he looks in a tuxedo. He must have had it custom made because it fits him perfectly.

And the bow tie, God the bow tie is sexy too.

This man can wear swim trunks to this thing and he will still be the hottest man there.

Once he's put together, he comes over to me and places another kiss against my lips.

A kiss that will have me applying my lipstick before we get to the party.

"I'll give you everything your sweet cunt desires when we get home." He pulls away, giving my ass a slap in the process.

Even though I feel like stomping my foot and telling him that he needs to fuck me now, I don't. Instead I concede.

"Fine. Let me go get my clutch from my room and we can go."

We walk out of the room hand in hand, splitting when we reach the stairs. Dante going downstairs and me going to grab the one and only clutch that I own.

I'm so glad I thought of bringing it with me when I moved in. It would have been a hassle if I had to go back to my apartment to get it.

The apartment that I haven't stepped foot in four months.

Maybe if Dante and I continue on this amazing path, I will let the place go, but that's an idea for another day.

I grab the clutch and as I'm walking out, a ringing sounds out.

The ringing makes me stop in my tracks.

Opening the clutch in my hands, I pull out my phone and see that the screen is blank. No incoming calls.

If it's not my phone, where is the ringing coming from?

It couldn't be coming from the burner phone, could it?

I haven't used that phone since my last text to Gallo telling him that I was out. That was back in November. It's been a whole two months since then, why would he be calling me now? Sure, I keep the phone charged, but I do that as a "just in case."

Just in case I find something that could be incriminating, but I had no real plan to use it.

Until now, I guess.

Walking to the dresser where I keep the phone hidden, the ringing becomes louder with each step.

As I open the drawer and reach for the phone the only thing that I can think of is, *Why the hell is he calling me now?*

Once the phone is in my hand, I see that it's indeed Gallo.

For a long minute, I debate even answering the call. I could just ignore it and go on with my night.

But if I ignore it, he could call again, and instead of me hearing the continuous ring, it could be Dante. And if Dante finds the burner phone, it will be over. Everything we've built these last two months will be over.

It's because of that that I answer.

"Hello?" I say into the device, hoping to God that this is just a routine call from Gallo, trying to convince me to go through with the plan.

"Ms. Vitale. It's happening."

I feel all the oxygen leave my body. "What is happening?"

"The takedown of Dante Rosetti of course. How can you forget, Ms. Vitale? It's the reason you paid me. Which, by the way, I'm going to need more money."

"What? No, I told you back in November that I was done," I tell him, my voice shaking the whole time.

I have to convince him to not do anything. I have to.

"Ah yes, the text message. I don't do text messages like that, so I ignored it."

He ignored it.

He ignored the message and continued with finding information even when I told him not to.

Not only has the oxygen left my body, but all my blood feels like it has dropped from my head to my feet.

"Then listen to me when I say this. The deal is off. I want nothing to do with it anymore. We are not taking down Dante Rosetti or anyone else for that matter," I hiss out as quietly as I can.

No way do I need Dante hearing this conversation.

"Oh, you mean because you're a little whore that is sleeping with him? I know I told you to make him trust you, Ms. Vitale, but that's low even for me."

I think I'm going to puke. "How do you know about that?"

I try to think of maybe someone seeing us together, but I wouldn't be able to pick Gallo's men out of a crowd.

He lets out a chuckle that sounds more like an evil villain than a guy that runs his business out of the back of a Laundromat.

"I have my ways. Just like I have my ways of getting a picture of Rosetti leaving your father's house the day he was killed. It's happening, Ms. Vitale. You can send me the money once it's done."

The call goes silent.

Bile starts to run up my throat, and I run to the trash can that I have next to my bed and throw it up.

Dante was at my father's house the day he died. There's a picture of him. He did it, he really did it.

My heart is pounding so hard that I feel like I'm going to faint.

Gallo's call was cryptic; he didn't say what he was going to do, all he said was that it was happening.

What was happening? And when?

Tonight? Tomorrow? Next week?

I don't know, but I know I will never be prepared for it.

Knowing that Dante is probably seconds away from

coming to look for me, I stash the burner phone back in its place and situate myself as best I can.

I look quickly in the mirror to make sure that I don't have any vomit on me and then take a few deep breaths.

Tonight.

I'm going to take tonight. I will have one last glorious night with Dante. I will have one last night with him and tomorrow I will worry about Gallo and what he is going to do.

Just one more night with the man I love.

32

DANTE

She hasn't said a word the whole car ride into the city.

I thought that the whole ride would be filled with the same teasing she was bringing out in the bedroom. But the most she has let me do is hold her hand as she looks out the window.

If I had my way, her pointy heel would be digging into my dick like it was as I was strapping on her shoes, and I would be finishing up what I started.

But instead, we are sitting in silence.

I would much rather hear Lorenzo talk about how much of a pussy I am for not working with the Muertos Cartel a lot sooner.

"Everything okay?" I break the silent streak, bringing her hand up to my lips and placing a small kiss on her knuckles.

Arianna turns to face me, giving me a small smile. "Yeah, everything is great."

"Then what's with the silence?" I probe, squeezing her hand.

She lets out a sigh. "I'm just nervous about tonight, that's all."

"What is there to be nervous about?" Is she worried about leaving the kids? Since we've been together, we've left them a few times but never overnight.

I figured that since there might be some drinking, it would be better for us to stay in the city and go back home tomorrow morning.

Arianna takes a second before she answers the question. "I just don't want to embarrass you. You know, since I'm a lot younger than you, and since it's only been a short amount of time since your wife passed. I'm sure people will start talking the second we walk in."

Dropping her hand, I move mine up to her face and cradle it so she can look up to me. She leans into my touch.

"You have nothing to be nervous about. People will not judge you, they will judge me. If they say anything to you, tell me and I'll take care of it."

Just like Helen Baker. If anyone says anything or even looks at her the wrong way, there will be hell to pay.

She gives me a nod before closing the distance between us and kissing me. "Thank you."

For the remainder of the ride, I kiss her. Mostly for good measure but also to relax her as best I can.

By the time that we are pulling up to the venue, Arianna is flushed, smiling and can't stop giggling. Just the way I like her to be.

I open the door and hold out a hand for her to take.

Once I have her hand cradled in my elbow, we make our way inside.

"Okay, now I really do feel like a princess. Holy crap, this place is beautiful," she exclaims the second we walk into the ballroom.

The place is littered with elaborate flower arrangements that leave no inch untouched. Looks like a place that someone could get lost in if they wanted to. This one hundred percent was all Ella.

"I guess beautiful is one word for it," I say, looking around and finding even more flowers.

Arianna marvels at the decor some more before I guide her over to the bar. If I'm going to be surrounded by flowers and an easily impressionable girlfriend, I'm going to need scotch.

With drinks in hand, we walk around the ballroom, Arianna squealing at every little thing. The silence from the car completely gone.

"We should throw a party and have decorations like this." She's literally shaking with excitement as she talks.

I shake my head before she can finish. "No."

"Why not? It would be fun. Maybe we can do it for Alessandra's birthday, since you didn't let me throw one for Angel."

"No, and he didn't need a party." I take a drink, silently thanking Bennett for providing the expensive scotch and not going for the cheap shit.

"He was turning one. He needed a big celebration." She narrows her eyes at me, the same way she did when we first had this discussion.

Angel's birthday was in December and she still won't let me forget that I didn't give my son a first birthday party.

"He didn't need a party that he would never remember," I throw back at her.

"We would remember," she says, fluttering her eyelashes at me.

I take a sip of my scotch. "Maybe for your birthday."

"Really?" Her eyes brighten up and her smile grows.

I nod. "Maybe. We'll see how you behave when we get closer to the day."

"Oh, how I behave?" Arianna's eyes not only light up with excitement but also with lust. Not only that, but her grin has morphed into a full-on smirk. "I promise you, Daddy, I'll be a good girl. I'll be a good girl whenever you want me to be."

"Jesus fucking Christ," I mutter into my glass. I walked into that one.

Arianna flutters her eyelashes and steps closer to me, her lips brushing my earlobe.

"I can also be the naughtiest girl you want me to be."

A growl forms in the back of my throat as I finish up my drink.

"You should really behave," I say, taking her by the hip, letting her feel the hardness starting to form behind my slacks.

"Maybe you shouldn't have teased me earlier. Things would have been a whole lot better if you would have gotten me off."

My fingers dig into the material of her dress.

Where the hell did the quiet girl from the car go? This

is definitely a different version of Arianna, and I fucking love it.

I'm about to suggest we find a random closet so I can do what she wants when I hear my name being called out.

Letting out a frustrated grumble, I turn to the voice and find Bennett Lane approaching.

If I could strangle the man for his timing, I would, but it's his party after all.

"Bennett," I say, shifting to hide my hard-on as best as I can. Thank god for the black tuxedo.

I hold out a hand for him to take, which he does as the distance between us closes.

"I'm happy you could make it. I didn't know if you would, what with the time of year and everything," he says.

I nod. "Yeah, well, this one wanted to come and I can't seem to say no to her."

Bennett looks over at my date and gives her a smile. "Bennett Lane," he says introducing himself.

I hear Arianna let out a small gasp, but she composes herself before taking his extended hand.

"Arianna Vitale," she says, her voice shy and a slight blush creeping up her cheeks.

Great, even my woman has a thing for Lane.

"It's nice to meet you, Arianna. Thank you for coming and thank you for forcing this bastard to come too. He can be a little hardheaded when it comes to things like this."

"He can be hardheaded about a lot of things," Arianna says, a sweet smile on her lips.

I swear, if my kids don't leave me with a full head of gray, Arianna definitely will.

Bennett laughs at my expense. "I like you. Let me introduce you to my wife."

Both Arianna and I watch as he turns and looks around for Ella before he finds her and waves her down.

Ella, dressed in a champagne gown, comes over to us with a small smile on her face. To be honest, she looks a little stunned, but I don't feel like asking why.

"Babe, I want you to meet Dante's date, Arianna." Bennett waves over at Arianna, giving her a smile in the process.

As I look over at her, though, she has a smile on her face, but it's tight. Like she's in an uncomfortable situation that she doesn't want to be in.

"It's nice to meet you, Arianna. I'm Ella," Ella says, the stunned look completely gone from her expression.

"It's nice to meet you too," Arianna responds, her voice tight, just like her smile.

What caused her to go from happy and excited to be here to looking as if this is the last place she wants to be?

"Hello, Dante," Ella greets me, a closed-lipped smile on her face.

Okay, something is definitely going on.

"Ella," I say, leaning down and giving the woman a peck on the cheek. "You look lovely as always."

"Thank you. It was a last-minute decision."

"Well, it suits you well and I'm guessing you were the one behind all the decorations for tonight?"

Ella gives me a nod. "I am because we both know that Bennett wouldn't be able to pull it off."

"She's right on that count," Bennett chimes in, praising his wife.

I nod. "Arianna was just telling me how she loves everything."

I feel her stiffen next to me, which tells me that something is definitely up.

"Oh really? Well, Arianna, do you want a look around? I would love to explain a few of the flower arrangements to you," Ella offers, holding out a hand for Arianna to take.

I look over at the woman that has quickly become the second woman in my life to capture a part of my heart and see her hesitating.

Maybe she's afraid to leave my side.

Giving her hip a reassuring squeeze, I bend down to her ear and speak to her.

"Go. I'll be right here when you get back," I say.

Even with a few inches separating us, I can hear her swallow audibly as if she's not sure, but eventually she nods her head.

"I would love to," she says, composing herself and taking hold of Ella's hand.

As soon as the women leave, Bennett waves over a waiter and grabs two glasses of scotch from the tray.

It's when we both have glasses in hand that he shoots me a question.

"You didn't tell me that your nanny was Joseph Vitale's daughter," He accuses.

I give him a shrug. "You never asked who she was."

Like me, Bennett had a strange relationship with Detective Vitale. They weren't close by any means, but the detective made sure he had friends in high places just in case he needed to cash in a favor.

Bennett and I both know what the detective was up to when he met his untimely death. Just like we also know what it was that killed him.

Given that he knew Joseph, it's no surprise he knew who Arianna was the second she introduced herself.

"Maybe I should have." He takes a swig of his drink. "Why did you hire her in the first place?"

"She came to the club, thought I was holding auditions for dancers. Evelyn thought that she was a good fit and she needed the money. So I took her on."

I take a drink myself, not really wanting to explain myself to the richest man in Chicago.

"She needed money?" Bennett asked, an eyebrow raised in my direction.

"Yeah, she needed money. Her dad had just fucking died, what was I going to do, tell her no?" Now it's my turn to raise an eyebrow at him.

"When did you hire her?" Bennet throws out.

Without stopping to think about the reasoning behind his question, I answer. "Beginning of October."

Bennett just nods at my answer as he continues to take small sips of his scotch.

Because curiosity killed the cat and all that, I ask. "Why?"

My friend takes a second to finish up his drink before setting it down on a nearby table. The man squares his shoulders and looks out to the room instead of meeting my questioning glare.

"Because a week after Vitale's funeral, I donated half a million dollars to his daughter. Unless there are two Arianna Vitales in Chicago that had a father who was murdered and Ella handed the check to the wrong person, that girl lied to you. She has money to keep her settled for a while."

A whoosh of air leaves me, like I was just hit by a boulder. Not only does the air leave me, but all of the sudden I'm hit with this wave of anger.

"Was the check cashed?" I ask, nothing else seems relevant.

Bennett nods. "It was. From what I know, she used some of it to pay off her parents' brownstone and pay for the debt she acquired from the funeral and a few months of her rent. Other than that, the money hasn't moved. Well, expect five thousand dollars."

I don't even want to ask how the actual fuck Bennett knows all of that information. One thing he said has grabbed my attention though, and it's making me question everything.

Five thousand dollars.

That was the same amount Lorenzo told me Gallo received through wire transfer.

The same amount that I blew off and thought nothing of it. Hell, I even told Lorenzo a few days after that conversation that I didn't want to know who sent the money. That whoever sent the money wasn't worthy of my time.

I guess I was so fucking wrong on that account.

"Does she know that you knew her father?" Bennett asks, taking my mind out of the dark spiral it's going into.

"No," I say, my voice clipped. "Never felt the need to. I guess the fact that she didn't need money isn't the only thing that we have to discuss."

Without another word to the man, I down my drink and leave him to go straight to the bar for another.

As I'm finishing up my third drink, I try to wrap my head around everything.

Yes, I didn't tell Arianna that I knew her father, but that was to protect her. I knew that if I told her, hell if I tell her now, she will have questions. Questions that she's not ready to hear the answers to. Me keeping that piece of information to myself was nothing more than me caring about her.

And I fucking cared from the first time I saw her.

Me telling her about her father and his actions now would only open a wound that seems to be closed.

As for her lying to me about needing a job, that is something that I have to ask her about. There was and is, no reason to lie.

I gave her the truth, all the fucking truth. Why couldn't she give me the same?

And the five thousand dollars? I don't want to believe that the two points connect. That Gallo didn't receive the wire transfer from Arianna. I want to believe it, but there is something in my gut telling me that I'm wrong. That I'm wrong for wanting to believe that because there was a reason why I didn't trust Arianna in the first place. This theory just cemented that.

I drink one more glass of scotch before making my way over to the table and taking a seat for dinner. Arianna shows up a few minutes after me, still wearing that tight smile on her face.

A tight smile that I return.

For the rest of the dinner, Arianna and I don't speak. We simply exist next to each other and only talk when one of us is asking a question.

By the time the dancing starts, I'm not in the mood to stay much longer and hopefully Arianna feels the same way.

"Are you ready to go?" I say in her ear, my hand already on her elbow to pull her away.

"Yes." Just a simple word and I'm guiding us out of the ballroom and the hotel until we reach the car.

Once we're in the car and I direct the driver to the hotel, we are back to the silence that encased us on the way here.

I always hate silence when it comes to her.

So I break it. "You lied to me."

A small gasp fills the back of the SUV. I watch as Arianna turns to me, tears forming in her eyes, trying to find words to say.

"Dante, I—" she starts, but doesn't finish.

Because her words are replaced with a high-pitched scream.

One second I'm looking at the woman that I love, then the next the only thing I see is glass.

And darkness.

33

ARIANNA

I'm jolted awake and right away I see that I'm no longer in the back of the SUV with Dante next to me.

No, instead of being surrounded by darkness, I'm in a brightly lit room that looks like a staged living room at a furniture store.

What the hell happened?

How did I even get here?

Sitting up, I try to rack my brain for something that will tell me how I got here and where I am.

I remember being back at the manor and getting ready for the gala. I remember Dante zipping me up and then helping me with my shoes. I remember the call with Gallo, the call that made me so sick that I had to throw up. I remember being in the car and walking into the gala and trying my hardest to just be with Dante.

Then I remember the gala itself.

For the first twenty or so minutes, it was fun and exciting. Dante and I were flirting and acting like any other couple.

Then I was introduced to Bennett Lane, and the second I said my name, I knew that he knew who I was. He hid it well, but he knew.

And when Ella came by, I knew that was when everything that I worked so hard to keep a secret, was going to come out.

Ella told me herself when she pulled me away.

"I told you to stay away from him," she hissed, her grip on my hand growing tighter.

"You did, but I had questions that I needed answers to. I needed to know if he was the one that went after my father," I told her, my voice shaking in the process.

"And did you? Did you find out if he was your father's killer?" Ella's voice is no longer sweet. There's a bite to it that I would have never thought her capable of.

I shook my head. "No, I didn't."

"Does he know why you're in his life in the first place?" she hisses this time.

"No."

"Then why are you still with him then? If you didn't find the answers you wanted, why are you still here?"

"Because I love him."

She was the first person, besides myself, that I admitted it to.

I remember she gave me a stern look after that and when I went to go sit at the table, I knew Bennett said something to Dante.

There was a coldness flowing between us, and I knew the time was coming for me to come clean.

Then we got in the car. We got in the car and he said those four little words that broke every single inch of me.

"You lied to me."

I started to cry instantly. He knew. He knew why I really took the position as his nanny and that I had been lying to him the whole time.

He knew.

So it was time for me to come clean and tell him everything.

That's when everything goes dark.

I don't remember anything after those words, and the harder that I try to think, the more my mind fills with nothing.

Absolutely nothing.

Sitting up from the cloth couch I'm lying on, I try to piece together my surroundings,

Nothing about this place looks familiar.

Where the hell am I?

And where's Dante?

Pushing myself off the couch, I cringe at the pain radiating off my ribs. I look down and see that my dress is ripped, and I can see dry blood on my ribs going down to my hips.

As I stand to full height, the pain shifts from just my side to my whole body, causing me to double down and dry heave from the pain.

Fighting through it, I stand back up again and make

my way over to the door that's on the other side of the small room.

There are tears rolling down my face when I finally make it over. But the tears of pain are quickly replaced with ones of despair when I turn the knob and the door doesn't budge.

"Fuck," I pant out, the pain becoming unbearable. "Hello?" I start yelling out, hitting the door with as much force as I can muster.

I hit the door a few more times and then stop to listen for any noise, but nothing comes through.

Trying to keep myself as calm as possible, I turn back to the room to give me some sort of hint at anything.

Nothing stands out and there are no windows to look out. The one door looks as if it's the only way in and out.

Something about this place doesn't feel right. It's too staged, too clean, too bright, and it's freaking me out.

I go back to banging on the door, hoping that there's someone on the other side of the door that will hear me.

The more that I knock, the more I want to fall to the ground and succumb to the pain, but I don't, I keep knocking.

I keep knocking until I hear footsteps on the other side.

When the door is pushed open, I almost fall to the ground, but somehow I'm able to keep myself steady, even with my heels still on and see who is about to walk in.

Roberto Gallo stands in the doorway, looking over at me with a smirk that makes my stomach churn.

"Ms. Vitale, it's good to see that you're awake," he spits out, coming farther into the room.

As soon as Gallo is in the room, a man, not the one that was always at the Laundromat, comes to stand in the doorway.

They're keeping me in.

"What's going on?" I say, trying my hardest to not let the pain seep through.

"I told you that it was happening. That it was time for us to follow through with our plan." His smirk grows even more sadistic.

"There was no plan," I say through my teeth. "We only agreed that I would bring you any information that I could find and then we'd figure something out from there. That's it. There was no concrete plan."

"That's where you're wrong. You paid me to do a job, and I'm doing it. I'm taking over. Since, you know, you were fucking the bastard and were taking too long to me.

"I sent you those pictures," I say, my voice is starting to fail me.

Gallo scoffs at my comment. "You really think random pictures are going to tie Rosetti to your father's murder? Those pictures were complete garbage."

I take a deep breath and try to power through the pain as I speak.

"I told you that I no longer wanted any part of this."

It's the way that Gallo laughs that tells me that I should have never gone into business with this man.

I should have trusted my gut instinct that day in the Laundromat and walked away.

Too late to do that now.

"Do you really think that I'm going to stop trying to

take Rosetti down just because a little twat like you told me to? Sweetheart, I've been trying to do this since the bastard took over for Falcone. I just needed something to make it happen, and that's when you came in. You were my opening."

Gallo closes the distance between us, grabbing me by my arms and pulling me to him.

The way he jerks me forward, has me seeing black spots and biting down on my bottom lip to hold in a scream of pain.

"Such a pretty girl. Now I know why Rosetti couldn't keep his hands off you," Gallo states, one of his hands moving from my arm down my body until he is cupping me at my core. "I bet this pussy is tight and hot. It would be perfect for me."

I let out a whimper when I feel his fingers dig through the fabric of my dress.

My body is in so much pain that I don't know if I will be able to push Gallo off me if he tries anything. But I have to do something.

I have to push the pain down and get out of here, alive if possible.

And the only way I can think of doing that is to keep Gallo talking.

"Why?" I say, my face is still too close to him.

"Why what?" Gallo spits out, moving his fingers along me.

"Why do you want to take Dante down? What did he do to you?"

The question must have been the wrong one to ask

because Gallo lets out an angry growl, causing his fingers to dig deeper.

"He stole my seat from me. I was supposed to be me sitting at the head of the table, not him. The fucker only got that seat because of his blood, I should have gotten it because of my loyalty. That chair was fucking mine and the only way to get it back is to kill him."

Tears burn at the back of my eyes at the thought of Dante being killed.

They burn even more when I think that he might be dead already.

"What did you do?" I ask, mustering whatever force is left in me and pushing Gallo off me. Thankfully this time, his hands fall from my body.

Gallo gives me yet another sadistic smirk. "Had you followed? Paid one of your dad's neighbors for his camera footage? Dodged Rosetti's men? Hired someone to ram their car into your SUV tonight? Is that what you want me to say? Because I did all of those things. I'm honestly surprised you made it out of there alive, the driver didn't."

He's the reason I'm in so much pain. That's why I don't remember anything after Dante's four last words, because somebody slammed into the SUV.

Memories of the crash that took my mom start rolling in instantly and soon the tears I'm trying to hold in escape when the memories morph into something else.

Instead of pictures of my mom's lifeless body, I see Dante's right next to the driver's. I picture his body, bloody and lifeless, and all the pain it will cause Angel and

Alessandra as they lose yet another parent to a car accident.

No, Dante can't be dead. No way in hell will that man let himself take his last breath that. No, he would fight to continue to live, if not for himself, then for his kids.

Dante has to be alive. He has to be.

I will not accept that he died. Not for the kids. Not for me.

"Where is he?" I say through gritted teeth, anger flowing through my body.

Gallo laughs, legit cackles at my question. "Where is who? The Devil himself? Your lover? Why don't you see for yourself?"

He waves a hand to the door guarded by his man. Keeping my eyes on Gallo, I move slowly past him and walk over to the door.

The guard surprisingly lets me walk through without a fight, but as I step over the threshold, I wish he hadn't.

Sitting in a chair in the middle of this warehouse-style building, is Dante.

Bloody.

Battered.

And looking as if he is barely holding on.

A sob escapes me and I'm right back to when I found my dad, in the same position.

This is what I wanted.

From the very beginning, I wanted Dante in this very position so I could see him suffer, just like my father did.

But seeing him like this shatters me beyond repair.

I want to run to him. I want to forget about all the pain

that my body is experiencing right now and run to him to make sure he's alive.

To make sure that he's still breathing and okay.

And I'm about to when a hand lands on my arms and pulls me back to a stop.

"Not so fast. He's still alive, if that's what you want to know, but he won't be for long. Especially after I show you my little gift," Gallo says into my ear.

"I don't give a shit about what you want to show me. Let me go!"

Gallo just continues to tighten his hold on me as he reaches into his pocket and pulls out a piece of paper.

I watch as he unfolds it and turns it for me to see.

It's a picture.

A picture of Dante leaving my parents' brownstone. I'd recognize the stupid little elf by the front door anywhere.

I'm about to ask when this picture is from, but that's when I see the date stamp.

The day my father died.

This is what I've been looking for all along. A piece of evidence that ties Dante to my father's killing.

I should feel elated that I have this picture in my hand. A picture that can put Dante away for good.

But all I feel is anger.

Anger at myself, because I should have never let it get this far.

Because now, I'm going to lose Dante for good and it's all my fault.

"Time to kill your father's killer, Ms. Vitale."

34

DANTE

I've said it before, if someone was successful in getting close enough to take my last breath from me, I would let them.

I've done some heinous things in my life and I don't deserve to continue to walk this earth. I deserve to pay for all the fuckery that I've done.

But that statement didn't apply to Roberto Gallo.

No way in fucking hell am I letting this sad, pathetic excuse for a man, for a Mafia man at that, take my last breath away.

Hell, I'm willing to die at the hands of Arianna before I let this fucking rat take my last breath from me.

He can try like he has many times before but like all those times, he won't succeed.

I should have trusted my instinct from the very beginning. I shouldn't have let it get this far, yet here I am. Tied to a fucking chair, beaten up, and waiting to see if it's going to be Arianna or Roberto to pull the fucking trigger.

Closing my eyes, I remember everything as if it were still happening.

I can clearly see Arianna looking at me with tears in her eyes and with my name on her lips. She was going to tell me the truth. What truth that was, I don't know because that's when the car headlights came crashing in.

Then I remember clearly hearing her piercing scream and wishing that it was me taking the brunt of the hit and not her. Then it's the car rolling and glass going everywhere that comes to mind next.

Somehow the car that hit us was able to hit us hard enough to cause the SUV to roll, but not hard enough to kill anyone in the car.

The three of us were still breathing, still aware. Arianna was looking at me with worried eyes and for a straight minute not a single word was said. It was as if this eerie silence passed by and encased us. No sound, not even from the city around us, was heard. It was complete silence.

Until I heard the footsteps.

At first, I thought it was a passerby coming to tell us that they had called the cops but when I heard the gun go off, I knew I was wrong.

I can clearly hear Arianna scream after that as if she were still screaming next to me and as much as I tried to go to her, I couldn't.

Everything after that comes back a bit of a blur, but not enough of a blur that I don't know that it was Gallo and his men that pulled us out of that car and brought us here.

To some warehouse.

One that Gallo doesn't own, so he must be leasing it from someone under a fake name.

I should have caught this. I should have had more men keeping track of Gallo, his men and his dealings, because my gut told me that he was up to something. Yet, even with all the men and surveillance I have on him, I missed this.

I never miss anything.

You were blinded by beauty.

That's what pisses me off more. The fact that my men showed me pictures of Arianna at Gallo's Laundromat and instead of destroying her like I had planned, I ended up fucking her.

And then loving her.

I should have been more vigilant, I should have pressed more, but I believed her. I believed her and loved her and now her I am, fucking tied to a chair.

"Isn't this what you had in mind when you came to me, Ms. Vitale? Have the bastard tied to a chair and let him suffer like your father?" Gallo's voice echoes through the empty space.

I've heard enough of their conversation to piece together what has led us here.

Arianna thought, or thinks, I'm not sure which, that I'm the one that killed her father. My guess is that she came to this conclusion and went to Gallo for help to take me down.

How she connected me to Gallo, I have no clue and I really don't want to know, but she did.

She's smart, my woman.

I'm still trying to piece all the in-between from her father's death to here but I could only take wild guess.

Arianna lets out a yelp and I try my hardest to not look up and see what happened.

"Isn't it, Ms. Vitale? Isn't it what you wanted?" Gallo growls out and I can only assume he's grabbing her by the hair.

A sob fills the room. "Yes."

"So why the fuck are you crying? You got your fucking wish."

"Because I changed my mind. I don't want this to happen anymore," Arianna says through her sobs.

There's fear in her voice, but I don't know if it's fear for my life or for hers.

"It's too late now, sweetheart. The bastard is as good as dead."

"No! Please don't do this! Please!" Arianna begs as they move closer to me.

From the sound of her heels, Roberto is dragging her, and the closer they get to me the more Arianna screams.

"Shut up, you entitled bitch," Gallo growls, this time a slap following his words.

She may have lied to me about every single thing and our relationship may be a sham, but once I'm free from this chair, I will kill the bastard with my own hands for laying a hand on her.

"Take the fucking gun and finish him," Gallo orders and there is more scuffling.

"Wh-why? Wh-why does it have to be m-me?" Arianna asks him, her voice shaking uncontrollably.

Because he doesn't want blood on his hands.

He wants her to be the one to shoot me because then it will be her fingerprints on the gun and not his.

I should have given the bastard more credit.

"Because I fucking said so. Now do it!"

Another sob escapes from Arianna and echoes through the room

"Do it. Kill your father's killer. Fucking do it!"

I sit completely still as Arianna's sobs continue and she moves closer, a gun most likely in her hand.

Her beautiful face must be red and covered in tears. Her gorgeous eyes must be bloodshot.

My eyes open and when her dress comes into view, I can't hold back anymore. I have to look up at her and talk her into doing what she is told.

Killing her father's killer.

My voice cracks a bit as I speak for the first time. "Do what he says, Arianna. Kill your father's killer."

At the sound of my voice, she falls to her knees in front of me, the gun leaving her hands and sliding a few feet away.

I lift my head slightly, enough to catch a glimpse of her face and I see the despair that lies in her expression.

"Do it, Arianna," I tell her once more.

She's shaking her head before I can get the order out. "No. I won't do it. I won't kill you."

Time to give her my own truth.

"I wasn't talking about me," I say, looking into her eyes before looking over her shoulder to the cowardly man standing a few feet away. "I was talking about the fucker standing behind you."

"Wh-wh-what?" she stutters standing back up and looking at Gallo.

"I wasn't the one that killed Joseph Vitale," I spit. "No, Detective Joseph Vitale was killed by the one and only Roberto Gallo."

35

ARIANNA

oberto Gallo.

The man I went to for help in bringing down Dante. The man that I thought was on my side in bringing powerful people down. The man that I sent information to is the man that I should've been going after all along.

Roberto Gallo killed my father.

This whole time I was trying to pin it on Dante. Trying to find something that told me that he did it, but I was looking in the wrong direction. I should have been looking at the man that was encouraging me to find information that wasn't there.

"He's lying to you. You saw the picture, he was at your father's house the day he died," Gallo argues, his face red with anger, the picture he showed me, crumpled up in his hand.

"Dante?" I turn back to the man that owns every piece of me.

When he spoke, I thought that I was dreaming. For a few short moments, I thought that he was dead and I would have to untie him, just like my father.

He was so still.

I thought that Gallo was just putting on a show and wanted me to pull the trigger so that I would suffer the repercussions that came with killing The Devil.

For a second, I thought of doing it.

I figured I'd done so many wrongs when it came to this man that I deserved to pay. I deserved to serve time in prison for putting a bullet in his head.

Then he spoke.

He spoke and it was like this wave of relief traveled through my whole body.

I was no longer crying tears of pain and desperation but tears of joy.

Because he was still alive and I didn't have to go back to the manor and tell Alessandra and Angel that their *papi* was never coming back.

Dante lets out a groan as he shifts, his arms trying to loosen some of the straps.

He looks at me straight on, his handsome face bloody and swollen but I can still see the sincerity in his features.

"Yes, I was there the day he died, but not because I was the one that beat him to a bloody pulp. I was there to fucking warn him that he was in too deep."

Dante struggles to get the words out and by the sound of the wheezing that is coming out of him, something may be wrong with his lungs.

I go to move closer to him but I'm stopped when Gallo

yanks me back. A pain shoots through my arm and I have to fight the urge to let out a scream.

Dante catches sight of this and even though he is beaten himself, he looks like he wants to kill Gallo for even touching me.

"He's lying to you. Don't listen to the fucker. He's just trying to get out of getting executed," Gallo throws out, his grip on my arm telling me how pissed he is.

"I've never lied to you, Arianna," Dante wheezes out, his chest moving more rapidly. "You know that. Yes, I've held information from you but never lied."

He's right, he hasn't.

In all the time that I've worked for him and been with him, he hasn't lied. At least not that I know of. Whenever and whatever I asked, he always told me the truth.

He opened up about Angelina, and he told me that he was the head of the Mafia.

But is he really being truthful about this?

He has no reason to lie.

The one that has every reason to lie through his teeth is Gallo. Dante is already beaten, probably has a collapsed lung, and is close to death. He has no reason to give me lies. But Gallo does.

Gallo has every reason to lie.

He wants power.

He wants recognition.

And he will probably do anything to get it.

Like kill a detective that is looking into him. Or better yet, kill anybody he sees as a threat.

From day one, my gut told me that this man was slimy and conniving and yet I didn't listen.

But I was so blinded by wanting to take Dante down that I didn't see the warning signs that were in front of me the whole time.

I look over at Dante, inspecting the way that he is tied down, everything about it looking oddly familiar.

During my first meeting with Gallo, I told him how my father was killed. I told him that he was tied to a chair and beaten to death.

But I didn't tell him how he was tied.

I didn't tell him that he was tied with his legs apart and each tied to a leg of the chair.

I didn't tell him that my father's arms rested on the armrest, while all circulation was cut off from his wrists.

I also didn't tell him what he was tied down with.

I didn't tell him anything, and yet Dante is tied down the same way. Same position, with the same material, exactly the way that I found my father.

Those details weren't publicized, so the only way one would know those details was if they were the one that did it.

Dante is telling the truth.

The man I fell in love with didn't kill my father. It was Gallo.

"He wouldn't lie to me," I say, my voice small, my eyes never leaving Dante. "He's telling the truth."

At my words, Dante seems to let out a sigh of relief.

But that relief is short lived because soon I'm on the ground and with something heavy pressing me down.

It's Gallo's foot, and it's pressing right into my injuries.
"Then you will die with him."

DANTE

THERE'S a lot of shit me and Arianna have to work through. There's a lot that both of us have to come clean about, but at this moment, none of that matters.

What matters is getting the fuck out of here alive and me putting a bullet in Gallo's head for thinking he can get away with this.

What matters is making sure that Arianna doesn't get buried next to her parents and my kids don't become orphans.

I watch in fury as Gallo stomps his foot on Arianna's back. From the way her scream pierces the air, she has something broken or dislocated.

If I was free, the bastard would have a few broken bones himself, but the fucker had to tie me to a chair.

Whoever tied these fucking knots must have been a damn Boy Scout, because no matter what I do, they don't budge.

"Let her go, Roberto. Your shit is with me, not her." I say as best as I can through the stinging I'm feeling in my chest.

My body has gone through a lot of shit in its lifetime to know when I have a collapsed lung. Trying to get us out of here is going to have to be expedited.

"Why? So she can run off and tell her daddy's friends who killed the bastard. I don't think so. She dies here. Maybe I'll kill her just like I killed the detective. Nice and slow. Maybe I'll even fuck her before she takes her last breath."

Something that Roberto hides well is the sadistic bastard he really is.

He doesn't give a fuck about what he has to kill or burn to gain power, he will do whatever it takes to get what he wants.

And if he wants to make me suffer, he will do exactly what he says and make me watch before deciding to put a bullet in between my eyes.

"You touch her and I will feed you your dick before slitting your throat," I say through my teeth, trying my hardest not to take too deep of a breath.

Gallo looks at me, a sick smile on his face. "I already touched her. She doesn't like to wear panties, does she?"

Arianna sobs into the concrete. Hearing her in pain and hearing Gallo's words on top of it makes me see red.

Something animalistic brews up inside of me. Something deadly and dark. So much so that a growl escapes me and I'm able to find enough power in me to do what's necessary.

With all the force I can muster, the pain coming from my chest all but forgotten, I throw myself back. The amount of force causing the chair to shatter as soon as it hits the concrete.

Gallo may be a wizard with tying knots but he sure as hell is stupid to use a wooden chair.

Pain travels through my back as the knots come undone.

My whole body screams out in agony as I shift to stand on my feet.

Roberto's eyes are wide, like he didn't expect me to do such a thing. His two men look just as surprised.

See, if these were my men, they wouldn't be fucking surprised. They would be ready with guns drawn, waiting for a signal to shoot me dead.

The motherfuckers are fucking morons.

Not giving a shit anymore, I charge at Gallo, and slam into his body causing us to fall to the ground.

The motherfucker lets out a groan, and as much as I want to succumb to my own pain, I don't.

No, I start to pummel at the bastard's face. Landing punch after punch until his face is a bloody mess. Just like he left mine.

When that's not enough, I grab him by his stringy gray hair and start slamming his head against the concrete.

I'm slightly aware of what is happening behind me, all my concentration on Gallo. I hear some shuffling and Arianna letting out a yell, but I don't turn around and look.

No, my sole purpose right now is to finish Gallo.

That is until a gunshot rings out, and a scream quickly follows.

A scream very similar to the one I heard before I was surrounded by darkness.

I forget Gallo. I forget and turn to see the aftermath of the gunshot.

And a body on the ground.

36

ARIANNA

"Oh my god. Oh my god. Oh my fucking god." The gun falls from my hand to the floor.

The one shot that was released is still ringing in my ear. The vibration of pulling the trigger is still moving through my body.

My breathing is erratic, my heart is pumping in my chest and I can feel tears starting to roll down my face.

I shot a gun. Not only did I shoot a gun, but I shot a person.

A person that is currently face down, not ten feet away from me.

My dad has always kept guns in the house, he was a policeman after all, but he never made me shoot one. He taught me all the safety, all the proper hand placements and what to do, but never did I shoot one.

Now I have, and I'm freaking out.

"Arianna." Dante's voice makes it's way through the ringing.

Slowly, I look from the body over to where he's currently hovering over Gallo as he tries to get up.

"I just shot someone," I state, still trying to digest what I just did.

"You did. I'm proud of you," he states.

He's proud of me.

He's proud I shot someone.

I'm about to run over to him when my body once again hits the floor. This time because of Gallo's second body-guard, the one that was guarding the room door earlier, slams me down.

His body slams into mine and once on the floor, he pins me down with his own body. All his weight on me, making it hard to move.

"Get off of me." I try to thrash out of his hold, but he won't budge.

"No, you little bitch. You've caused enough trouble." The guard reaches for something hidden in his jacket.

I realize too late that it's a gun and it's pointed right at my face. It's a handgun, and I've seen enough action movies to know that the barrel in the front is a silencer.

Within a second of the gun being pulled, I close my eyes and say a silent prayer. A silent prayer that hopefully this man has a really bad aim and misses. I pray that Evelyn takes care of Alessandra and Angel because there's no way Dante and I are both making it out of here alive.

I should have told them that I loved them.

I should have held both of them in my arms before we left for the gala and told them that I loved them as if they were my own. They wouldn't know what my words meant, but I would. I would know that I told them how much they meant to me.

I should have also told Dante that I loved him. That my heart has never belonged to a man like it has belonged to him. That he has been and will be the only man that will ever hold my heart like this.

When the shot rings out, I let out a scream, waiting for the impact to hit me. For the bullet to hit me and for me to die without another thought.

But it doesn't happen.

My eyes shoot open, and I'm met with the eyes of Gallo's guard. They are wide and all life seems to be disappearing from them.

Soon, he's falling on top of me, his whole body limp. Before I'm crushed by the man's weight again, he's being pulled off me by Dante.

As soon as there is enough distance between me and the dead guard, I scramble from under him and Dante lets the body fall to the ground.

Blood seeps onto the concrete and it should make me sick to see, but the more I watch it spread, the more I'm relieved that it wasn't me.

What the actual hell has this night turned into? Is it even nighttime anymore?

"Are you okay?" Dante asks, crouching down to my eye level, one of his hands reaching out and gently touching my face.

It's when his fingertips meet my skin that I step out of the out-of-body experience that I was just having.

Looking up, the first thing I see is for just how bad his

face is swollen, but even through the swelling, I can still see the concern in his eyes.

This man is wheezing, bruised and bleeding, and he's concerned about my well-being.

I don't deserve him.

I give him a nod. "I'm okay. I'm in pain, but I'm okay." I raise my own hand and gently glide my fingers against his face. "Are you okay?"

He flinches a little at my touch and his face shows so much pain that I have no idea how he's still standing up.

Gallo and his men must have beaten every single inch of him while I was locked in the room.

Dante nods, even while his face contorts with discomfort. "I will be."

"Dante." I step closer to him but not close enough to plaster my body to his. I don't know just how far his injuries go.

"I'll be fine, Arianna," he urges, but I can hear the pain in his voice. "Let's just concentrate on getting out of here," he states, holding out a hand for me to take.

I want to fight him on it, but I know I won't win so instead I just take his hand and let him pull me up.

When I'm settled on my feet, surprised that I've lasted this long in my heels, I survey the both of us.

We look like we were grabbed by a tornado and flung around the ground a handful of times.

Our clothes are completely trashed and covered in blood. My dress is destroyed and there is not a chance that I will be able to wear it again.

From the looks of it, Dante's injuries are worse than

mine, but he is trying to tough them out. His face is starting to go pale and standing this close to him, I can hear his breathing get worse.

"I think we need to get you to a doctor," I say, placing a hand on his hip, as if my small body can hold his up if he falls.

Dante shakes his head. "I'm fine."

"No, you're not. You need to see a doctor," I argue. It looks like he's about to fall to the ground.

Again, he shakes his head. "No. Doctors ask too many questions. I'll be fine."

"Dante." I want to reprimand him like I would if he was a child, but when a chuckle sounds behind me, I stop.

A coldness travels through my body as I turn slightly and see Gallo sitting up on the floor a few feet away.

Like Dante, his face is bruised and bloody but he wears a sadistic grin instead of a grimace of pain.

How is he still alive?

I saw his head get bashed into the concrete multiple times. I saw his body go still and not moving an inch.

So how the hell is this man still able to breathe, let alone sit up and let out a chuckle?

Gallo makes the effort to stand up but ends up falling to the floor a few times before giving up on the task.

"I guess this is how Detective Vitale felt before I tied him to the chair." Gallo lets out another laugh before turning to look at me. "Couldn't keep his balance. The fucker fell more times than I could count."

Tears start to form at the mention of my dad, but I've cried enough already, and I won't let them fall.

Pushing all my emotions to the side, I move toward him, Dante's hand landing on mine to stop me, but I pull away.

"Why did you do it? Why did you kill my father?" I say through gritted teeth.

I need to know. I need to know why he was really killed. I need to know before I let Dante finish the fucker off.

"Because he was looking into things he shouldn't have. I was making all kinds of money with the girls, but then the detective came in and ruined everything. He had it coming. You're lucky I didn't do it sooner."

Girls.

The sex trafficking from the note.

That wasn't about Dante and the mafia he runs; it was about Gallo and his.

I step closer to him, silently aware of Dante walking a few feet behind me.

"You mean you killed him for doing his job?"

Gallo lets out another chuckle, this time one sounding a lot eviler.

"His job," Gallo scoffs at the two words. "Sweetheart, Joseph Vitale was as corrupt as they come. If I didn't kill him, someone else would have."

That's the tipping point for me.

I've heard people say that my father was a corrupt cop. At his funeral, after his funeral. I heard the word and I hear it now.

But I know deep in my gut that it's not true. If my dad

was working for the other side, he was doing it for a reason.

A really good reason.

Joseph Vitale didn't care about money or going up the ranks, he cared about making bad people pay for their crimes.

He probably wanted Gallo to pay for his.

And he will.

I will make him pay, and the way to do that is to finish this man once and for all.

I turn back to Dante, seeing that the gun that Gallo handed me, the one I used to kill the guard and Dante used to kill the second one, is still in his hand.

Dante's eyes find mine and he looks at me long and hard. As he looks at me, I feel it. I feel what I felt the first time I was in a room with him.

Power.

I feel power moving through my body, and much like our first meeting, I don't want to let it go.

Dante Rosetti makes me feel powerful, so I grasp it and hold it as close as I can.

"Kill him. Kill the fucking bastard." I order.

Surprise fills his eyes but quickly turns into what looks like pride.

Like he's proud of me for giving him the order. Like he's proud of me for finding my power and demanding that he kill Gallo.

A smirk shows through his swollen features as he comes to stand next to me.

"I think you should be the one to pull the trigger," he says, holding the gun for me to take.

But I don't take it. "No, you have to do it. I don't know if I can shoot someone again."

"You can. He's hurt you more than he's hurt me. You should be the one to do it." This time instead of holding out the gun for me, he grabs my hand and places the metal piece in my palm.

I look down at the gun in my hand.

I can do this. I can point it at a man's head and shoot him dead.

I did it before, even if that was different. Gallo's man was charging toward me, and I didn't have time to think. Now I do.

But Dante is right. Gallo has hurt me in more ways than I can comprehend. He needs to die at my hands.

So I give him a nod and turn to face Gallo one last time.

I step closer to him so I don't miss his beady eyes on me the whole time, teasing me.

"You don't have it in you to pull that trigger," he taunts, shifting again trying to get on his feet, but yet again he fails.

"I do," I throw back, raising my arms into position, gripping the gun and trying to keep it steady.

"My men will come after you. I have men in high places. They will find out, and they will kill you," he spits, his whole body shaking with anger.

"No, they won't." I say, my finger releasing the safety.

"And how can you be so sure?"

"I just am." I pull the trigger. Then again, and again and again, until more blood seeps out of Gallo and his body slumps over.

Wanting to make sure that he doesn't live, I shoot the remaining bullets into his body. The last one going into his head.

Once the magazine is empty, I drop the gun to the floor.

I did it.

I killed Roberto Gallo.

I killed my father's killer.

"It's okay." Dante's voice sounds in my ear. As I feel his hand slide against my hip, I realize that I'm crying.

They aren't tears because I killed Gallo; no, they are tears because I finally got revenge for my dad's death. I got what I wanted since the funeral.

I continue to cry in Dante's arms and after a few minutes, I hear his breathing get a lot more labored than it was before.

He really needs to go see a doctor.

"We need to get you out of here," I say, turning in his arms and seeing beads of sweat traveling down his temple.

Surprisingly, this time, he doesn't fight me on it. Dante just nods. "We need to find keys to a car or something."

Right, because our phones are probably in the wrecked SUV.

Quickly, I move out of Dante's hold and head to the lifeless bodies of the two bodyguards. One of them has to have keys to a car.

Patting all of their pockets, I finally find a set of keys on the one that Dante shot down.

With the keys in hand, I make my way back to Dante, who looks like he's seconds away from passing out.

I slide an arm around his waist and throw an arm over my shoulder and make our way out of the building.

Thankfully Gallo and his men were smart enough to leave an SUV right outside the door.

Pressing the key fob, I unlock the doors and as I'm opening the door, Dante sags into my arms.

The both of us almost fall to the ground, but somehow, by the grace of God, I'm able to pull him back up.

"C'mon, baby. I need you to stay with me, okay? I need you to help me get you in the car and stay with me until we get you help."

"No." He takes a shallow breath. "Hospital."

"I won't take you to the hospital, I promise. Just please let me get you in the car."

It's a struggle, but I'm able to slide Dante into the back seat. But as I slide my arm from around his waist, I see just how bad his injuries are.

Not only can he not breathe properly, but his whole side is also covered in blood.

"Crap."

I slam the back door and quickly make my way over to the driver's side and as soon as the SUV is on, I'm high-tailing it away from the warehouse.

So many driving laws get broken as I make my way through the city and to the manor.

Dante doesn't want me to take him to the hospital, but

one of his men has to be a medic, right? This can't be the first time that something like this has happened. He has to have someone that can fix him.

I speed all the way until I reach the gates to the estate, and once I'm there I hop out and start calling the guard, whose name is Alec, that is always on watch.

"Ms. Amato?" The voice.

"Dante is hurt. I need the door opened and for someone to meet us at the main house. He's bleeding heavily and has trouble breathing."

"Yes, ma'am," Alec says, buzzing open the gate.

Getting back in the driver's seat, I don't wait until the gate is fully open to speed through. As I move through the property, I see men on either side of me racing toward the house and when I get to the driveway, they don't waste any time.

The SUV isn't even parked, when Bruno comes running out of the main house straight to us, opening the back door and pulling Dante out.

"He's wheezing. I think he has a collapsed lung. He's also losing a lot of blood." I yell at anyone that can hear as I get out of the car.

"I got him, Ari," Bruno tells me before rushing inside the house with his boss on his shoulder.

Soon everyone is running behind Bruno and Dante and leaving me in the driveway.

I did this.

This is happening because I wanted to take down him and now, he may very well die.

I may not have been the one to throw the punches, but

I was the one that wanted this to happen.

I wanted to take down The Devil. I wished for this.

And I have no right to be here.

A sob tries to escape me, but I hold it in as I turn around and head back to the SUV.

"Arianna." My name is yelled out and I look over my shoulder and see Evelyn standing in the doorway with Angel on her hip and Alessandra at her side. "Where are you going?"

Tears spring into my eyes as I see the three of them and they fall when Angel sees me and holds out his arms to me.

I can't do this.

I can't continue hurting them.

I need to leave.

"I'm sorry, but I have to go," I tell Evelyn and continue to the driver's door.

"Arianna!" she yells right before I close the door and speed away.

The farther away I drive away from the house, the more I cry. The more I want to look out the rearview mirror.

But I don't.

The kids, Dante and Evelyn, they deserve more than what I did to them.

They deserve everything and more.

Dante and the kids own my heart completely and the only way to make things right is to take myself out of the equation.

I should have never started this.

37

DANTE

"I told you not to strain yourself," Evelyn reprimands me as I make my way over to Angel's room.

It's five seventeen in the morning and he's awake.

"I'm fine," I say, trying not to let out a groan as I walk down the hall.

"You're not fine. You have a damn hole in your chest from a damn needle to repair your collapsed lung so you can freaking breathe. You also have three broken ribs and thirty-two stitches in your side. Tell me how the hell you're fine."

"You sound like a mother," I say, walking into Angel's room.

"And I will act like your freakin' mother until you listen and go back to bed."

There is no winning with her. "Let me get my kid, and then I will gladly go back to bed."

"Fine, but I swear to God, Dante, if you start jumping

him up and down, I will puncture a hole in your other lung."

Honestly, she's worked for me long enough to learn a few things, I wouldn't put it past her.

"Yes, ma'am," I say.

Leaving my assistant at the door, I walk into the room and find Angel standing up in his crib already with his arms outstretched.

Even though there's excruciating pain when I lift him up, I do it without complaining, walking us out of the room and heading back to the master.

"See, back to bed," I say as we pass Evelyn.

"It better stay that way," she says, following behind us, but stopping at the doorway, not stepping inside.

"If you're hovering this much after less than a day, I wonder what a pain in the ass you'll be for the rest of the week," I mutter, mostly to Angel but I know she heard me when she lets out a snort.

"Enough for you to give me a raise," she throws back.

All I do is shake my head at her as I place Angel in the middle of the bed and let him cuddle into the pillows.

Arianna's pillows.

It's been less than twenty-four hours since we left the warehouse and Arianna brought me to the estate and had my men fix me up.

I passed out somewhere between the warehouse and here because once I woke up, Evelyn told me that I was out for a good ten hours.

Evidently, I did have a collapsed lung, one that Bruno

was able to help relieve by stabbing a needle in my chest. Something I wasn't conscious for, thank fucking god.

Apparently while I was out, a lot happened.

They called one of the doctors we have on call to come and take a look at me. After he checked Bruno's work with my lung, he set my ribs, stitched me up and told my staff that I was going to live. That I had to take it easy, but that I would live.

The other thing that happened while I was out from the pain, Arianna left.

After I came to, I asked two questions. Where were my kids and where was Arianna?

I needed to see that she was okay. I needed to see that her injuries weren't as bad as mine and that she was okay after everything that happened. But Evelyn told me that she had left soon after arriving.

Evelyn told me that she looked scared and had tears in her eyes as she pulled away.

Now twenty hours later, I have no idea where she is, or how to get a hold of her since her phone was left at the scene of the car accident and then brought here by my men.

According to Bruno, they got wind of the accident as soon as it happened, making it to the scene before the paramedics and the cops, but not before Arianna and I were taken.

Because Gallo covered his trail, he couldn't locate us or even figure out if we were still alive. He didn't know what had happened to us until Arianna pulled up to the gate yesterday morning.

We calculated it from the time we left the gala to the gate, me and Arianna were in Gallo's warehouse for eleven hours.

After telling Bruno all that happened, we dispatched men to the warehouse to burn it to the ground and to make sure all three bodies were accounted for.

Once that was taken care of, I rested and spent time with the kids. Trying my hardest not to think about why Arianna would leave.

"I'll give you the raise," I say as I take a seat on the bed, letting out a groan in the process. "Not because you asked, but because you deserve it."

"Much appreciated," she says, the hard-ass she was a minute ago gone. "Rest for a few more hours."

I give her a nod as she closes the door and I slowly try to lie back on the bed.

My chest hurts and my ribs are killing me, but I'm alive, and at this moment, that's all that matters.

I'm home with my children, and they don't have to go through the pain of losing their father a year after losing their mother.

I close my eyes a bit, waiting for sleep to take over. Angel is fast asleep next to me, and I hope to follow his lead.

And I'm almost there when I hear the bedroom door creak open. Opening my eyes, I half expect it to be Evelyn coming back to reprimand me for the way I'm lying, but it's Alessandra.

Her little body squeezes in through the small opening, and she just stands there silently asking to come in.

I sit up slightly and wave her in. "Come here, *gioia mia.*"

Alessandra abandons her post at the door and comes into the room, climbing into the bed and settling between me and her brother.

I brush her hair away as she lays her head against my chest. "Did you have a bad dream?" I ask her.

She nods against my chest, curling into my side a bit more.

I let out a sigh.

Of course, she had a bad dream. This time last year, she was doing this with her mother, and then a few hours later, she lost her.

"It's okay. The bad dreams will go away soon," I say, hoping that I'm not lying to her.

After a few minutes, I think that she has fallen asleep since she doesn't move, and all I can hear is their breathing. I'm about to lay Alessandra's head on the pillow next to her brother's when she says something.

"Ari." It's a faint whisper, so faint that I think I imagined it.

"Did you say something?" I ask her, brushing her bangs away from her eyes.

Alessandra nods.

"Can you repeat it for me?"

The last time she spoke, she said *papi*, and ever since then, Arianna and I have been trying to get her to speak more, but she won't budge.

"Ari," she says, a bit louder this time.

I know if Arianna were here, she would have the

biggest smile on her face and plant a boatload of kisses on Alessandra's cheeks to deal with her excitement.

"Are you asking where Ari is?" I ask my daughter, hoping she answers with more words.

Unfortunately, Alessandra gives me another nod. I try to think of an answer to tell my four-year-old. I can't very much tell her that Arianna almost got killed and decided to leave because she might have been scared.

"Ari," I start, using the nickname I said I would never use. "Ari, is just taking a short break. She misses her *papi,* like you miss your *mami.*"

Alessandra looks at me, her mouth opening slightly like she wants to say something but doesn't know how.

"Ari," she lets out, her mouth moving a bit more, trying to find the right sounds. "Back?"

Two words.

She spoke two new words today.

Today of all days.

"Do you want Ari to come back?" I ask her, giving her a small smile, trying to contain my emotions.

Another nod from Alessandra, this time an eager one, and I don't care that she didn't say any words this time around. She said two, and that's progress. Amazing progress.

"Then Ari is going to come back. We just need to give her time, do you think we can handle that?"

She looks at me for a long minute as if she is trying to make sense of my words, but eventually she gives me another nod and a smile.

"Go to sleep, okay?" I tell her, patting her little body until her eyes are closed.

She noticed that Arianna wasn't here, and of course she did. Arianna has been a constant in this little girl's life for almost six months. She spent time with her every day, she talked to her, and she was involved in her school activities. Arianna has become a major part of Alessandra and Angel's world.

Of course they would notice that she wasn't here.

As I listen to my children fall into a deep sleep, I make the decision to find Arianna and talk to her.

Talk to her about everything and make her come back.

For the kids.

And selfishly for me.

38

DANTE

One year.

One year ago today, I saw my wife alive for the very last time.

If I had known that was going to be the last time I was going to kiss her in the morning, I would have savored it a bit more.

It's only been one year, but it feels like it's been ten and, at the same time feels like it's only been days.

I place the flowers, white roses since they were her favorite, in the little flowerpot in front of her grave. I try to arrange the bouquet as best I can, but all the roses just seem to flop in their own directions.

"I should have brought a bigger bouquet," I say, to myself, to the gravestone, to nobody in particular.

Giving up, I let the flowers be and plop down on the ground, not caring about the mud.

"I saw people on the hill below with some chairs and

blankets. Maybe next time I come and visit, I will do that," I say, this time directly to the gravestone.

"Maybe next time, I'll also bring the kids. They should know where they can come to visit you. Or maybe I should wait until they're a little older and they can comprehend what's going on."

I nod as if she can really hear what I'm saying and would be agreeing with me.

Is this what people do? They come to visit their loved ones' graves and talk to them as if it were normal. As if they were still here.

Maybe if this wasn't the first time I've come here since the funeral, I would know if this is what's done.

"*Amore*, I'm sorry that I didn't come sooner. I'm sorry that I just put you in the ground and didn't visit you for a whole year. That wasn't right of me."

I should have made more of an effort. Visiting her should have been something that I did on a regular basis, not just once a year on the anniversary.

"I hope you forgive me."

The February wind moves around me and if my mom were here, she would tell me that Angelina is here and listening.

"Hopefully you can forgive me for everything else too. Hopefully you can forgive me for letting myself fall for someone not even a year after your death."

I let my head fall forward in shame.

I didn't come here to tell her about the woman I've been sleeping with for the last four months. I came here to tell her about how much the kids miss her and how Alessandra looks just like her.

But here I am, using my wife's gravestone as a confessional.

"Her name is Arianna, and she started out as the nanny a few months ago. Somehow, she was able to get under my skin and I became intrigued by her. Believe me when I tell you that I didn't want to. After you died, I was just going to live life without another woman. Without anyone besides the kids, because I loved you too much to do that to you."

I can feel tears start to form in my eyes.

I just don't know if it's because I'm here and I miss her, or because of all the guilt eating at me.

"I tried, Angelina. I tried to stay away from her, to not fall for her, but I couldn't. I fucking fell and I didn't know how hard until yesterday."

My mind goes back to how I felt when that fucker was on top of her and pointing a gun to her head or when Gallo threatened her.

All I felt was rage and the only thing in my line of vision was blood.

Nobody was going to take Arianna from me. If I was going to lose her, it was going to be of her own accord.

"I thought I was going to lose her, and in that moment, I felt the same way I felt when I lost you. Despair, guilt, rage. Never did I think that I would have felt that way again, especially for a woman, yet I did."

Closing my eyes, I speak the words that I wanted to say right before the gala.

"I love her, Angelina. I shouldn't, not this close to you passing. I shouldn't because she's too young, and I shouldn't because she lied to me, she was betraying me and was working with my enemy to bring me down, but I do. I love her. I love everything about her. I love how she is with the kids and how she treats them as if they were hers. I love how she expresses herself and how she holds this power within her. I love her, and I tried to push it away, but I couldn't. Loving her just seems like second nature. Like breathing. I love her, and just because I do, doesn't mean that she is going to replace you. She won't. Not in my eyes or in the kids'. You will always be in our hearts, minds, and souls, and I will spend the rest of my life telling the kids everything about you. But we need Arianna. We need her to bring laughs and smiles and life back into our world. We need her to bring back everything that we lost when we lost you, and she's done that. Hopefully, if I can get her to come back to me, she will continue to do that. I love her, the kids love her, and I hope that you are okay with that. I hope you can forgive me for moving on so quickly. I never wanted to hurt you. I love you, Angelina. I hope you know that, but life has to continue, and I hope you are looking down at me and see that the kids are happy, that we are happy."

I stand up from the ground and place my fingers against the rock. Closing my eyes, I try to embrace the air moving around me.

Finally, I let out a sigh and open my eyes again.

"I love you. Say hi to my parents for me."

With one last look at the gravestone, I start to walk away, silently leaving with the promise to come back a lot more and not wait another year.

Angelina was my everything for large portion of my life, and I have to do everything in my power to keep her memory alive.

As I'm walking back to the car, no bodyguards with me today, I look around the cemetery.

Angelina is buried a few miles out of the city, mostly at the wishes of her parents, so it's a lot less crowded than the cemeteries within city limits.

And if I remember correctly, someone else was buried here.

Ignoring my car, I decided to walk around the cemetery, with hopes that I find the gravesite that I'm looking for.

After an hour and kindly asking the groundskeeper for some help, I'm able to find the gravesite. Except, I'm not the only one there to pay a visit.

I stop in my tracks, not wanting to spook her, so for a few minutes I just watch her.

Much like me, she has bruises and cuts on her face. Hers are just not as bad as mine. She also has her left arm in a sling.

I'm guessing she went to the doctor after dropping me off.

Her back is leaning against a headstone and she's looking at what I'm guessing is her father's, and from what I can see, she's talking. Just like I was talking to Angelina.

For a few minutes, I watch her.

She looks sad even from a distance. I want to take that look off her face and make sure she never looks that depressed again.

Which is why I decide to walk toward her.

As I close the distance between us, Arianna looks up, the rustling sound of my footstep must have caught her attention.

As soon as she sees it's me, she gets up immediately and starts playing with her hands.

She's nervous.

Or scared.

I don't have time to ask, before she speaks.

"How did you know I was here?" she asks, her eyes looking a bit sad.

"I didn't," I say, sliding my hands into the pockets of my slacks. "I was visiting Angelina, and remembered Joseph was also buried here. Thought I would pay him a visit."

She nods, but it's more of a nod that you give someone when you don't know what else to do or say.

Her eyes travel up and down my body before she speaks. "I don't think you should be walking."

Now it's my turn to give her a nod. "Evelyn told me the same thing, but I needed to visit the cemetery today. Besides, I'm not a stay-in-bed kind of person."

"Did someone drive you here?" Her eyes go wide with worry at the possibility of me getting behind the wheel when I have a hole in my lung.

"I did."

"Dante," she starts to say. Without a doubt about to scold me for my decision.

"I'm fine. Bruised up and still with chest pain, but I'm fine. I'm alive." I want to say thanks to her but I don't. I don't know if she would see it the same way.

She probably blames herself for everything that happened.

Actually, there's no "probably" about it, I know she does.

"You should still be resting," she tells me, not dropping it. Her eyebrows still bunching up in concern.

"I will."

The Devil of Chicago never rests. There is so much shit to get done that there is never time to just rest. But I want to.

For her.

Arianna continues to look at me with concern, except now she is starting to bite her bottom lip and play with her hands a lot more.

Knowing she's not going to say anything else unless I force her, I ask the one question that has been circling in my head since I woke up.

"Why did you leave, Arianna?" My voice is stable.

Her face shifts a bit as she contemplates how to respond to my question.

Eventually she speaks. "Do you want the honest truth?"

I nod. "No more lies. I think we both know how deadly those can be."

She nods in agreement. "Okay, I'll tell you why I left yesterday, if you tell me something in return."

"What do you want to know?"

"How did you know my father, and how the hell did he get involved with the Mafia?"

39

ARIANNA

"I met Joseph when I was a teenager. I was eighteen and he had just been promoted to detective, if I remember correctly," Dante starts off.

After I told him what I wanted to know, he agreed. So now we're sitting on the ground, both of us with our backs to the headstone that faces my parents'.

He pauses for a moment as if he expects me to speak, but I don't.

I won't speak until I know the whole story, then I will tell him mine.

A few seconds later, Dante starts talking again.

"At the time, I wasn't the head of the Mafia. Hell, I didn't even want anything to do with the Mafia or the *famiglia.* The only reason I was even involved was because the boss, Alberto Falcone, was my uncle. My mother's brother. Alberto never had a wife, so everyone that worked under him treated her like their queen. My father was a capo, so it was evident that I would be involved too. I mostly took care of little things. Never really having a seat at the table," he says as if he has drifted off and is in the past.

"I met Joseph one night as I was finishing up a job for Falcone. Delivering a "package" to a city council member. A tongue. I thought he was going to arrest me when he pulled up next to me, but no. He just rolled down his window and asked if I knew a good place for some Italian lemonade. So I pointed him to one in Little Italy."

Dante showed my dad that place? I thought he just found it one day.

I try to think back to when the first time my dad took me there, but I can't remember. That place has been a staple in my life for so long that I don't even remember when I went there for the first time.

With the story Dante is telling me, I had to be around five.

"He loved Italian lemonade. He would always take me and then when I moved out, once a month, we would make a trip into Little Italy just to grab some. It was our monthly date."

I say the words and instantly regret that I didn't keep up with that. Yes, I didn't have him with me anymore, but it could be something I do for myself.

Keep his memory alive, in a way.

Dante gives me a nod, as if he knew that small piece of information, before continuing his story.

"He offered me some that night, saying that he would pay. I tried to blow him off, I knew he was a cop from the second he pulled up, but he continued to follow me and nagged at me until I finally agreed. The second I got in the car, I saw his badge and we went off to get Italian lemonade. He didn't try to get me to talk. The whole way to the place he stayed silent, just talking when he needed directions. When we got to there, I was going to book it, and he knew it, so he said the one thing that would hold me back."

Dante pauses as if he remembers that day like it was yesterday and not nearly twenty years ago.

"What did he say?" I ask, curiosity taking over.

"'Falcone is threatened by you, Dante,'" he lets out.

"What does that even mean?" Was my dad keeping a close eye on Dante? Why?

"It meant a lot of things," Dante tells me before pausing and continuing. "Falcone, like I said, didn't have a wife. He thought that having a woman would take too much time away from the *famiglia* and not make him as rich and powerful as he wanted to be. So he stayed single, and because of that, he didn't have any kids. And since his sister was the closest thing he had to a queen, I was treated as if I was the heir to the throne. Essentially, I was since I was his only male nephew. So the crown would fall to me when he met his demise, but I wanted nothing to do with it. Sure, I did jobs for the family here and there, but I always had one foot out the door and Falcone hated it. He thought that I was going to get cocky one day and take it all away from him. That continued for years. Everyone knew he hated me, his men, my parents, even your dad. So that night after he told me that, he asked me to work with him to take Falcone down and put him behind bars."

"Did you?" I turn my body to face him fully, but he keeps his eyes on my parents' grave.

Dante shakes his head. "As much as I wanted to, as much as I hated the man, I couldn't do that to my mother and your dad understood that. But just because I said no, doesn't mean that I didn't tell him when shit was going to go down. Drug deals, murders, when a body was going to pop up somewhere, whatever I knew, I would tell your dad. We would meet every once in a while, and I would tell him everything. All over Italian lemonade."

"How long did that go on for?" I ask, intrigued by all of this.

Dante finally turns to look over at me. His eyes filled with sympathy. "Until his death."

I wasn't expecting that answer. I was thinking he was going to say until he took over the mob. Not tell me that it continued into last year.

"What?" I ask, trying to speak through the shock. "Why?"

One of his hands lifts up and he goes to brush a few strands of my hair away from my face.

I close my eyes for a few seconds and marvel at his fingertips grazing my skin. When I open my eyes, Dante drops his hand and answers my questions.

"I asked the same thing. Why did we keep it up for so long? Thinking about it now, I think at the beginning, it was a kid just trying to placate a cop. In my head, if I had a cop that knew me, then he would help bail me out if I did stupid shit. After a few years went by and my hate for the Falcone family grew with each passing day, we had a common goal we both wanted to destroy. He wanted Falcone behind bars, and frankly I had no respect for the man, so I was happy with whatever happened to him. We became friends in a way. He told me about his wife and you and what it was like to be a cop. He was there for my parents' funeral at twenty-three, was there for Angelina's funeral, was one of Perversa's first clients—"

"Wait, my dad was a Perversa client?" How did I not know this?

Oh my god, I let Dante fuck me in a club my dad was once a member of.

"He signed up opening night, but he didn't step foot in there until a few years after your mom died."

"Seriously?" The picture is forming in my head of my dad sitting on one of the leather couches and getting a lap dance.

I gag at the image.

"He mostly went to drink and de-stress. Not once did I see him get a lap dance."

"The image is still in my head. Why would he become a client?"

Dante shrugs. "To support me, I guess. After my parents died, or should I say when Falcone killed them, I didn't have a whole lot of people, and the people I did have wanted me dead. Your dad sort of was one of the few people I had, even if we did only meet once every two months."

"Wow," is all I can say in response.

"Yeah," he says before continuing. "When Falcone died, and I took over, the meetings stopped for a bit. Me taking over as boss was something that he wasn't expecting because then he would have to put *me* away. We clashed for a few years, and didn't talk a whole lot. We mostly just talked when I crossed the line, or he arrested one of my men. Things got slightly better about five years ago but never really got back to how things were before I took over."

"What changed?"

Dante goes silent for a long minute, just looking at the headstone. "We came to an agreement. He would still be the cop in the friendship, and I would keep my men in check as best I could. He would also tell me if anyone was looking into me and who to stay away from. I did the same."

I run through his words, and I understand most of them, but they are still leaving me confused. "That just sounds like he was looking out for you. How did he get involved with Gallo?"

He takes a deep breath before answering. "Gallo was one of Falcone's men. His most loyal, I guess you can say. When Alberto died, Gallo thought that he was going to be the one to take over, and honestly, I would have been fine with it. But the *famiglia* voted, and they all voted for me to be the new boss, something that Gallo didn't like. So he left and took a few of his men with him and formed a *famiglia* of his own. From day one, Gallo had been trying to find things that would make him more powerful. First, it was laundering money, then with getting into the drugs and arms business. But his biggest one was sex trafficking.

That's what started the cops' interest in him about four years ago."

Dante continues to tell me everything. He tells me how my dad was put on the case, and instead of him going to Dante for help in taking down Gallo, my dad decided to do it himself. Like going undercover and getting information from Gallo.

According to Dante, dad spent years getting close to Gallo until he was able to get enough to put him away.

But being on the inside with Gallo, changed my dad. Dante tells me that he became harder, angrier, and it wasn't just with him, it was also with his coworkers.

He tells me that I probably didn't notice it because I was out of the house, and when I did see my dad, he probably tried to hide it.

I agree. My dad was a completely different person around me than what Dante is painting him to be.

The story continues with Dante telling me that my dad wanted to do everything in his power to get the individuals that were getting sex trafficked out.

"In the end, he got some of them out, but he wasn't able to save all of them. I think that was the tipping point for him, because three months before his death, he came to me and told me that he was going to pull the plug and arrest Gallo. That he had enough to put him away for life. Gallo found out somehow what Joe was planning, how I have no idea, but I heard from some of my men what was happening. So I went to him. I went to the brownstone and told Joe that he needed to pull away from this. That he needed to step away and hand the case to someone else.

That his life was on the line. He said he would, because he couldn't take it anymore and all he wanted to do was spend time with his daughter. That he was tired of thinking that his daughter was going to be the next one to be taken."

That's why he would walk me home every night from the bar. Because he was scared. He was scared that I was going to be the next one to be trafficked.

"Oh my god," I say. The thought of my dad being scared for me brings tears to my eyes. "Then he…"

I can't even say the words. So Dante says them.

"Then Gallo killed him. In the worst way possible."

For months, I wanted to know why my dad was killed. Why someone would take a man's life in such a way, but now I know.

My father got involved with the wrong person, and he got in so deep that even Dante couldn't save him.

All day yesterday, I kept thinking about how I killed two people and I even started to regret it. But now, I'm happy that I pulled the trigger. I'm happy I killed Roberto Gallo.

"I wanted revenge," I start. Dante gave me the truth. Now it's my turn. "I wanted my father's killer and everyone that had that type of power, to pay for what was done to him. People at the funeral were talking and the name The Devil was mentioned, so I told myself that I would start off there. That I would find out who this devil person was and bring them down. Then I found out it was you and even after a few warnings to stay away, I was determined to do what I felt I needed to do. I found out about the interview and I thought that it would be a good way to insert myself.

A good first step. But then I walked into that room with you and instantly felt like I shouldn't have been there. And I shouldn't have. Even if it did bring me to you and the kids."

The tears start to flow out faster and they become uncontrollable when Dante closes the distance between us and wraps an arm around me.

But even as I'm being tucked into Dante's side, the words don't stop.

I continue to tell him everything.

From the first meeting with Gallo to how I paid him from the money I received from the Lane Foundation. I even tell him how I went snooping around in his office and found the pictures and note in his bottom drawer. Then I tell him about how I told Gallo I no longer wanted any part of it. That I didn't want to take down Dante Rosetti anymore.

"I told him, Dante. I told him that I wanted to stop it. I told him that I wanted no part of it. I wanted no part of it because I love you, and I love the kids and I couldn't stand hurting you any longer."

I sob into his shoulder, slightly cringing when he lets out a groan from his injuries.

But even with his injuries, I don't make a move to pull away. I don't want to pull away from this man anymore.

I continue through the sobbing and tears and tell him that the guilt I told him I felt was real. So real that I had to pull away from him even when I didn't want to. That even the night of the gala, I was sick to my stomach with thoughts that Gallo was going to do something to him.

"I'm sorry. I'm sorry that I couldn't stop Gallo earlier. I'm sorry that I lied to you from the very beginning and continued to lie. You had every reason not to trust me, but yet you did. You let me inside your house, near your kids, and I betrayed you in every way possible. I'm so fucking sorry I deceived you. So sorry."

"It's okay," he says into my hair.

His words cause me to pull away. "It's not okay. You should hate me. You should hate me for all the shit I put you through. I almost got you killed. That's why I left yesterday, you were dying because of me. I did this to you. You need to hate me. Why don't you hate me?"

Dante shifts, taking my face in his hands and looks me right in the eyes as he says the next words.

"Because I love you. I don't hate you because I love you. I understand why you did what you did, I do, and yes, it pisses me off. But my love for you still is stronger than my hate. I love you, Arianna."

More tears escape from my eyes at his words, this time no sobbing accompanying them.

"You love me?" He said the words more than once, but I still need confirmation.

He gives me a nod. "I do."

"I love you, too," I tell him, a small smile on my face.

Not being able to hold back any longer, I lean up and slightly place my lips against his. Even though I want to spend hours kissing him and getting lost in him as he touches me and kisses every inch of me, I pull away.

We're in public.

In a cemetery, for crying out loud. Time and place.

"Where do we go from here?" I ask, nervous that even with my confession, I've lost Dante and the kids.

And if I lose them, I won't have anything left.

Dante lifts a hand and cradles my face.

"Well, I have a little girl and boy that are asking if you are coming back to them, so what do you think about going to go see them?"

"They asked about me?" I give him a tear-filled smile.

Dante nods, brushing a strand of my hair away from my face. "Alessandra said your name. She said your name and asked when you were coming back. She said two words, and all I wanted was for you to hear them."

He leans in and places his lips against mine. It's sweet and gentle like the last one and nothing like the kisses I'm used to from this man.

"Come back to the house, Arianna. The kids want you there. I want you there. Don't leave me, *amate*. We need you. More than you will ever know."

A small gasp leaves my lips.

Don't leave me.

"I won't. Never again."

"Then let's go home."

40

DANTE

There's a calmness. Circulating through me and surrounding me.

It's a calmness that I haven't felt in a very long time. If I had to pinpoint when, I would say the day before Angelina died.

That was the last time I felt this way and now a year later, I'm feeling it again.

And it's all thanks to the twenty-four-year-old woman that is currently lying in my daughter's bed. The woman that is sandwiched between both my children and even in her sleep wears a smile.

The woman that, even when lies were trying to eat at her, gave me her heart.

A heart that I will hold and protect as long as I can. A heart that I know holds mine in the same regard.

Never did I think that my heart would be given to another woman, but like I told Angelina, I was wrong.

Arianna took it and is grasping it so tight that at times it's hard to breathe.

But I'm okay with that.

I'm also okay with letting my heart belong to two separate women because it does. One half to Angelina, the other to Arianna.

And that's how it will be for the rest of my life.

The second Arianna and I walked to the house after the cemetery, Alessandra came running toward us. Well, came running to Arianna, I should say.

Alessandra was so happy she even yelled out Ari, which caused Arianna to cry. So much happiness radiated off of Arianna when she heard Alessandra say her name.

Her smile grew even more when Evelyn came down with Angel on her hip.

Once Arianna had both kids with her, something hit me. This is where she is supposed to be.

I couldn't help but wonder if somehow, Joseph sent his daughter to me because he knew I needed her. My kids needed her, and he sent her to us to be in our lives in some capacity.

After their little reunion, Arianna spent the rest of her day playing with the kids and just enjoying them. So much so that she told me to go rest and not disturb her time with them.

So I did.

And now they're all asleep after their tiring day.

Looking at the time on my watch, I step into the room and head over to the bed.

I gently shake Arianna's shoulder, trying not to wake

the kids.

Her eyes open right away, a panicked look coming across her face.

Once she sees it's me, she relaxes.

Without a doubt, she's still in shock with what happened with Gallo. That's not something that is going to go away anytime soon. It's going to take her some time to get through it.

"Time to go to bed," I say to her.

She gives me a nod and starts to detangle herself from Alessandra and Angel's hold. When I go to pick up Angel, she slaps my hand away.

"What the hell?"

She gives me a stern look like I'm one of the kids. "No lifting. Your stitches can come out, and your breathing isn't back to normal."

I roll my eyes at her. "I'm fine."

She sounds like Evelyn.

"Nope, sorry. Go to bed, I will make sure that Angel is put in his crib and Allie is tucked in."

I open my mouth to fight her on it, since she's injured to, but she slaps a hand over my mouth. Stopping me. "Go."

When the actual fuck did this woman become so damn bossy?

She ordered you to kill Gallo, remember?

Damn, I may need to find more ways to bring that side of her out more often.

But for now, I comply.

"Fine," I say, giving her a small kiss before I make my

way over to my own bed.

She's right though, I'm nowhere near healed. I'm going to be out of breath walking to the bathroom for a few weeks.

Even though I rested most of the afternoon, I still get ready for bed. My body is still tired from the events of the last two days.

Fucking Gallo and his men. If the fucker wasn't dead already. He would be.

This morning, after things quieted down from yesterday, Lorenzo came over and told me that Gallo's men are fearful that they will be next.

They should be. They worked for the bastard. That's not something that I'm going to easily forget.

He also told me that a few of them wanted to pledge their loyalty to me and our family.

It's interesting how when the boss dies, men start to frantically search for a new one to work under.

It happened when Falcone died, and it is happening with Gallo.

I asked Lorenzo what he thought about bringing them on. His response was that we should burn them to a crisp, that they should have never pledged their loyalty to a rat like Gallo. His words, not mine.

Hearing his words, I couldn't help but agree.

So I gave him the green light to do exactly what he suggested.

Which is why as I get into bed, my phone goes off with a text message from Lorenzo.

. . .

LORENZO: Job is done. Damn fuckers.

JUST ANOTHER LESSON TO not fucking mess with The Devil.

Arianna walks into the room and instead of answering Lorenzo, I place my phone on the side table and give my girl all the attention she deserves.

She sees me already in bed and instead of getting completely naked, she stands at the foot, just staring at me.

"What's on your mind, *amate*?" I ask her.

Her bottom lip gets clamped down by her teeth, which makes me want to crawl over to her and release it.

"Are you sure you still want me? That you still want to be with me? Especially knowing everything that I did against you?"

Her questions somber me up.

I let out a sigh. "Why are you asking me this?"

"Because I don't want to cause you any more

pain." She lets out, almost like she's in pain herself.

I can see why she may think that. Why she may think that she may cause me more pain.

Because of the lies and who she was working with, there was a possible chance that I wouldn't have made it back yesterday. I could have died and it would be because of her actions.

But that's not the way I see it.

And I don't blame her for what happened. Not once was that a thought.

I answer her question as honestly as I possibly can.

"Yes. I still want you," I say, getting up from bed and

walking over to her.

"Even if I'm just the nanny?"

"You were never just the nanny. You have always been more."

Breathless and in pain, I get out of bed. I take her face between my hands and make sure she looks me in the eyes as I say the next words.

"I still want to be with you. As long as the deception stops here. On both of our parts. That's the only way that this will work. No more lies, no more omissions. Just trust and love. That is all."

Her hand comes up and covers mine as she moves her head slightly to place a kiss on my palm.

When she turns back to look at me, she gives me a teary smile.

So much crying has been happening today.

"No more deception," she agrees, before standing on her tiptoes and placing a chaste kiss on my mouth.

As much as I want to continue the kiss, I pull away from her, my forehead settling on hers.

"If I didn't need to take it easy, I would be fucking you right now."

Arianna lets out a hum. "I know, but I might have a solution."

"Oh yeah? What's that?"

Her hands land on my body, sliding against my bare chest, her fingers softly gliding against my stitching.

"Let me take care of you," she purrs, leaning and in and placing kisses against my skin. Her lips following the path of her fingers.

"Go right ahead," I say, marveling at her light touches.

She covers my chest and the other edge of my stitches with kisses before taking my hand and guiding me back to the bed.

Once I'm on my back, she does what I wanted to do when she first walked in. She strips her clothes off.

"Too bad there's no music playing, like there was at the club," I say as I lean up on my elbows to watch.

Our night at Perversa is something that has popped in my head so much since it happened that if I wasn't injured, I would be driving there right now. That night deserves to be repeated nightly.

"Maybe when you're better," Arianna answers as if she was reading my mind.

"I'll hold you to it," I say, reaching out and taking one of her nipples between my fingertips.

Her tits are fucking glorious and have my mouth watering.

I've covered them in my cum so many times it has become my favorite sight.

Arianna slaps my hand away. "No. Tonight is about me taking care of you. Of me showing you how much I love you. Let me do that."

"Okay," I say, letting her take all the control.

She gives me a shy smile before falling to her knees and ridding me of my sleeping pants.

I'm not a sleeping-in-boxer type of person, so as soon as she pulls my pants down, she comes face-to-face with my cock.

A hum escapes her as her hands slide against my

thighs.

I watch as she slowly leans in and places kisses against the insides of my thighs, just like she was doing to my chest.

The more she kisses, the closer she gets to my cock, and when she finally kisses on the pulled skin, every inch of me is awake.

She continues to kiss, then her kisses turn into sucks and licks until she takes me in her mouth. Her movements are slow at first, but with the warmth of her mouth driving me crazy, I say fuck slow.

She said to let her take care of me so I don't slide my hands into her hair like I want to. Instead, I lift my hips and thrust ever so slightly into her mouth.

Her eyes look up to mine, but she doesn't move to slide me out of her mouth.

No, instead of pulling away, her eyes fill with lust and are encouraging me to continue.

So I do.

Arianna tries to keep stable as I thrust up into her mouth. I start up slow, but then after a minute or two, I start to really move.

My injuries aren't letting me give her everything that I want, but I don't give a shit.

"Such a pretty mouth, and it's all mine," I groan. "That's it, baby. Take each thrust. Your throat can take it."

As my cock meets the back of her throat and I hear her gag, I think about how wet she must be. Arianna loves sucking my cock and every time, her pussy is wet and needy and always ready for me.

"Turn and sit on my face. I need to lick your pussy," I order, finally letting my hands go to her hair.

Even through my thrusts, Arianna shakes her head.

I let out a growl. "I won't say it again, Arianna. Sit. On. My. Face. Now."

My thrusts stop, and she gives me one last suck before letting me out of her mouth with a pop.

Drool is covering her mouth and tears from my attack are spilling out of her eyes. She looks absolutely beautiful.

"I'm supposed to be taking care of you," she says as she climbs on the bed and maneuvers herself so that she straddles me with her ass positioned toward my face and her mouth hovering over my cock.

"You are. Me eating this needy pussy of yours is taking care of me. Now finish sucking me off. I need to come down your throat." I slap her ass for good measure.

I know how much she likes it when The Devil comes out to play, so I will use him whenever I can.

Arianna takes me in her mouth again and I spread her ass cheeks and lick up everything that she has to offer.

My fingers dig into her ass as I tease her pussy entrance with my tongue.

She's salty and sweet, and I need to drink up every last drop.

One of her moans fills the room and she cradles my balls, making me harder and fighting the urge to come.

Needing her to get there before I do, I slide my fingers against her pussy lips until I reach her clit and give her a good pinch.

With fingers on her clit, I continue to tease her with my

tongue and mouth.

Arianna starts to grind against me, pulling off my dick. "Dante. I'm getting there."

"What do you need to be there?" I ask, not relenting my attack on her pussy.

"Eat my ass and finger my pussy," she orders, another moan escaping from her sweet mouth.

"Mm, such a dirty girl. I like it when you order me around, but you will remember who the boss is here." I give her pussy one last lick before moving my mouth right where she wants it.

"Yes, *daddy*."

A growl slips out and I don't give her any time to adjust to anything as I do what she says.

I eat her ass and fuck her pussy until she is letting out a scream and tightening around my fingers.

"Yes. Yes. Right there. Yes, Dante. Fuck," she chants as her orgasm takes over and she comes all over my fingers.

Before she comes down fully, I give her my own order. "Finish me off."

With a moan, she does what she's told and takes me back in her mouth.

I lick up her release and two minutes later, I'm shooting my own release down her throat.

Fuck, that felt good.

But I still need more.

As Arianna sags against my body, I shift until she's on her back and I'm hovering over her.

"What are you doing?" Her eyes go wide with concern.

"Fucking you," I state, leaning down and taking her

lips captive.

"Dante, no, your stitches," she says against my mouth.

"Fuck my stitches. It's my turn to show you how much I love you." I pull back from her to show her with my eyes the sincerity of my words.

She watches me for a bit, but eventually she gives me the sexy smile that I love so much.

"Okay, then show me."

With no waiting, no warning, I situate myself between her legs and show her.

I show her that I love her.

I show her how much she means to me.

I give her everything as I thrust into her, hard and fast.

Even with the awful pain at my side and my breathing becoming uncontrollable, I don't stop.

I continue fucking her, making love to her, until we are both at another breaking point.

This woman might have come into my life with all the wrong intentions, but that didn't stop her from making me fall for her.

From making me mark her as mine, because she is mine.

Our relationship may have started with deception, but from here on out it will be filled with love and honesty.

She loves me and my kids, and we love her, and a year after tragedy struck, it feels as if our lives are whole again.

It looks as if The Devil of Chicago has a queen yet again, but she's not a replacement for his first. She's an addition.

And a powerful addition she is.

EPILOGUE

ARIANNA

"Angel, baby, it will just be for a little bit, I promise. Just put on the pants, and I promise as soon as we're done, you can take them off."

I'm currently crouched down on the floor in Angel's room, clutching a pair of black little-kid slacks fighting with an almost three-year-old.

"No," He yells out as he continues to run circles around his room pretending to be a tiger or something.

I let my ass fall to the ground. "I liked you better when you couldn't walk or run," I grumble, feeling defeated.

If you told me that at twenty-six, I would be fighting with a two-year-old over wearing pants, I wouldn't have believed you, but here I am.

Dante is hosting a dinner tonight, a fancy dinner at that, that he wants the kids to be a part of. I told him in not so many words that having the kids attend a fancy, adult-only dinner is not a wise idea.

I think I used stupid but that was just my age showing.

He told me that it would be fine and here I am, fighting to dress one of the said children.

At least Alessandra was easy.

"Angel, how about ice cream? Do you want ice cream? If you put on your pants, I promise to get you some," I throw out at the child in the sweetest voice I can muster.

"No," he yells out again and I swear I see a smirk on his face, just like the one his father wears.

I think it might be time to pull out the big guns. Pulling out my phone, I dial Dante's number. Thankfully he answers after the second ring.

"You okay?" he asks, instead of a greeting. He's used to these types of calls, especially now that Angel is in his terrible twos phase.

God, what awaits us when they're teenagers? I may need regular vacations.

"Your son won't put on his pants. Can you come up here, please?"

"My son? If I remember correctly, you're the one that told me when he started doing that to just let him be. He's having fun, I think, were your words."

I let out a small growl, which I know he hears because he lets out a laugh.

"Can you just come up here, please? I'm on the floor, my dress is getting wrinkled and I'm hungry. And yes, your son, he's your spitting image."

Dante just laughs at me. "I'll be right there."

I hang up the phone and continue to watch Angel run in circles.

I wonder if he'll eventually burn a hole in the ground because this kid does not tire out.

Two minutes later, Dante appears in the doorway, with a stupid smirk on his face.

"Here," I say, holding up the pants. "You try it."

Dante continues to smirk as he walks over to me and takes the pair pants. The man has the audacity to wink at me before turning to the moving tornado.

"*Angioletto,* come here. Now," Dante orders, and within seconds, Angel stops.

The kid stops.

What the hell?

I watch, dumbfounded, as Angel smiles up at his dad as if he were a superhero or something, walks over to him and lets him put on his pants.

Unbelievable.

"Why are you giving Mama a hard time?" Dante asks his son as he situates his shirt and small bow tie.

As I watch Dante dress Angel, my mind drifts.

It's almost two years to the day since my dad died. Two years since I walked into Perversa and pulled down my dress for Dante for the nanny position. Almost two years since I met Angel and Alessandra, became their nanny and fell in love with them in ways I can never comprehend. Almost two years since Dante and I started the journey that we are in now.

A lot has happened since that day I agreed to work for Dante as his children's nanny.

After the situation with Gallo, and then Dante and I declared our love for each other, I was officially fired as the nanny and officially became Dante's stay at home girlfriend.

As much as I wanted to work, Dante wouldn't let me, so we came up with a compromise. I'd stay home with the kids and if anything came up where he needed help with anything that Evelyn couldn't handle, he would come to me. I agreed.

That worked for the better part of a year and a half, but earlier this year, I decided to go back to school to get my master's in business.

The idea came to me one day as I was helping Alessandra with her words. She is speaking a bit more than what she used to, but it's definitely not the same as other six-year-olds. As I was helping her, I thought about kids in her situation that didn't have the same resources that she did. So I looked into it and found that while there are a lot of charities that help kids for a number of things, speech therapy wasn't one that was heavily available.

So I decided to go back to school to open one and learn all the ropes.

Dante was okay with it.

I was able to get into some night classes and stay with the kids during the day, and so far, it's working out. I stay with the kids during the day, and when Dante comes home from the club or from doing *famiglia* things, he stays with the kids while I go to school.

"Because I wuv her," Angel responds, taking me out of my headspace.

With a smile, I get up from the floor and make my way over to my little man.

"And I love you too," I say as I lift him up and plant kisses on his chubby cheeks.

"Mama!" Angel squeals as I kiss him and when I put him on the floor, he runs right out of the room.

Mama.

That's what the kids have been calling me for almost two years as well. It started when Angel first started to say words and he must have heard the word from somewhere because he repeated it.

The first time we heard him say it, we were in shock. Never had I told him to call me mama, but yet here he was saying it. I tried my hardest to teach him another word, but all that would come out of Angel's mouth was mama.

After a week or so of me panicking, Dante told me that it was okay if they called me mama. I was helping raise them, I was in their lives, and in a way, I was a mother figure to them.

I thought about it, and after a few days, I was okay with it, but I was even more okay with it when I explained to Alessandra that Angel may call me mama, but I would never be *mami*. I didn't want to replace Angelina, and I wasn't going to.

So the kids have their *mami* and their mama, and I'm happy with that.

"You ready to go downstairs?" Dante asks me, wrapping an arm around my waist.

"I still think that the kids will be bored out of their minds around adults," I say, leaning into him.

"Leo is bringing his wife and son, so they won't be the only ones," he says, placing a kiss on my bare shoulder.

"Fine, but if Angel decides to take his pants off in front of all your friends, that's all on you." I pat his hand and give him a smirk before leaving the room and going to grab Alessandra from her room.

My princess is all dressed and ready when I walk in, so when I hold out my hand, she takes it, and we make our way downstairs.

Like fighting a two-year-old to put on pants, never did I think that I would be attending a black-tie event in my own house, but yet here I am.

Alessandra and I make our way downstairs, and instantly my eyes land on Dante and Angel, talking to a set of men in suits.

Tonight, Dante is hosting a business dinner, as he called it, so the house is filled with billionaires, Mafia men, and even a few cartel men sprinkled in.

They are people that Dante trusts and if he trusts them, then so do I.

Allie and I make our way around the room, greeting people until we find Evelyn, who is talking to Lorenzo.

The two of them are making sexy eyes at each other and I'm about to call them out on it, but dinner is called.

Next time then.

I'll give it to Dante, he sure knows how to throw a party. Even with a room filled with people that can be deadly, things went off without a hitch, and I tell him so when we are in bed a few hours later.

"I told you that it would all work out, and Angel didn't take off his pants once." He gives me that sexy smile I love so much as he hovers over me, ready to slide home.

Opening my legs and wrapping them around his waist, I give him a small nudge to slide into me.

"I know, you were right," I say through a sigh as I feel his cock against me.

"I did get asked one question though, that has been on my mind," he says, right before he thrusts into me again.

I let out a moan at the delicious sensation.

"Hmm, and what was that?" I ask, sliding a hand into his hair and pulling his face to mine.

I try to tell him with my tongue and with my hip movements that we should drop the conversation, but he doesn't get the memo.

"One of Leo's sisters asked me, when I was going to make you my wife," Dante says right before moving his mouth down to my chest.

Suddenly, I go completely still, only being able to concentrate on his words.

He must notice it because Dante looks up at me, devilish grin and all.

"And what did you say?" I ask, my voice barely a whisper.

Dante lifts up a hand and caresses my face in the most tender way, my heart flutters a bit at the movement.

"I told her that I was just waiting for the ring to arrive from the jeweler, and then I was going to do it."

He's serious.

Oh my god. Oh *my* god.

I try to push down the lump in my throat. "And when does the ring arrive from the jeweler?"

This is definitely not a conversation we should be having while his penis is in my vagina.

Dante shrugs. "It could be a couple days, a few weeks, maybe a few months. Can't really tell with a custom ring."

I gasp, and at the gasp, Dante starts to thrust into me again.

"Now the question is, will you say yes?" Another thrust, followed by another.

I don't know if it's the way he's pounding into me or the question itself, but I respond.

"Yes," I say, throwing my head back in euphoria.

Another thrust. One that hits the right places.

"Say it again, *amate*."

"Yes, Dante. The answer is yes."

Another thrust.

And that's how it continues. I yell out a hundred yeses until I see stars and I'm tightening around Dante and he is spilling his seed into me.

My life changed two years ago when I lost my father. At the time, I never thought that I would ever be able to move on from that.

But I did.

It took a different direction to be able to achieve it, but I was able to move on from losing the most important man in my life. I was able to find his killer and make him pay for his crimes. And in the process, I was able to find the love of my life and help him raise two beautiful children.

I didn't think that after my dad died that I would have a family again, but now I have a promise of a future with my little family.

I'm going to grasp it, and I will hold it close to my heart and protect it.

There's a new man in my life that gives a shit about me and brightens up my darkest days.

Who knew I was going to get all this by falling in love with the most dangerous man in all of Chicago?

I fell in love with the man that they call The Devil, and I'm never going to let him go.

THE END.

PLAYLIST

Walls Could Talk - Halsey
Don't you know - Jaymes Young
Seven Nation Army - Future Royalty
Money - Tara Carosielli
Toxic - 2WEI
Chains (Remix) - Nick Jonas, Jhené Aiko
Darkside - Oshins, Hael
Temptation - Becoming Young
Closer - J2, Keeley Bumford
Set Me On Fire - Estelle
Collide - Rachel Platten
Wicked Games - Ursine Vulpine, Annaca
Lucifer - XOV
Take Me To Church - MILCK
Like that - Bea Miller
Joke's On You - Charlotte Lawrence
I Wanna Be Your's - Arctic Monkeys
I Fell In Love With The Devil - Avril Lavigne
I'll Make You Love Me - Kat Leon
Hurts Like Hell - Fleurie, Tommee Profitt
Talk - Salvatore Ganacci
Walk Through The Fire - Clergy, BELLSAINT
How Villans Are Made - Madalen Duke
Devil Knows - Armen Paul
The Night We Met - Lord Huron

ACKNOWLEDGMENTS

After what feels like a long time coming, Dante and Arianna are finally out in the world!

It feels as if I've been waiting for this day for a very long time, and I'm glad that it's finally here and I can share Dante and Arianna's story with you.

This story came about sometime in late 2021. I wanted to write a story that was involved in the Flor de Muertos world, I just didn't know what I should be. I knew I wanted to introduce new characters and have it set in Chicago. Finally the idea came to write a mafia romance that had a nanny falling for the boss.

I didn't want to make Arianna just your typical nanny, I needed her to have a reason to be there besides the kids, and that's where the story line of her father came in.

I won't lie this story was hard. Writer's block was real through out this whole process. There were times where I wanted to quit and give up and I didn't it. There were obstacles of course, some that made me move back the release by a few weeks, but in the end it all worked out.

This story has a lot of elements to it, including new characters that you will be seeing later on. For now, I hope that you loved Dante and Arianna (and Angel and

Alessandra). They have a special place in my heart. So much so that this will not be the last you see of them.

Dante and Arianna are special to me and I hope they are to you too!

Now onto the thank yous!

Ellie and Rosa - Thank you for staying me with me through out this chaotic journey. From moving dates around to last minute crunches. I appreciate both of you with everything that I have!

Shauna and the team at Wildfire Marketing - thank you so much for your help through the promo of this book. I would be completely lost without you.

Cassie - Thank you for creating an amazing cover. It fit the story perfectly.

Emily - Thank you for the beautiful special edition cover. It ties in to perfectly that I can't get enough.

Reviewers - Thank you for your support with this book and taking a chance on me.

To my readers - thank you for your constant support, especially when I was feeling down about this book and kept moving things around. You guys are the real MVPs.

Thank you all for your support! Now onto the next one.....

I'm thinking a certain baseball player.....

BOOKS BY JOCELYNE SOTO

<u>One Series</u>

One Life

One Love

One Day

One Chance

One for Me

One Marriage

<u>Flor De Muertos Series</u>

Vicious Union

Violent Attraction

Vindictive Blood

<u>Standalones</u>

Beautifully Broken

Worth Every Second

Powerful Deception

Fake Love

Salutis Meae

ABOUT THE AUTHOR

Jocelyne Soto is a writer born and raised in California. She started her writing journey in 2015 and in 2019 she published her first book. She is an independent author who loves discovering new authors on Goodreads and Amazon. She comes from a big Mexican family, and with it comes a love for all things family and food.

Jocelyne has a love for her mom's coffee and writing. In her free time, she can be found reading a romance novel off her iPad or somewhere in the black hole of YouTube.

Follow her website and on social media!
www.jocelynesoto.com

facebook.com/authorjocelynesoto

twitter.com/AuthorJocelyneS

instagram.com/authorjocelynesoto

pinterest.com/authorjocelynesoto

tiktok.com/@authorjocelynesoto

goodreads.com/jocelynesotobooks

bookbub.com/profile/jocelyne-soto

JOIN MY READER GROUP

Join my ever-growing Facebook Group.

https://www.facebook.com/groups/jocelynesotobooks

NEWSLETTER

Sign up for my Newsletter!
You will get notified when there are new
releases to look out for, giveaways and more!

https://www.subscribepage.com/
authorjocelynesotonewsletter